D1564406

OF MUSHROOMS AND MATRIMONY

OF MUSHROOMS AND MATRIMONY

Amy Patricia Meade

SEVERN
HOUSE

First world edition published in Great Britain and the USA in 2023
by Severn House, an imprint of Canongate Books Ltd,
14 High Street, Edinburgh EH1 1TE.

Trade paperback edition first published in Great Britain and the USA in 2023
by Severn House, an imprint of Canongate Books Ltd.

severnhouse.com

British Library Cataloguing-in-Publication Data
A CIP catalogue record for this title is available from the British Library.

ISBN-13: 978-1-4483-0654-1 (cased)
ISBN-13: 978-1-4483-0663-3 (trade paper)
ISBN-13: 978-1-4483-0662-6 (e-book)

All Severn House titles are printed on acid-free paper.

Typeset by Palimpsest Book Production Ltd.,
Falkirk, Stirlingshire, Scotland.
Printed and bound in Great Britain by
TJ Books, Padstow, Cornwall.

ONE

'I can't believe it. My café is closed, and once this job is finished, my catering business is on hiatus until I can find a new kitchen,' Tish Tarragon, owner of Cookin' the Books literary café, lamented as she loaded a crate of dishes into her bright red van in preparation for a book-themed wedding weekend at Abbingdon Green Bed and Breakfast. 'When I opened this business, I knew there was a chance it might close because it wasn't successful, but I never imagined it would close because I'd been evicted.'

Julian Davis, Channel Ten weatherman and one of Tish's dearest friends since college, slid a box of crystal stemware into the spot beside the dishes. 'Well, you did tell your landlord to shut up, honey. And rather angrily, too.'

'When I said that, I wasn't talking to Schuyler Thompson, my landlord. I was talking to Schuyler Thompson, my ex-boyfriend and Hobson Glen's crummy new mayor who was working with the town council to cover up the identity of a murderer.'

'Clearly, Schuyler doesn't compartmentalize these matters as well as you do,' Jules deadpanned. 'I've gotta say, though, you got the crummy mayor part right. Do you know that man is imposing a town tax on vehicle registrations in addition to the state fee we already pay?'

'Yes, I heard. The tax would be on a sliding scale, with owners of larger vehicles paying more than those with smaller cars. I can't wait to see how much it will be to re-register this van.'

'Disgraceful. I'm proud to say I didn't vote for him. Although I have a bit of a confession to make – even before you and he split up, I'd decided not to vote for Schuyler.'

'I have a confession to make, too. Even before he and I split up, I'd decided not to vote for Schuyler either,' Tish replied, eliciting a loud cackle from Jules.

'Well, let's forget him. Now you have yourself a hot, hunky man who treats you like a goddess.'

Tish thought back to the previous night and the lovely candlelight dinner Sheriff Clemson Reade had cooked in the kitchen of his cozy circa-1930 bungalow. 'He really is wonderful,' she gushed. 'He's been so incredibly supportive through all of this. Helping me scour real estate ads, listening to my fears . . . he even arranged for his friend Shirley – remember, she owns Justine's, the restaurant by the Canal Walk in Richmond? – to buy leftover stock from me. I don't have a lot to sell, but it's good to know that food won't go to waste. It will also be nice to have a little extra pocket money.'

'Mary Jo and the kids are staying with Celestine until they can find a new apartment,' Jules said, referring to their other college chum who had been living in the apartment above the café after a nasty divorce and was now rooming with Tish's recently widowed baker. 'The café is closed to the public, you're selling off extra supplies, and you're completing the last of your catering gigs this weekend. You also need to be out of here before the end of the month which – need I remind you – is mere days away. So why are you still staying here?'

Tish gazed at the flower-and-plant-festooned porch with its wide cushion-lined swing and blinked back her tears. She had put so much time and care into transforming the café into not just a thriving, welcoming business, but a comfortable home, that it was difficult to imagine leaving it all behind. 'I suppose I'm not ready to let go quite yet,' she confessed. 'There's also the matter of Tuna—'

'Tuna will be fine. Out of all the porches in Hobson Glen that cat could have wandered on to, he chose yours. He's your cat, honey. Wherever you go, he'll follow and he'll adapt.'

'So long as he *can* follow. Do you know how difficult it is to find an apartment that allows pets?'

'No, luckily, my landlady loves Biscuit.' Jules glanced down at the Bichon Frisé sniffing the ground at his feet. 'But why are you even bothering to look at apartments? I'm sure Clemson wouldn't mind Tuna coming along for the ride. He *has* suggested that you move in with him, hasn't he?'

'He has,' she confirmed. 'I told him I'd think about it.'

'What's there to think about? You love him, and he's loaded to the gills with love for you. What else do you need?'

'Assurance. The last time I moved in with someone so quickly, things didn't end very well.'

'Your relationship with Schuyler didn't break up because you moved in with him too soon. Your relationship ended because Schuyler's a jackass.'

'I understand that, but—'

'But what?'

'I don't want to do anything to put my relationship with Clemson in jeopardy. I'd like us to progress to the next step naturally, instead of being pushed into it by circumstance.'

'Sometimes circumstance is simply fate lending a helping hand,' Jules philosophized. 'Considering it took five murder cases and a totaled car before the two of you even started to date, I'm thinking y'all should grab on to any helping hand that comes your way.'

'I didn't say no, Jules,' Tish reinforced with a sigh. 'I just need some time.'

'Time for what? To perfect your shadow-puppet skills on the empty walls of your tiny bedroom?'

'To grieve a little.'

Jules folded his arms across his chest and rolled his eyes. 'This space is gone, but your business isn't.'

'To find a new location for the café,' she added to the list of excuses.

'A new, improved, and possibly expanded location,' he added with a broad grin.

'I agree with you on the new, but I'm afraid the improved and expanded isn't quite in the stars at the moment. The only place I can afford is nearly a third the size of this one. I'll have to limit my business to takeout only.'

'Oh, you mean that little storefront for rent over in Coleton Creek?'

'If you're talking about the one in the strip mall between Jenny Craig and the check-cashing place, then yes, that's the one.'

'Well, being next door to Jenny Craig probably won't help sell Celestine's fabulous cakes, but the check-cashing place might bring in some business, what with all those people with money in their pockets waiting to be spent.'

'Yeah, the check-cashing place also runs a pawn service, which means after you hock that engagement ring you no longer need or cash in your late Aunt Hattie's pearls, you can swing by my place and treat yourself to a scone,' she said, her voice dripping with sarcasm. 'The ads will practically write themselves.'

'OK, so maybe it's not the ideal location,' Jules admitted. 'But I know one that is – the Hobson Glen Bar and Grill building. It's bigger than this place, has plenty of parking, a newly renovated living area upstairs, a back room you could rent out for parties, and enough surrounding property to expand into an outdoor eating area. Plus, a little birdie told me that the owner turned the deed back over to the bank who, in turn, is selling it for a song.'

'Yes, I heard the same news, so I took a look online. Even with the discounted price, that song is still way out of my key.'

'Oh, but it's perfect! You worked in finance for years. Surely someone you know back at the bank might be able to help you.'

'Maybe. It's Friday morning – the work week isn't over yet. I'll email my old boss this morning and see if some new financing options have opened up,' she thought aloud. 'But I'm not holding my breath. In the meantime, we need to pack this van. I have a wedding weekend to cater.'

'Not just a wedding weekend, but a bookish wedding weekend. Ever since you started your business, I've been waiting for you to get a gig like this one. Romance, reading, great food . . . sounds like it could be *your* wedding.'

'I already had a wedding, remember?'

'How could I forget?' Jules asked dramatically. 'In addition to feeling like an oversized eggplant in that suit you made me wear—'

'Aubergine was a hot color for bridesmaids that year!' Tish interrupted.

'—I spent most of that morning in the ladies' room with Mary Jo while she suffered from morning sickness.'

'That's right. She was pregnant with Kayla. It's hard to believe that was nearly sixteen years ago.'

'It is, but you're missing my point. A wedding isn't a funeral, honey. A person can have more than one.'

'A person also can also have more than one best friend,' Tish volleyed, 'but sometimes that additional best friend can be a real nag.'

Jules gave a mock laugh. 'Haha. And here that additional best friend was going to invite you to join him in some food from Bombolini once you finished with the welcome dinner tonight.'

Tish did a double take. '*Bombolini?*'

'Yes, I'm covering a story downtown today and I know how you love their smoked salmon and peas over fusilli. I thought maybe, if you were nice to me, I might bring back some dinners to reheat. You know, seeing as you said tonight's buffet should wrap early and you've given away everything but the food you're cooking for the wedding weekend.'

Tish pasted on a broad smile 'I didn't say that *you* were the additional nagging friend, Jules. I was talking about Mary Jo.'

'Yes, she can be a real pain, can't she?' he joked. 'OK, well, since you've made amends, I *suppose* I could pick up some of that pasta you like. We could watch a movie and have a spa night, just like old times. Why don't you pack some things and stay over? It's not like you need to start baking at six in the morning, like you did when the café was open.'

Tish sighed. *As if she needed reminding. She had only just shuttered the café after serving the lunch crowd that last Sunday.* 'No, but what about Tuna? I was out all last night. I'd feel bad leaving him alone again after spending the day prepping for tonight's welcome dinner.'

'*All* last night?' Jules raised an eyebrow. 'Simple, leave his carrier out and I'll come by after work, feed him, and bring him to my place. We can keep him and his litter box in the spare bedroom with you, like we did when Schuyler had the café repainted – no doubt so he could sell the place as soon as you were out of it.'

Tish pulled a face. 'That did work out well, didn't it? Biscuit didn't even know Tuna was in your apartment.'

'He hadn't a clue. And Tuna slept with you in a deluxe queen bed in glorious air conditioning.'

Tish thought of the lumpy twin futon in her makeshift office-cum-bedroom. 'Since the café closed, it is a bit sad around here. OK, we'll join you,' she capitulated.

'Hooray! What time can Biscuit and I expect you?'

'Oh, let's see. The dinner is set to start at six – it's buffet style, which makes things easier. I'll stick around to refill platters as necessary, but Glory Bishop's staff is taking care of clean-up, and

I'll need most of those platters for the wedding on Sunday so they'll be staying at the B and B. Given all that, I shouldn't be any later than seven thirty.'

'Sounds good. I know the wedding-day menu focuses on regional specialties – I have a glorious vodka and grapefruit-based Virginia Black Bear cocktail in store for when I tend bar on the big day – but what are you serving tonight?'

'Tonight's regional as well, so I'm doing a Tidewater riff on the New England clambake. I have an outdoor feast of local blue crabs served with brandy mayonnaise, chilled marinated shrimp, steamed potatoes, succotash, and coleslaw. The bride's parents will have coolers of beer and other beverages on hand and, for dessert, there's a tray of Celestine's Pecan wedding cookies and, because late August is the height of plum season, a large tub of greengage plum ice cream. A laidback meal for twenty people, just perfect for kicking off a long wedding weekend.'

'And here my mouth was watering for Bombolini.'

'My mouth is still watering for Bombolini. I don't have to cook or do dishes afterward.'

'Speaking of cooking,' Jules segued as he remarked upon the appearance of a black SUV in the café parking lot, 'here comes Sheriff Reade. You were together all night and he's already missing you at eight thirty in the morning? Girl, I'm gonna need a scoop!'

'A scoop? Your Channel Ten news credentials don't work with me,' she said with a laugh. 'My lips are sealed – even for Bombolini.'

'We'll see about that,' Jules teased before heading off to his car. 'Hi, Sheriff. Bye, Sheriff.'

Clemson Reade, tall and handsome in aviator sunglasses, a dark gray T-shirt, and a pair of fitted jeans, waved to a passing Jules as he strode across the gravel lot toward Tish. 'He's in a good mood this morning,' Reade observed as he slid an arm around her waist.

'He's trying to get me to talk about our date last night by bribing me with takeout Italian food, but I am not a woman to kiss and tell.' She planted her lips squarely on Reade's as if to demonstrate the veracity of her statement.

'Just two of the many things I love about you,' Reade said when she pulled away.

'Two?'

'Your kisses and the fact you don't talk about them.'

She smiled and, with an arm entwined in his, led the way back to the café porch. 'So what brings you by? I thought you had a meeting this morning.'

'I did. It ended early, so I thought I'd stop by to say good morning. I felt bad leaving without saying goodbye, but you were sleeping so peacefully I didn't want to wake you.'

'I appreciate that. It was the best night's sleep I've had in a long time. I didn't even wake up at five thirty in anticipation of the alarm going off like it did when the café was open. All that pampering you treated me to last night must have worked.'

'There's a whole bunch more where that came from if you're interested in coming by after your catering job tonight,' he invited.

'I'd love to, but how about a rain check? I'm joining Jules for Italian food tonight.'

'So you were telling the truth about him trying to bribe you.'

'Partly. I'm sure Jules also wants to pick my brain about his annual end-of-summer party. He hosts it at the rec park the second week of September. Jules provides the burgers, hot dogs, or whatever main he's decided to serve. Everyone else brings a side or dessert to share. It's gotten quite popular – I think his guest list has tripled in the past few years.'

'I'm glad you're spending some time with Jules tonight. It's been a while since the two of you hung out together. Just do me a favor and make sure I'm on this year's party list as a plus-one.'

'Don't worry. If you don't go, I don't go,' she promised, confident that she'd never have to act on her ultimatum, since Jules, ever in search of the latest story, knew the sheriff was a valuable source of police information.

'Deal,' he agreed. 'Since I won't be seeing you this evening, how about I lend you a hand in bringing your gear over to Abbingdon Green?'

'Really? That would be terrific – it would cut my load-in time in half. But are you sure you're not busy right now?'

'Positive. Since we covered everything in our meeting, and in record time, I gave everyone involved an extra-long coffee break. The perks of being the boss,' he said with a wink. 'Besides, even if I was busy, I'd like to be able to see you for at least a few minutes today.'

Having spent so much time with Clemson the night before, Tish was surprised to realize that she had actually missed him upon waking up that morning. 'Yeah,' she replied, 'I'd like that, too.'

Located on the main road, halfway between the neighboring towns of Hobson Glen and Ashton Courthouse, Abbingdon Green was an expansive Victorian dwelling with a wraparound porch, a three-story corner turret, pale yellow clapboard siding, green shutters, and copious amounts of gingerbread trim. Built in 1890, the house had been in Glory Bishop's family since its construction but had only been converted into a bed and breakfast in the late eighties, when Glory, left by her husband to raise two young sons on her own, determined that she needed a source of income that didn't require her to be away from home for forty to fifty hours a week.

Using her small savings, Glory converted the property's carriage house/garage into a living space for herself and her children and opened two of the home's several bedrooms to guests. More than thirty years and hundreds of favorable reviews later, Abbingdon Green now offered eight well-appointed queen-sized bedrooms with private baths, one luxury king turret suite with Jacuzzi and waterfall shower, sumptuous three-course breakfasts, and immaculately landscaped grounds to travelers looking to escape busy city life.

Tish steered the van up the driveway and behind the privet hedge that separated the guest parking lot from the B & B's trash collection and delivery area, pulling to a stop just outside the back steps. Extracting two boxes of supplies from the rear of the van, she and Reade walked up the steps and through the back door.

Inside and straight ahead, a narrow archway led to the servants' staircase. To the left, a wider archway opened to the home's charming farmhouse kitchen. Updated with stainless steel industrial appliances, a deep country sink, state-of-the-art dishwasher, and marble countertops for pastry-making, the space not only exceeded the health and safety standards of the county health inspector but also ensured that Glory and her staff were able to satisfy the palates of her guests both quickly and efficiently.

Glory, carrying a tray of dirty dishes from the morning's breakfast service, entered the kitchen mere seconds after Tish and Reade's arrival. She was dressed in a beige linen shirtdress and a pair of ballet flats, and her silver hair had been trimmed into a sleek bob.

'Mornin', Tish,' she greeted as she passed the tray to the young woman loading the dishwasher. 'I see you've brought your young man with you.'

Reade looked playfully over each shoulder. 'Tish has a young man? Who? Where?'

'Well, you're certainly not an old man, Sheriff,' Glory chided with a giggle.

'Eh, some mornings I feel like one.'

'Just wait until you get to my age. With the exception of George, my gardener, I used to take care of this place all by myself. Then I turned sixty and I hired a girl part-time to help make beds. When I turned sixty-five, the part-time bed-maker became a full-time housekeeper. I turned seventy and decided I needed someone to help serve and clean up in the mornings, so I hired Esmeralda.' Glory gestured toward the young woman loading the dishwasher. 'I turn seventy-five next month and I hate to think who I'll have to hire next. Probably a nurse to roll me around in a wheelchair.'

'Nonsense,' Tish scoffed. 'I see how you zip around this place. There aren't many people half your age capable of getting up at the crack of dawn to fix plates of fresh fruit, baskets of home-baked pastries, *and* a fully cooked breakfast for eighteen people every morning, three hundred and sixty-five days a year.'

'Three hundred and fifty-one,' Glory corrected. 'The B and B is closed for two weeks after New Year's. And what I do isn't impressive. You served more people than I do each day when your café was open.'

'With the help of two other people,' Tish clarified. 'Now, enough silly talk. This place is your life's blood. It keeps you going.'

'Ain't that the truth. My oldest boy asked me about retirement the other day. Retirement! What am I supposed to do with my free time – play bingo? I told him that if I have any say in it, I'll be running this place until I die.' She led the way to the B and B's dining room. 'My guests are dining on the front porch this morning, so you can keep everything in here.'

'OK. If it's nice out this evening, I think I'll set up the food for the welcome dinner outdoors as well,' Tish suggested as she placed the box she was carrying on one of the dozen or so cherry-wood Queen Anne-style dining tables that filled the space.

'That's a lovely idea. I'll have George move some tables and chairs into the garden this afternoon. There's more room for people to mill about and mingle out there. And there's a fire pit, too, just in case—'

Glory was interrupted by a man's voice booming from outside the front door of the B & B. 'What do you mean you're no longer serving breakfast? It's only nine o'clock in the morning. Don't you know who I am?'

With Tish and Reade in tow, Glory rushed to the front porch to find Esmeralda quietly, and unsuccessfully, trying to defuse the situation. 'Sir, it's Abbingdon Green policy. When you checked in, you were told—'

'It's OK, Esmeralda. I'll handle this.' Gloria dismissed the young woman to the kitchen. 'I know precisely who you are, Mr Randall. Now if you'd please keep your voice down, you're disturbing the other guests.'

Randall continued to shout. 'You mean the other guests who were served breakfast this morning? Let them be disturbed!'

'Mr Randall, I've been both preparing and expecting to serve you breakfast with the other guests since you arrived, but this is the first time during your stay that you've ventured downstairs in the morning. Perhaps she failed to inform you, but when your assistant checked you in two days ago, I told her that breakfast was between seven o'clock and eight thirty. She said you would have no issue whatsoever with that schedule.'

'So you're putting the blame on *my* people instead of taking responsibility for a completely ridiculous and inflexible policy?'

'In all my years of business, no one has ever called my policy ridiculous. In fact, I have over one thousand glowing Tripadvisor reviews that rave about my service. Nor is my policy inflexible. If a guest can't make breakfast at the scheduled time, I'm always willing to make other arrangements. Had either you or your assistant communicated to me that you wanted a late breakfast this morning, I'd have set aside a basket of pastries and fruit salad and kept your breakfast warm until you arrived. However, I had no idea you were dining with us, or that you were sleeping in this—'

'Sleeping in?' he thundered, the vein on the left side of his blond head bulging. 'Sleeping in? Is that what you think I was doing? I'm not here on some senior citizen bus trip. I'm here on business. I don't have the luxury of sleeping in. Successful television shows don't just create themselves. But, of course, you have no idea, do you? The way you go on about your meaningless reviews as if that gives you the right to treat your guests however you like. Well, how about I tell my one *million* viewers about the terrible service in this place? Then we'll see just how much your one thousand positive reviews help your business.'

Glory, on the verge of tears, took a step backward. 'I don't have any pastries left, but I have plenty of sliced melon. For the entrée, I can cook you a mushroom omelet.'

'A mushroom omelet?' he sneered. 'Is that what your other guests had, or did they actually get to choose what they wanted to eat?'

'They had a choice between the mushroom omelet and vegan blueberry pancakes. But I used all the batter and I'm out of blueberries,' Glory explained, her voice quavering.

'Still, they had a choice,' Randall challenged.

Tish had heard enough. 'The other guests had a choice because they clearly communicated their morning plans,' she said, stepping forward from behind Glory. 'Are you able to eat an omelet?'

'What do you mean, am I able to eat an omelet?' he asked with a derisive laugh. 'I have a mouth and two hands, don't I?'

We're all fully aware that you have a mouth, Tish thought. *An extremely active one.* 'What I mean is do you have any dietary restrictions that might prevent you from eating a mushroom omelet?'

'Clearly, you don't watch my show. I don't believe in the recent spate of food allergies. Man is an omnivore. All this "I don't eat gluten, or dairy, or anything that has a face" tripe is for wimps.'

Tish refrained from rolling her eyes, as it only would have elevated tensions. However, she couldn't help but emit a tiny sigh, as the man's denunciation of legitimate health concerns and his indignation over the lack of availability of a second breakfast option – a 'wimpy' vegan breakfast option he would have rejected anyway – were infuriating. 'Sounds as if the omelet is perfect for you. And Glory makes such delicious ones.'

Glory took Tish's praise as her cue to retreat to the kitchen.

'Considering how you people tried to cheat me out of my breakfast, that omelet had better be the best I've ever tasted,' Randall threatened.

It was Reade's turn to step forward. 'With the exception of some baked goods, Ms Bishop is making you the exact same breakfast you would have ordered had you made it downstairs during serving hours. She's upholding her commitment to provide you with a full breakfast. Now it's your turn to do your part as a respectful guest and quietly take a seat.'

'Fine. I'll wait outside and catch up on emails.' A reluctant Randall trudged toward the front porch. 'But I'm putting you all on notice. Another slip-up and I'm mentioning this place on my show.'

When the television host had disappeared through the front door of the B & B, Tish and Reade retraced their steps to the kitchen.

'You didn't tell me Gunnar Randall was part of the wedding party,' Tish said to Glory, who was in the process of melting butter in a small skillet.

'Because he isn't. About a year ago, a woman by the last name of Fisher called to reserve the Turret Suite – the best room in the B and B – for her boss. She never mentioned Randall's name, only that he was a well-known personality and that he required a quiet place to stay that was close to Richmond but away from prying eyes. I told her that Abbingdon Green was very much off the beaten track and took the reservation.

'About a month or so later, the Spencers called to book the B and B for their daughter's wedding. Well, I needn't tell you that wedding parties aren't the quietest of guests, so I called Ms Fisher to apprise her of the situation with the wedding and explain that although the first part of her boss's stay might be quiet, the atmosphere at the weekend might not be quite as tranquil as originally promised. I fully expected her to cancel the reservation – at which point I could have offered the Turret Suite to the bride and groom, who are staying in another B and B down the road. To my surprise, Ms Fisher kept the booking, citing the fact that although the B and B might not be as quiet as anticipated, it was in an ideal location.'

'Yeah, it's an ideal location because Randall's probably banned from Richmond's upscale hotels,' Tish remarked.

'I should have known something was wrong with that booking.' Glory clicked her tongue. 'Even my most loyal return guests would have canceled if they knew a wedding was booked. If only I knew that Ms Fisher was working for Gunnar Randall, I'd never have taken her reservation.'

'Pardon my ignorance,' Reade spoke up, 'but who's Gunnar Randall?'

'Who's Gunnar Randall?' Tish and Glory cried in unison.

'You've never heard of him?' an incredulous Glory questioned.

'Not before today, no,' Reade confessed. 'Obviously, he's a jerk and works in television, but that's all I've gotten so far.'

'Gunnar Randall does more than work in television,' Tish explained. 'He's a celebrity chef and the host of *Taste of America*, one of the most popular shows ever to air on the Food Channel. In *Taste of America*, Randall travels to a different location each episode and critiques local restaurants and food purveyors, as well as the odd hotel or inn. His critiques are usually scathing.'

'If that's the case, why would anyone allow him to review their business?' Reade asked.

'Because a rare positive review from Gunnar Randall is a ticket to success. Viewers from every corner of the country will flock to a place with a gold-star *Taste of America* review. Even a negative review can mean an uptick in business for an eatery. It's the old "any publicity is good publicity" saw – curious people will go out and see for themselves whether they agree with Gunnar's assessment. It's sad, really, that a man like him possesses so much influence. I'm not sure what it says about the future of the restaurant industry.'

'Negative. Positive. I, for one, would like to avoid being mentioned on his show altogether.' Glory frowned and retrieved a carton of eggs from the nearby refrigerator. 'Abbingdon Green's done well enough without that sort of publicity.'

'I don't blame you. As much as I miss my café, I'm relieved that there's zero chance of it being on the show,' Tish said. 'So how can I help keep Abbingdon Green out of the limelight? What can I do to help make this omelet the best one Randall's ever tasted?'

Glory passed the carton of eggs to Tish and pointed to the large yellow mixing bowl that was drying on the drainboard by the sink.

'If you could whisk up three eggs while I go and get the mush-rooms, that would be terrific.'

Tish nodded and set to work as Glory made her way to the back door.

'Where are you going?' Tish asked.

'Out to the root cellar,' Glory replied as she gestured to one of three outbuildings on the property. 'I've found that storing the mushrooms with the potatoes keeps them fresher longer.'

TWO

After assisting Glory in producing an omelet that Gunnar reluctantly deemed 'better than average' – citing the quality of mushrooms used, rather than Glory's skills in the kitchen – Tish drove back to the café, bid an affectionate adieu to Reade, and set about preparing the wedding party's welcome feast.

Cracking six egg yolks into the base of a food processor, she added salt, pepper, Dijon mustard, and white wine vinegar, and then slowly blended the mixture with olive oil until thick and creamy. She then stirred in a squirt of lemon juice, a dollop of tomato paste, and several tablespoons of brandy to make a delicious, spiked mayonnaise for the local blue crabs she had steamed along with a sack of small, tender, red-skinned new potatoes.

After cleaning the food processor of the mayonnaise, Tish inserted the grater blade into the machine and shredded one head of green cabbage, a head of red cabbage, an onion, and three carrots. She then dressed the grated vegetables with smooth buttermilk vinaigrette, turned the finished slaw into a large serving bowl, covered it with plastic wrap, and placed it and the brandy mayonnaise in the refrigerator.

Working outside to minimize kitchen mess, Tish husked a dozen ears of corn on the front porch and then brought them inside, where she shaved their kernels from the cob and sautéed them in a hot skillet with butter, olive oil, diced red onion, lima beans, fresh thyme, and cherry tomatoes from the garden of her friend and romance writer, Opal Schaeffer. When the vegetables had just started to soften and brown, Tish placed them on an ovenproof serving dish for easy reheating and covered the dish with a tea towel.

With her cooking tasks done, Tish had just enough time to pack an overnight bag, enjoy a cold glass of water on the front-porch swing, feed Tuna an early supper, freshen her makeup, and change into her evening's uniform of black tee, black cropped trousers, and leopard print loafers, prior to loading up the van and setting off for Abbingdon Green.

Whereas the mood at the bed and breakfast that morning had been tense and anticipatory (mostly due to the presence of a certain television personality), the atmosphere in the evening was one of relaxed joviality. As Tish steered the van up the driveway, she spied two middle-aged couples happily chatting in the front-porch conversation area, and when she stepped through the back door, the sounds of laughter wafted into the kitchen from the adjacent front parlor. Even Glory appeared more at ease.

'Hello, Tish. George has all the tables and chairs arranged in the garden, and Esmeralda and Julie have already laid out the table-cloths, the napkins, and the floral arrangements. All you need to do is direct them as to how you'd like to set up the dishes, silverware, and chafing dishes.'

'That's wonderful, Glory. Thank you. I didn't expect your staff to get so much done, what with a full house of guests.'

'It was such a beautiful day that all those guests drove into Richmond for a walking tour of the city, leaving us plenty of time to clean up and prepare for this evening. Also, Mr You-Know-Who went out shortly after his breakfast and still hasn't returned. It's been blissfully quiet in his absence.'

'He's probably out filming,' Tish guessed. 'And making other people's lives miserable.'

'Ugh. I feel sorry for those people, but if they could tire him out so he's a bit mellower when he returns tonight, I'd be eternally grateful.'

'Maybe Randall's assistant will "accidentally" schedule him to tour a Xanax factory.'

With a hearty laugh, Glory reached out a freckled arm and patted Tish's shoulder. 'Honey, I should be so lucky! Now, what do you need from me? How can I help set up for tonight?'

'I don't need anything right now except to bring the food in and then meet Julie and Esmeralda in the garden.'

'Excellent. The bride's parents are on the front porch. Once you load in, I'll introduce you to them and then you can get to work.'

And work Tish did. As the succotash finished cooking in a low oven, she set the potatoes to warm over a pot of hot water while she directed Esmeralda and Julie to bundle the guest utensils and napkins and secure them with lengths of raffia to which had been secured leather bookmarks bearing the bride and groom's first initials.

With one task delegated, Tish set about arranging the buffet table. Unlike her plans for the wedding feast, which featured the use of fine crystal, bone china, the B & B's antique silverware, and an exquisitely decorated vanilla chiffon wedding cake, the vibe for the welcome dinner was elegant but informal. Using white ceramic baking dishes she had brought from the café, she inverted them, open side down on the tablecloth, to form pedestals of varying heights upon which she would rest the platters of food in order to create depth and visual interest.

Opting to forgo floral arrangements on the buffet table for fear it might distract from the food, Tish grabbed one pink-and-green-tinged Limelight hydrangea from each of the two guest-table centerpieces and scattered their petals around the pedestals and directly on to the crisp white tablecloth, saving their verdant leaves to adorn the food platters themselves. She then reached into the pocket of her apron for the finishing touch – a small plastic bag of literary confetti she'd created by shredding the black-and-white pages of an old *Readers Digest* magazine. Sprinkling the lettered fragments atop the blossom-strewn buffet table, she then scattered them on the guest tables, offsetting the silver bowls of hydrangeas centered upon them.

Stepping back to survey the scene, she smiled at her handiwork. The heirloom hydrangeas spoke of summers past, while their dusty pink trim blended with the warm, autumnal color scheme provided by the blooming tansies, asters, lilies, and coreopsis of the surrounding garden. Glory's small wrought-iron fire pit and the clusters of silver and glass lanterns her staff had arranged around the seating area would keep the romantic atmosphere glowing far into the evening. And the literary confetti and bookmarks tastefully brought to life the theme of the weekend – a theme that would be rounded out with the inclusion of a book wherein guests were invited to pen their wishes for the bride and groom and where the happy couple themselves could include their favorite passages and quotes about love and marriage.

Satisfied with the décor, Tish set off for the kitchen where she instructed her helpers to load the evening's beverage offerings into ice-filled coolers, while she poured her brandy mayonnaise into an elegant silver and mother-of-pearl dish and spooned the marinated shrimp into a deep white oval dish before placing the steamed blue crabs on to a large, rectangular platter filled with chipped ice. She then set to retrieving the succotash from the oven and mixing her potatoes with melted butter and fresh chopped dill before turning them both on to white serving vessels and placing everything on the buffet table.

As the stars of the menu, the platter of crabs was given the buffet table's highest pedestal and the shrimp the second highest. The vibrantly colored succotash rested upon a heatproof trivet at table level and the potatoes were placed into a chafing rack beneath which a heating element was ignited to prevent the butter from solidifying.

As guests trickled into the garden from the front porch where they'd convened for a champagne toast, Tish skedaddled back into the kitchen and readied the remaining crab and shrimp for platter replenishment – a replenishment that was required far more quickly than anticipated for a crowd who'd already enjoyed one of Glory's three-course breakfasts and lunch at a Richmond soul-food restaurant.

Less than an hour later, Tish helped Esmeralda and Julie put away the leftover food and serve the greengage plum ice cream and Celestine's pecan wedding cookies. She also offered coffee and tea, which were consumed by the older members of the party. The bride and groom and their contemporaries, however, made it clear that the party was just getting started.

'Why don't you head on home, Tish?' Glory suggested as the guests consumed the ice cream. 'The girls and I can take it from here.'

'Are you sure?' Tish checked.

'Absolutely. No use in you waiting around for those serving dishes to run through the dishwasher when you'll be back here the day after tomorrow. Besides,' Glory added with a grin, 'we've been through these parties before. There's going to be very little eating or sleeping going on tonight.'

Esmeralda chimed in, 'And there will be lots of glasses to wash tomorrow.'

'OK.' Tish capitulated. 'I'll check in with you tomorrow to make sure you ladies survived.'

'Oh, we'll survive,' Glory assured her as she gave Tish a farewell hug. 'Though we might be licking our wounds a little.'

With a goodbye and thanks to Esmeralda and Julie, Tish left the B & B through the back kitchen door and climbed into her van. It was a little past seven thirty. *Not too late*, Tish thought as she recalled the time estimate she'd given Jules.

Pulling the van from its spot behind the privacy hedge, she drove down the driveway, her mind focused on getting to Jules's apartment – and her dinner. She'd been so busy all day that she hadn't stopped to eat, and she hadn't realized until now just how hungry she was.

Tish's stomach rumbled noisily. Thankfully, she would be at Jules's apartment in approximately five to seven minutes. *Just a few minutes*, she thought with a smile. *Just a few minutes until air conditioning, good food, a glass of wine, crisp pajamas, and one of those cleansing avocado face masks Jules always—*

As Tish daydreamed about her evening plans, she was surprised by a small sports car speeding up the driveway and heading directly toward her van. After blasting her horn in warning, she swerved sharply to the right and slammed on the brakes, bringing the van to an abrupt halt on a section of adjacent lawn.

She watched as the sports car whooshed past her, its driver gesticulating wildly.

It was Gunnar Randall.

THREE

'I can't believe Gunnar Randall is that mean in real life, too,' Jules exclaimed, the green of his moisturizing avocado and oatmeal face mask making his blue eyes appear even brighter than usual. 'I thought it was just an act to boost ratings. You know, like Simon Cowell.'

'Well, if it is an act, someone ought to tell him to try breaking character when he's off set.' Tish, wearing a similar mask, placed her empty plate on the coffee table and picked up her glass of chilled chardonnay. 'The man's an absolute menace.'

'Did you tell Glory that he ran you off the road?'

'No,' she answered after taking a sip of wine. 'I called her from my cell to warn her that he was coming in hot, so to speak, but I didn't go into detail. I figured she had enough on her plate with the wedding party.'

Jules, having finished his dinner seconds prior to Tish, picked up his own glass of wine. 'Poor Glory, and, oh, that poor bride! All that dreaming and planning only to have some self-absorbed, attention-seeking TV host show up at your wedding. That has to be worse than the drunk uncle.'

'Or the mother-in-law who wears black.'

Jules nearly spat the wine out of his mouth. 'Oh my God, I almost forgot about that! Your ex-mother-in-law totally looked like Morticia Addams – if Morticia had been outfitted by Sears.'

'Come to think of it, she and my ex-father-in-law did purchase a new dishwasher right around the same time she bought that dress,' Tish said with a laugh.

'I knew it! Haha . . . Oh, Tish, I'm so glad you came by tonight. I've missed our little get-togethers.'

'I have, too.' She pulled her feet up on to the sofa and tucked them beneath her. 'Things have been so chaotic that I haven't had much time.'

'I understand, but not all of that chaos has been bad,' Jules said with a raised eyebrow.

'No, it hasn't all been bad. In fact, some of it's been quite lovely. And that, Jules,' she said as she raised her glass to him, 'is all I have to say on the matter.'

'Oh, come on, Tish,' he urged. 'You're not going to dish even a little on your romance?'

'Nope. How about you, Jules? What's going on with you?'

'Me? Oh, hectic – like you – but good. The station has been giving me more human-interest stories to cover when I'm not doing the weekend weather, which is nice. My mama is *finally* redecorating her downstairs powder room. Remember the one near the kitchen, with the silver foil wallpaper from before I was born? Yeah, she's going for warm oak cabinets and gold taps – not exactly modern, but at least she's moved from the seventies to the nineties. So now when I visit, I'll be tinkling in a thirty-year-old time capsule instead of a fifty-year-old one. Oh, I should be getting the proofs of my Christmas cards next week. I know it's early, but I can't wait to see the photos of Biscuit in his little plaid vest and bow tie.'

'I look forward to seeing them, too, as well as the photos of your mom's bathroom reno. But what about *you*?' Tish prodded.

'What do you mean?'

'I mean, when I first moved to Hobson Glen, you were social-izing, dating, and nagging me to put my personal life first and go out and meet people. Now it seems as if you're the one who's putting your career before your social life.'

Jules pursed his lips together. 'You're right. I have become more of a homebody lately. But it has nothing to do with my career. Ever since I got Biscuit, I just feel bad going out and leaving him alone.'

Tish was unconvinced. 'That's it? That's the only reason?'

'You always could read me like a book, couldn't you?' He placed his wine glass back on to the coffee table. 'OK, I suppose I have been focusing more on my career. I think it's because I can control what happens there. If I try harder and work harder, I eventually see progress, whereas in my personal life, I try and . . . well, I've pretty much given up on ever meeting the right man.'

'You're not going to meet him by sitting around here. Isn't that what you told me? "A white knight isn't going ride down the middle of Hobson Glen's Main Street, Tish."'

'I did say that,' Jules acknowledged. 'But your white knight did kinda ride down the middle of Main Street, didn't he?'

'Maybe, but I wouldn't have known Clemson was my white knight if I hadn't gotten out in the world and seen, through my relationship with Schuyler, what I really wanted in a partner.'

'And solved a murder. You only met Clemson because you solved Binnie Broderick's murder. However, you probably still would have met him when he came for breakfast at the café.'

'OK, so maybe my white knight *did* ride down the middle of Main Street,' she allowed. 'The point is I was out and about and doing things when I met him. And although I wasn't looking for him, I wasn't at home watching Regency romances on the BBC, wondering where he was, either. Not that there's anything wrong with watching Regency romances – heck, I'll watch one with you tonight – but I think you understand what I'm saying.'

'I do, but where am I supposed to go? What am I supposed to do? I am far too old for the club scene. And I did actually check out some online dating sites, but they just didn't seem right for me. I'm not interested in hooking up – I want a long-lasting relationship. I want to get married someday and maybe even adopt a child before I'm too old.'

'I didn't know you wanted children.'

'I didn't, either. I mean, I've always loved children, but I never thought – as a gay man – that parenthood could ever be on the cards for me. But with the changes to adoption laws these past few years and after seeing other LGBTQ parents doing a great job out there, I've decided it's something I might like to pursue.'

Tish reached for Jules's hand. 'You'd be a terrific dad.'

'Aw, thanks.' He blushed as he took her fingers in his. 'I know I have the heart, but I sometimes wonder about my organizational skills.'

'I'm no expert, of course, but I'm pretty sure if you have the heart, the rest will follow. You do realize, however, that if you have sufficient income, you needn't wait for a partner to adopt a child.'

'Oh, I'm aware. Five years from now, if I still haven't met someone, maybe I'll pursue being a single parent, but for now I'd like to have it all: spouse, house, job, child, and a dog.'

'The good news is you're two-fifths of the way there.'

'True, but it's the last three that are the toughest.'

Tish pulled her hand from Jules's and placed it on his shoulder. 'Let's see if we can't help you on your way. You know that Clemson plays in a band in his spare time, don't you?'

'Yes, I remember thinking how weird it is to have a cop playing at a club instead of raiding it.'

'Well, he doesn't really play clubs – more like pubs and restaurants who add live music to their roster. He's playing at Justine's next weekend, and I'm going to go watch him. Why don't you join me? I can't guarantee you'll meet someone, but it's a pretty diverse crowd. Plus, it's fun.'

'That does sound like fun,' Jules agreed. 'And the following weekend is my annual Labor Day barbecue.'

'That's right. What do you want me to bring?' Tish asked, even though Jules always requested the same thing.

'Oh, I couldn't ask you to bring anything. Not this year, with your café closing and you needing to set up shop elsewhere.'

'I may not have a café, but I should still have access to a kitchen, even if it's yours or Celestine's.'

'Or Clemson Reade's,' Jules slyly suggested, prompting Tish to wrinkle her nose. 'Sorry, not sorry. Look, I don't want to impose on you to bring a dish. Not with what you're dealing with right now. So, if you need to back out at the last minute, I'll understand.'

Tish nodded. Every year, no matter what was happening in Tish's life, Jules also went through the same spiel. *I hate to be boring, but . . .*

'I hate to be boring and predictable, but it's simply not Labor Day without a giant pot of your homemade baked beans.'

Jules's request for Labor Day baked beans was one of the few things about him that was predictable. 'Of course. To be honest, I may or may not have already purchased a few bags of pintos.'

'You probably bought them August first, didn't you?' he said with a chuckle. 'This is exciting, Tish! After weeks at home, I'm attending two social events on two consecutive weekends. I'm going to need to plan my outfits. Oh, that reminds me.'

Jules took a swig of wine, wandered to the closed door of the spare bedroom and opened it.

'Reminds you of what?' she asked.

'That I need to look my best!' He emerged from the spare bedroom with a small box in his hand.

'You're already wearing an exfoliating and moisturizing mask. What else could you possibly need to do?'

'Just a little hair tonic to keep the locks looking luscious,' Jules answered before disappearing into the bathroom.

Hair tonic? Since when did Jules use hair tonic? Tish wondered, but she'd long since learned that Jules's beauty regimen was aggressive, comprehensive, and ever-evolving. Rather than question his behavior, she took the remote from the coffee table and checked the television for a film they could watch while their various spa treatments worked their so-called magic.

Jules emerged from the bathroom five minutes later, just as Tish had decided to give *The Last Letter from Your Lover* a whirl. A thick, inky substance had been combed through his normally chestnut hair – a substance that now dripped from his sideburns and was about to comingle with his avocado hair mask.

'Jules,' she started, 'your, um, hair tonic is—'

Tish's warning was interrupted by the sound of a cat screech followed by a loud bark.

Jules gasped. 'Oh no! I must have forgotten to shut the guest-bedroom door all the way. Biscuit!'

'Tuna!' Tish shouted as she leaped from the sofa and ran to the bedroom, stumbling over Jules, who was also rushing to corral his pet.

'Biscuit,' he cried as he and Tish squeezed their bodies through the guest-bedroom door at the same time. 'Biscuit, leave the kitty alone!'

The long-haired black-and-white cat was backed into a corner, his ears back and hackles raised. As a curious, yapping Biscuit poked his nose toward Tuna and sniffed, the feline hissed.

'Tuna! Don't you touch that doggie,' Tish warned. 'He's just trying to make friends.'

Tuna paid no mind to his owner's admonitions and instead gave Biscuit's nose a claw-laden swat before running between Tish and Jules's legs and out of the bedroom door.

'Biscuit!' Jules lunged forward to grab the fluffy white Bichon Frisé, but the dog bolted off after Tuna, leaving his master to fall, face forward on to the carpet.

'Careful, Jules,' Tish cautioned before chasing after the two pets. 'You'll get hair dye on the rug.'

'It's hair tonic,' he shouted after her. 'Hair tonic!'

Tish didn't respond. She was too busy chasing Biscuit who, in turn, was chasing Tuna into the kitchen area of the open-concept living space. 'Biscuit! Tuna! Stop!' she shouted as they ran laps around the center island, Biscuit barking and nipping at Tuna's heels.

Jules suddenly appeared in the kitchen and, with a deft motion, bent down and scooped the barking dog into his arms just as Tuna hopped on to the kitchen counter and then jumped to the top of the refrigerator.

'Is Biscuit OK?' Tish asked.

'Yes, he has a scratch on his nose, but otherwise he's fine.'

'Are you sure? I'll happily pay the vet bill if you think he needs to be examined.'

As if to prove his fitness, Biscuit tilted his head back and licked the avocado facemask from Jules's chin. 'Um, yeah, I don't think that'll be necessary. I'll just clean his nose and get his leash so he doesn't run off again.'

'And I'll get Tuna down and put him back in the bedroom where he belongs. Do you have a stepladder, Jules?'

'I do, but why don't you just let Tuna be for now? He obviously reacted the way he did because he felt trapped. Let him relax and calm down in a safe spot while you and I camp out on the sofa with Biscuit.'

'He did seem terrified, didn't he?' Tish agreed. 'I just don't want him slinking off where we can't find him.'

Jules pointed to Biscuit. 'With Mr Super-Sniffer here to ferret him out? Doubtful.'

'You're right. Tuna could probably use some time to chill.'

'He's not the only one. Come on.' Jules turned on one heel and headed toward the living-room sofa.

'Wait. You'd better wipe your forehead and sideburns,' she instructed, ripping a sheet of paper towel from the roll on the counter and handing it to him. 'Your hair dye is dripping into your mask.'

'For the last time, Tish, it's hair tonic. Hair ton—'

Just then, Tuna opened his mouth wide and began to caterwaul.

'What's the matter with him?' Jules asked.

'I don't know, but considering he was chased around the apartment by a dog and is once again cornered, I'm going to say stress.'

'Then let's back away and head to the sofa,' he suggested as he mopped his hairline with the paper towel in his right hand and held Biscuit firmly with his left. As they stepped away, Biscuit replied to Tuna's plaintiff cry with an equally mournful yowl.

'Shh! Biscuit, quiet.'

As Jules attempted to silence Biscuit, Tish stepped forward and stroked Tuna's head. 'Hush, now. You're OK. It's OK.'

Neither of their efforts had the desired impact. Rather, the pair of animals grew louder and more vociferous.

'This isn't working, Jules. I'm going to grab my things and take Tuna back to the café.'

'Oh no, don't go. Let's give them some time to quiet down and maybe we can salvage the evening,' Jules insisted.

There was a series of knocks on the floorboards from the apartment above, no doubt in response to the noise.

The audible complaint changed Jules's mind. 'On second thought, you're right. You should probably go. I'll get your overnight bag and the cat carrier.'

'You think I'm getting this cat in the carrier?' she challenged.

'Right. Nix the carrier. I'll get your bag and your purse.'

After placing a restless Tuna in the passenger seat of her van and quickly slamming the door so he couldn't escape, Tish tossed her bag and purse into the cargo area and set off, avocado mask still in place, for the café. Tuna burrowed his way beneath the passenger's seat and meowed for the duration of the short journey.

'Shh . . .' She tried to soothe the traumatized cat. 'We're almost there. We're almost—'

For some reason, Tish couldn't bring herself to say the word 'home.' Probably because it really wasn't home any longer. Her clothes, her bed, and her personal kitchen gear were still there, but the heart of the white clapboard building had stopped beating the moment the café closed its doors.

Tish pulled into the empty café parking lot with a pang of melancholy. The Cookin' the Books sign had been removed from the building's facade, the window curtains stripped and packed away, the pendant lighting dismantled, and the tables, chairs, and counter stools removed and sold to a restaurant supplier. All that was left were her few belongings and the food and equipment needed for Sunday's wedding feast.

When the café was in full swing and the upstairs apartment occupied by Mary Jo and her children, Tish would have loved to have enjoyed a solo evening in her room, watching cooking shows in bed. But now, after spending the past twenty-four hours at Clemson's cozy Cape Cod, Glory Bishop's homespun inn, and Jules's well-appointed apartment, returning to her tiny, windowless bedroom at the back of an empty fluorescent-lit restaurant did feel, as Jules had once described her living arrangement, like returning to a prison cell.

Forgetting about her avocado facemask, Tish took her phone from her handbag and sent a simple text: *Would you mind some company?*

Within seconds, she received a reply: *I'd love it.*

FOUR

Clemson was waiting on the brick front porch of the tidy whitewashed house as Tish pulled her van to a stop at the front curb.

'Hey, what happened to you?' he asked, taking note of her still-green face.

Tish emerged from the driver's seat and described the debacle at Jules's apartment.

'Hair tonic?' Clemson questioned. 'Where'd he buy it? At the old medicine show?'

'Either that or somewhere in 1957,' she said with a laugh. 'Thanks for letting me come here tonight. I'd actually gone back to the café, but I just couldn't stomach it. I'm not sure why, but I couldn't.'

Clemson slid a hand around her shoulders and pulled her close. 'No need to thank me. I love having you here. I'd have you here all the time if I could.'

Full of love and forgetting her avocado mask, Tish leaned in and gave him a kiss.

He licked his lips afterward. 'Tasty, but could use a little more garlic. And maybe a couple of chips.'

She fake-punched him, but she wasn't at all annoyed by his comment. On the contrary, his light-hearted support was precisely what she needed.

'So, where's Tuna?' he asked.

'Under the passenger seat. I brought his food, spare dishes, and bed from the café, but I don't think he'll be coming out anytime soon.'

'Grab your overnight bag from the back and go inside and get cleaned up. In the meantime, I'll get Tuna settled.'

'Oh, but he's really wedged in there, Clemson.'

'I know. That's what they do when they get loose in a moving car. I've gotten cats out of that spot before.'

Tish was notoriously bad at admitting when she needed help,

but she was at a loss as to how to lure Tuna from the car without getting clawed to pieces. She also trusted Clemson implicitly.

'All right,' she capitulated before going into the house to deposit her bag in the master bedroom, wash her face in the adjoining bath, and get settled for the evening. When she emerged from the bathroom a few minutes later, she followed the sound of soft music downstairs and to the rear deck, where Clemson sat near a small fire pit drinking a beer, his own long-haired tuxedo cat, Marlowe, curled at his feet.

Tish took a seat beside him on the vintage metal porch glider.

'Here.' He passed her a perfectly chilled glass of New Zealand Sauvignon Blanc. 'I thought you might need that.'

'Thanks. I only had a few sips of the wine Jules bought before all hell broke loose. Speaking of which, where's Tuna?'

'He's in my office with some fresh water, kibble, and his bed. I left the door slightly ajar so he can explore if he wants. The last thing I wanted was for him to feel trapped again.'

'The back door is open. What if he comes out here? What about Marlowe?' She reached down to pet the cat who'd migrated from Clemson's feet to hers.

'This guy? He might be double Tuna's size, but he's a lover, not a fighter.'

As if on cue, Tuna wandered out the back door of the bungalow and sniffed his way, tentatively, across the deck, investigating everything he encountered – plants, barbecue grill, chairs, and glider. Coming upon Marlowe, his ears went flat back against his head.

Tish knelt beside him and stroked him. 'It's OK, Tuna.'

Clemson, meanwhile, perched beside Marlowe. 'Easy, big fella. Don't go trying to make friends too fast. Let him check you out first.'

Marlowe heeded Clemson's words, for he remained serenely coiled by Tish's feet while Tuna poked an inquisitive pink nose in his direction and then slowly proceeded to groom the fur on Marlowe's head.

'That's a good Tuna,' Tish exclaimed. 'That's a good boy.'

'Atta boy, Marlowe.' Clemson cheered on his gentle giant of a cat as he and Tish slowly returned to their seats.

They sat in silence and watched as the two felines became

acquainted and then sauntered off together across the lawn to explore the garden in the dwindling twilight. 'That shouldn't happen so quickly, should it?'

He shook his head. 'Nope. I thought for certain we'd have to put Tuna back in the office, which we'll do before we go to bed. I don't want them alone together unless we're around. For now, let's see what happens.'

Tish nestled back into Clemson's arm and sighed in contentment. The fenced-in yard, with its collection of perennial plants, birch, willow, and Japanese maple trees, looked positively magical in the glow of the fire pit. And beneath the sound of music coming from inside the nearby living room, she could detect the chirps of crickets, the soft rustle of leaves in the breeze, and the faint laughter of children making the most of the last minutes of daylight on a late-summer Friday night.

'It's so peaceful,' she remarked.

'I've tried to make this house my haven – someplace to relax and shut out the world for a while.'

Tish glanced at Clemson and then her surroundings. The atmosphere was more than just comforting and serene. It felt like home. 'What do you think of the possibility of having a new roommate?'

'I think I already have one.' Clemson gestured to Tuna, who munched on a few tall blades of grass while Marlowe dozed in a patch of clover a few short feet away.

'All right, then, how about two new roommates? One furry and the other . . . not.'

Clemson turned to her, his gray eyes dancing with excitement. 'Really?'

She nodded. 'Really. I've spent these past few weeks clinging to the café, but that's all in the past. You – you're my future.'

'And you're mine.' He squeezed her tightly and kissed her hair. 'You know what else is in your future? A new café.'

'I hope so.' She sighed.

'I know so. We'll find a way to make it work.' He kissed her again. 'Together.'

After a sweet evening beneath the stars, Tish and Reade turned in for the night with plans to sleep late and then travel to nearby

Staunton for a celebratory breakfast before Tish returned to the café to prep for Sunday's wedding.

They were, therefore, both shocked and dismayed when not one but both of their phones awoke them at seven forty-five in the morning. After rolling over and exchanging puzzled glances, they each answered their respective calls and, minutes later, disconnected from them within seconds of each other.

'Your office?' Tish guessed.

'Yeah, there's been a death at Abbingdon Green. The coroner has some questions. Was that Glory Bishop on the phone with you?'

'Yep,' she confirmed as she rolled back the covers and stepped out of bed.

'She must be beside herself.'

'She is. The death your coroner is questioning is that of Gunnar Randall.'

FIVE

'So much for breakfast,' Reade lamented as he pulled his black SUV to a halt along the lower driveway to Abbingdon Green. The rear parking area and section of driveway closest to the house were filled with emergency vehicles.

'And coffee,' Tish added. 'But we need to be here. This is what we do.'

'It is, but I still owe you.'

'Do you? Well, luckily for you, you know where I live.'

They leaned over the center console and kissed each other before disembarking from the vehicle and walking up the driveway to the B & B's back door.

Twenty-four-year-old Officer James Clayton met them in the kitchen. He was dressed in a Saturday-morning-casual ensemble of jeans and checked chambray shirt and, from his unshaven countenance and uncombed hair, it was clear that, although assigned to work the weekend, he hadn't expected to be called away from the office. 'Morning, sir. Morning, Tish. The deceased is fifty-two-year-old Gunnar Randall. Housekeeper went up to his room this morning to give him a wake-up call. When he didn't respond, she used her key to access his room. When she entered, he was in the midst of convulsions. She called nine-one-one, but he was dead by the time paramedics arrived.'

'Convulsions?' Reade questioned. 'Was Randall epileptic?'

'Not according to his assistant. We called her, by the way. She's on her way here. The coroner felt we should ask about Randall's medical history as well as what he did yesterday.'

'Then he doesn't believe Randall died of a heart attack or stroke,' Reade surmised.

'He . . . has questions, sir. It's probably best if he explains to you why,' Clayton replied. 'He's upstairs in Randall's room. In the meantime, I've gathered the other guests in the dining room. We're taking their statements right now.'

'Great job, Clayton. Thanks.' Reade followed Tish as she made her way out of the kitchen and into the main hall, and stopped at the foot of the stairs.

'Mind if I join you?' she asked.

'I was hoping you would. After all, you are a paid consultant to the sheriff's office.'

'Yes, but this isn't a case.'

'Not yet, no, but I've worked with our forensic pathologist, Doctor Andres, several times through the years. If he has questions, you can bet by the end of the day we all will.'

After a quick check-in with Glory, who was in the dining room trying to calm her guests while police asked questions, Tish went upstairs and met Reade and Dr Andres in Randall's bedroom.

Gunnar Randall's body, clad only in a pair of boxer shorts, lay facedown on the carpet runner, his arms sprawled in front of him, and his head sideways, as if he had rolled out of bed and on to the floor.

'This is how the body was positioned when the paramedics arrived,' Dr Andres explained as he leaned down and rolled Randall on to his back. His position had already been photographed and marked. 'I moved him to examine him for signs of wounds or other bruising – there were none. While examining him in this position, I noticed a yellowing of the eyeballs and abdominal swelling, which are both indicative of acute liver failure. Then I noticed edema in the calves, ankles, and feet' – he pointed to the areas in question – 'which, combined with seizures, is in line with acute kidney failure.'

'Multiple organ failure?' Reade questioned. 'Was the victim ill?'

'Not that his assistant was aware of,' Dr Andres replied. 'Nor did your officers find medication or any paperwork supporting the idea that he was suffering from cancer or an autoimmune disease that would have increased his risk of liver and kidney failure. Likewise, although there is a faint smell of alcohol on his clothes from last night, there's no sign of alcohol in the room – be it empty bottles, a flask, or traces of it in a glass. Of course, if the man had been diagnosed with cirrhosis of the liver, he might have given up heavy drinking, but, again, he would have been prescribed diuretics and there aren't any in this room or in his vehicle. No, if Randall was healthy, the liver failure must have been caused by something he ingested – either an overdose of acetaminophen, herbal supplements such as kava or ephedra, or prescription drugs. However, as I said previously, your officers found no evidence of any of those things in the room or in Randall's car. Nor did they find the packaging from acetaminophen or the herbal supplements I mentioned. They did, however, find several over-the-counter anti-diarrheal and anti-nausea medications in the bathroom. When they might have been used, I don't know, but nausea can be a symptom of both liver and kidney failure. Diarrhea, on the other hand, is not.'

'I'll have my team look for a receipt. I'll also check Randall's bank and credit card statements to see when they might have been purchased,' Reade stated. 'The assistant is on her way to the B and B. I'll talk to her and see if Randall had any next of kin who might know more about his medical history, and I'll try to get a timeline of Randall's overall health this past week and when it may have deteriorated.'

'What we're looking for are symptoms of malaise, confusion or disorientation, drowsiness, abdominal pain, or a general sense of feeling unwell. If we can pinpoint when those started, we might be able to form a better picture of what may have happened,' Dr Andres explained. 'Now, if your people are done with the body, I'll take it to the lab and start some samples.'

Reade released Randall's body to Dr Andres and his medical staff, and walked with Tish into the upstairs hallway.

'You were right about having questions,' Tish remarked.

'Is your head ready to explode? Because Doctor Andres can have that effect on people.'

'It's not just Doctor Andres. I actually saw Randall last night. He was returning to the B and B just as I was leaving after the welcome dinner. In fact, I had to drive on to the lawn to avoid hitting him.'

'He nearly crashed into you?' Reade questioned.

'Yes, what with the Biscuit and Tuna drama, I forgot to tell you,' she explained.

'Hmm, I wonder if he drove directly at you on purpose or if he was experiencing the confusion and disorientation Doctor Andres described.'

'Either one is possible. He was gesturing frantically at me, almost as if the incident was my fault, but after seeing how he reacted to breakfast, that doesn't really go against character, does it? I'm going to talk to Glory and see what transpired the remainder of the evening. I know she's probably already given a statement to your team, but that was before we knew to ask about Randall's health and behavior. Also, talking to a friend rather than a police officer might help her remember something she may have missed.'

'I think that's an excellent idea. While you do that, I'll track down the purchase of the over-the-counter meds and talk to Randall's assistant.'

'How was Gunnar Randall last night? He was drunk – that's how he was,' Glory Bishop said as she and Tish made coffee for the police and the B & B's guests. 'He came back here just after seven thirty and crashed the welcome party.'

Tish frowned. Although nearly hitting her car head-on could have been a by-product of illness, crashing a party of wedding guests didn't sound like the behavior of a sick man. 'Are you sure he was drunk?'

'Absolutely. When I greeted him on the front porch, I noticed his breath had a sickeningly sweet, slightly musty odor to it. Like he'd been drinking port wine or cordials, or something like that.'

'Did he say anything to you?'

'Not really. I offered to serve him tea in the drawing room or up in his room. He pushed past me and said he wanted to sit outside in the fresh air. I reminded him that there was a private function going on at the time, but he wouldn't hear of it. He said he needed the fresh air and no one would stop him from getting it.'

'What happened then?'

'He went out to the garden and sat with the wedding party, chatted, drank, made a pass at the bride's mother, and generally behaved like an ass. When I heard he'd made a pass at Mrs Spencer, that's when I got involved. I was about to tell him that if he didn't go to his room, I'd call the police, but when I went out to the garden to confront him, he'd fallen asleep in his chair. He seemed fine. He was breathing regularly and sleeping soundly – so soundly I couldn't wake him. The drink most likely,' she whispered. 'So I called George, who lives nearby, and he and his son came by and helped him up to bed. That was the last I saw of him.'

'And did George and his son undress Mr Randall?'

'No. No, they told me they had a tough enough time getting him up the stairs. Said he was dead weight.' Glory drew her hand to her mouth 'Oh! I didn't mean he was dead. I–I mean he was so heavy they put him to bed fully dressed.'

'I understood what you meant,' Tish said soothingly. 'If I'm not mistaken, Gunnar Randall checked in on Wednesday, didn't he?'

'Yes. His assistant, Ms Fisher, arrived around noon that day to get Mr Randall settled in. Check-in, however, isn't until three – I like to give the girls and myself ample time to get the rooms and the rest of the B and B in order after guests check out,' Glory said, aside, 'so I took care of the paperwork and went over the rules with Ms Fisher and stored Mr Randall's luggage in the closet beneath the stairs until his room was ready. Mr Randall himself arrived in the evening.'

'Approximately what time?'

'Same as yesterday. Around seven thirty or so.'

'And how was he?'

'Couldn't say. He went straight up to his room without as much as a hello. Didn't come down for the tea and cookies I put out as guests return from dinner – you know I do that as a "perk," but it also buys me time to do the turndown service.'

'So Randall didn't even wait for turndown service,' Tish surmised.

'No. We knocked on his door to offer it, but he refused. Brusquely, of course!' Glory took one of the coffee carafes from its burner and poured a portion of its contents into two mugs – one for herself and the other for Tish.

Tish accepted the beverage with hearty thanks.

'You're welcome. As a flight attendant friend of mine used to say, "You can't help others with their oxygen masks unless you put yours on first."'

'So, going back to Randall. You didn't see him at all after he went to his room on Wednesday evening?' Tish prompted after she'd added some milk to her coffee and taken a sip.

'That's right. Ms Fisher saw him, though. She stopped by a little after eight. She was coming up the stairs just as I was about to head down after finishing turndown. She was carrying a white paper bag. Something for Mr Randall, I suppose, since she left a few moments later without it.'

'What time did you see Randall the next day?'

'Not until the afternoon. Maybe two, two thirty. He didn't come out of his room all morning, and neither the girls nor I heard him on the phone or walking around while we were cleaning the rooms below his. We assumed he'd been traveling and decided to sleep in, but you heard how he exploded yesterday morning when I suggested that's what he did.'

If Randall thought being vegan, dairy-free, or gluten-free was a sign of weakness, Tish could only imagine the low opinion the man might have held of those who succumbed to illness – especially something as small as a stomach bug. 'And what time did he get back to the B and B on Thursday?'

'Late. The headlights of his car shone through my bedroom window at eleven as he pulled into the lot. Woke me up from a deep sleep.'

'So you didn't actually see or talk to Randall.'

'Oh, I saw him. I got up and looked out the window to make sure it was him. He was whistling as he walked around to the front porch and let himself inside. There's a combination lock on the door for guests who get back after I'm in bed. Because Randall didn't check himself in, I was afraid he might not have known the combination, but he got in with no trouble.'

'And the next time you saw him was the following morning – yesterday – when he complained about breakfast?'

'That's right. It's a good thing you were here, Tish. I don't know what I would have done if I'd been on my own. He really rattled me with his threats.'

'Anyone would have been rattled, Glory. This place is not just your livelihood – it's your home, your family's legacy.'

Glory placed her mug on the counter with a trembling hand. 'I–I can't believe this is happening. I've had guests who needed to be hospitalized during their stay, but never – never did anyone . . . Oh! I've only just realized. What's going to happen to this place once word gets out? What's going to happen when people find out Gunnar Randall died here?'

'Your business will be fine, Glory,' Tish assured as she rested a hand on the innkeeper's shoulder. 'As someone whose first catering job was spoiled by murder, I can assure you that you'll be fine.'

'I almost forgot that you started your business "under fire,"
didn't you?' Glory flashed a wan smile. 'You poor thing. Why do
people have to be the way they are? Why do they have to try to
destroy other people's lives? As the daughter of a Baptist minister,
I was taught to be mournful for the passing of one of God's children, but I'm not. I'm not mournful at all. Gunnar Randall was a
wicked man and he got exactly what wicked men deserve.'

While Glory went to her quarters to rest and Tish worked with
Julie to rustle up a buffet breakfast for the guests, Reade met
with Shae Fisher at one of the many bistro tables that lined
Abbingdon Green's front porch.

Reade thanked Randall's assistant for her cooperation. 'Ms
Fisher, it's good of you to come here and speak with us.'

'It seemed like the right thing to do. Gunnar had no one else,
really,' Shae explained, tucking a few wayward purple strands of
her shaggy pixie cut hair behind a double-pierced ear.

'No next of kin?' Reade confirmed.

'He never mentioned anyone. He had a couple of friends he'd
hang out with at holiday time, but otherwise I'm pretty sure he
was alone.' She leaned forward in her chair. 'If you've seen the
show, you know my boss wasn't exactly a "people person."'

'I haven't seen the show, actually, but I did meet your boss
yesterday morning. I thought, perhaps, he was putting on an act
to drive up ratings.'

Shae moved her head from side to side. 'The Gunnar Randall
you met yesterday is the same Gunnar Randall audiences tune in
to watch each week. It's the same Gunnar Randall the crew and
I interact with on a regular basis. It's the only Gunnar Randall
we've ever known. If a gentler incarnation of the man ever existed
in this universe, I've yet to find anyone who's met him.'

'It must have been difficult, working as a personal assistant to
someone like him,' Reade asserted.

'Working for Gunnar was a great way for someone straight out
of college to establish themselves in the industry,' Shae replied,
deftly evading the question. 'If you could survive two years with
him, you were prepared for whatever any Hollywood diva could
throw at you.'

'And how long have you worked for Mr Randall?'

'Two and a half years.'

'You must have known him pretty well.'

'I don't think even Gunnar knew himself well,' she said with a sniff.

'But you did know his daily habits, routines, and such.'

'I did,' Shae confirmed.

'Would you say Mr Randall was in good health?' Reade asked.

She pulled a face. 'He had no health issues that I was aware of and he wasn't on any medication, but I wouldn't say he lived a healthy lifestyle. He never exercised. He ate just about everything – which I guess comes with the territory when you're a chef with a show like his – but he also had a thing for regional fast food. He ate pretty normally when we were back in California, but when we'd hit the road to shoot, he'd eat fast food every day for lunch or dinner. On the West Coast, it was In-N-Out. Southwest was Whataburger. Northeast was Dunkin Donuts and Legal Sea Foods. And here in Virginia, it's been Hardee's.'

'And how was Mr Randall's health this past week?'

She shrugged. 'Fine.'

'Really? We found a bunch of over-the-counter stomach relief remedies in his room,' Reade challenged.

'Oh, yeah,' she said as if she suddenly remembered. 'He wasn't feeling too great on Wednesday afternoon – vomiting, diarrhea, stomach cramps. I'd already checked him into his room during my lunch break, so he came back here to rest in the early evening, but wound up calling me for help. I didn't know what to do, so I basically picked up the entire GI range from the drug store and dropped it off in his room.'

'Was it common for him to feel ill?'

'Not common, but it happened occasionally. The guy ate for a living, and his body wasn't exactly a temple, so . . .'

'So you weren't alarmed?'

'Not really. When he called me, he told me he really had it bad, but then again, if you looked up the term "Man Flu" in the dictionary, you'd probably see his photo.'

'So Gunnar didn't suffer illness quietly.'

'Gunnar didn't suffer anything quietly,' she deadpanned. 'Well, not when he was around me and the crew, at least. In public, he was quick to pick on other people and call them wimps or babies, but he was the real baby. He'd throw a tantrum over just about anything.'

Having met Gunnar, Reade was not at all surprised. 'Let's rewind. Tell me about the show and Mr Randall's time here in Virginia this week.'

'As you probably know, restaurant owners apply to be on the show. Once we receive a sufficient number of "good" applications – meaning a spot with decent Yelp reviews and an OK local following – in a location, we schedule to feature that city or town on the show. I know everyone views it as a completion but it totally didn't start that way. It's just that food people saw it as a challenge to get one of Gunnar's positive reviews. They continually want to defy the odds and come on the show. It's crazy really.' Shae drew a deep breath. 'Anyway, after a two-month summer hiatus during which it was determined that Richmond would be the first town we'd visit this season, the crew and I arrived on Monday, checked into the Hampton Inn in Richmond and scoped out our locations to determine the best time of day to shoot, the best spots in which to shoot, what microphones might be needed, what questions Gunnar should be asking, etcetera. Gunnar took a red-eye on Tuesday and arrived at five in the morning on Wednesday.'

'Was that customary for him?'

'Yeah, he never wanted to be in on the scouting trips. He didn't have the patience for it. He wanted to taste the product, briefly meet and harangue the food producers, shoot his bit, and move on to the next stop.'

'Is that what happened on Wednesday?'

'Yes. Gunnar arrived as scheduled, and after we all had breakfast, we immediately started filming. We managed to finish all four of our scheduled locations before Gunnar started feeling queasy.'

'So he'd sampled goods from four different food purveyors that day?'

'Yeah, and he had some kind of cheffy lunch date. I forget who it was with. He made the appointment; I just made note of it on the schedule. I also used that time to check him into this place so I didn't have to drive out here after a long day.' She sighed. 'Of course, the moment I got to my room in the Hampton

Inn in Richmond after we'd finally wrapped up for the day, I got the call to come out here on a Pepto Bismol run. So much for *that* plan.'

'Did you check in with Mr Randall later that evening?'

'No, because he wasn't the type you checked in on. He would have viewed an unsolicited call as a disturbance. My job was to wait for him to contact me and respond appropriately, which I did, but the phone didn't ring until the following morning when he told me he was going to be late for the day's shoot.'

'What was his reason for being late? His illness?'

'Yeah. He claimed he had lived through a "night of hell."' Shae cast her brown eyes heavenward. 'Always with the drama.'

'So you don't believe he was as sick as he claimed?'

'Oh, I think he was sick. When I dropped off his meds, he looked terrible. It was also the first time in two and a half years that he canceled a shoot – not that the crew was supposed to know that; I told them he had an unexpected appointment. But I also think his illness was mostly self-inflicted. Gunnar had a fear of flying, so he always fueled up with liquid courage before boarding the plane. Then, when he arrived in Virginia on Wednesday morning, instead of eating a cereal bar or some granola like a normal human being, he took us to some strip-mall diner where he proceeded to order two eggs over easy, biscuits with sausage gravy, fried catfish, and grits. That breakfast was soon followed by tastings at a mushroom farm, a restaurant/winery, a vegan restaurant, a gastropub, and – in the middle of it all – lunch.'

'Could you provide us with a copy of his schedule, with names and addresses?'

'Sure,' she agreed before returning to her disgust for Randall's eating habits. 'Like, how he could have consumed another thing, I have zero idea.' She folded her arms across her chest. 'Anyway, it's no wonder Gunnar's dead, is it? He was a heart attack waiting to happen.'

'Is that what you think happened to him? A heart attack?' Reade inquired.

'Of course. He was the right age, the right personality type. Oh, and vomiting is one of the symptoms of a heart attack, too. I mean, isn't that what you guys think?' she asked eagerly.

'The coroner isn't certain yet,' he replied coolly. Something in

Shae Fisher's readiness to write Randall's death off as a coronary issue bothered him. 'Getting back to Thursday, Randall had called in sick in the morning. Did you see him at all that day?'

'As a matter of fact, I did. We'd pretty much written off getting any shooting done when Gunnar called us out of the blue and said he was feeling better and wanted to get to work. We'd already canceled with the food producers who were scheduled for the day, so we decided to record Gunnar's tour of Richmond. You know, the scenes between the interviews where he walks around the town, gives an overview of the food scene, the nightlife, regional specialties, that kinda thing.'

'And how was Gunnar?'

'He was fine. More than fine. He was supercharged. He had us shooting well into the night with hardly any break.'

'Was that usual for him?'

'When he had an axe to grind or something to prove, yeah. He could work you into the ground.'

'Which would you say was the case on Thursday?'

'The latter. Definitely,' she said without missing a beat. 'He wanted to prove to me that he was feeling well and could still manage the job. I mean, I was able to cover for him for the morning, but canceling shoots is a big deal. Fortunately, we were able to make up for the time lost, but if news traveled back to the bosses at the studio that we needed more production time, Gunnar's head could have been on the chopping block.'

'Why would the bosses fire Randall? He was a ratings success,' Reade pointed out.

'He was. But his show's like, what, eleven years old now? The Gunnar Randall style doesn't work as well as it did. People are woke – they don't want to watch him mock an Indian restaurant owner's accent or ask a middle-aged female chef if she needs to leave the kitchen when it gets too hot for her hormones. Gunnar appealed to a pre-PC, pre-"Me Too" audience that laughed when he teased an overweight restaurant owner about sampling their own goods. But that audience is no longer the norm. After numerous complaints about bullying, the network asked me and the crew – but me, mostly – to monitor and, hopefully, modify Gunnar's behavior on camera. Whatever behavior couldn't be modified would be edited prior to airing.'

'How did that go?'

'You met Gunnar yesterday. How do you think it went?' She smiled and rested her chin upon a small hand with a light blue manicure. 'The crew has learned to edit footage on the fly so that the bad outtakes don't even make it back to the studio. If you watch last season, it basically consisted of Gunnar eating food, looking at the camera, saying what he hated about it, and then thanking the food purveyor for their time before also telling them that they should find another job. It's totally bizarre and way different from the previous seasons – like *Taste of America* lite starring the zombie of Gunnar Randall. The network didn't receive any further complaints, but I'm sure Gunnar's diehard fans must have hated it.'

'So Gunnar was under pressure to keep his show afloat,' Reade surmised.

'Oh, yeah. He was stressed *and* angry. He literally could not understand why audiences might not want to watch some wealthy middle-aged white dude shout down hard-working people just trying to make it in the business. I tried to explain that with every-thing going on in the world, people might want to see a little bit of happy. I also tried to gently suggest that he was the epitome of white privilege and a symbol of the patriarchy we women are so desperately trying to smash, but he just didn't get it.'

'Yeah, I'm not surprised. So, how was he yesterday?'

'Irritable, like always. Whatever had given him so much energy on Thursday was there first thing Friday, but then it gradually dissipated throughout the day. He was yawning and messing up his lines. I even had to wake him from a lunchtime nap and get him back in the makeup chair and camera-ready. By the time we wrapped at a quarter to seven he was completely shot. Like dark circles under his eyes, no-amount-of-makeup-could-fix-him kinda shot.'

'Had he been taking any medication? Or possibly drinking?'

'I never saw him take any medication. And he definitely wasn't drinking. He'd get loud when he drank. No, he probably just overdid it the day before – we were at it pretty late. Oh!' She gave a start. 'Maybe his ticker was starting to give out then. That's what it must have been! I've never had to wake him up on a shoot before. Never.'

'Mmm,' Reade responded. Again, he was not about to disclose any details until the cause of death had been established.

'Well, however it came about,' Shae said, 'Gunnar's death did the studio a huge favor. Now, none of the bosses need to decide whether to keep him on as host of *Taste of America* or let him go.'

SIX

'Sounds as if Glory and Shae Fisher's accounts of Gunnar's behavior match,' Tish stated as she passed Reade a mug of coffee and scooped a pan full of scrambled eggs on to a waiting plate before pushing it toward him.

'Mmm,' Reade replied. Whether he was responding to Tish's statement or the arrival of breakfast was unclear.

'Gunnar became ill on Wednesday, recovered on Thursday, started to fade on Friday, and died late last night or early this morning.'

'There's one major difference between the two accounts,' Reade pointed out between sips of coffee. 'Glory Bishop claims Gunnar was drunk when he arrived here yesterday evening. Shae Fisher insists that Gunnar was both drug-free and sober when they wrapped filming – she was with him for most of the day.'

'Might Gunnar have stopped off at a bar on the way here?'

Reade shook his head. 'Shae told me the shoot in Richmond wrapped at quarter to seven. Glory said he arrived here at seven thirty. There's no way Gunnar could have made it here that quickly if he'd stopped along the way, especially not on a Friday night at the tail end of summer.'

'He might have had the booze stashed in his car,' Tish suggested, 'then tossed the bottle out the window when he'd finished. Once a person drives beyond the Richmond City limits, the road turns rural rather quickly. Gunnar could have gone miles without seeing another car and, more importantly, without another driver or cop seeing him.'

'That certainly is a possibility,' he acknowledged after swallowing a large forkful of fluffy scrambled eggs. 'It would explain not only the discrepancies in the stories but also why Gunnar nearly plowed into your car as he was pulling into the driveway.'

'And why we didn't find any booze in his room, despite his clothes smelling of alcohol.'

'Well, I emailed Doctor Andres about the timeline. He'll run a full toxicology screen and get back to us as soon as he knows anything, but I wouldn't bet on learning much more until tomorrow.'

Believing their investigative work at the B & B completed for the day, Reade finished his breakfast and ordered his team back to wrap up their inquiries and return to the sheriff's office. Tish, meanwhile, took care of the morning dishes and cleaned the kitchen while Julie made up the guest rooms. It therefore came as a great surprise when Reade's phone rang just as he and Tish were en route to Glory's cottage to provide an update and say goodbye.

He placed the instrument to his ear. 'Reade . . . yes, Doctor Andres. That's interesting . . . What does it mean? . . . I see . . . We'll, uh, we'll be right over.'

'Doctor Andres had some news? Already?' Tish asked once Reade had disconnected the call.

'Yeah, and you'll never guess this one. Gunnar Randall's cause of death was mushroom poisoning.'

'Mushroom . . .?' Tish's voice trailed off, and she felt a sudden chill. 'Glory made Gunnar a mushroom omelet yesterday.'

Reade drew a deep breath. 'Let's talk to Doctor Andres before we leap to any conclusions.'

'Yes, but there's something else.' Tish led him back into the kitchen and out of the door that led to the property's outbuildings. 'Look outside the door of the root cellar.'

Reade did as he was instructed. A sea of slightly domed olive-green caps resting upon off-white stems populated the ground surrounding the aged wooden doorframe. 'Toadstools?'

'Worse than that. Julie warned me about them today when I was making breakfast,' Tish explained. 'She told me if I wanted mushrooms, to use the ones in the cellar and not the ones outside the door. The ones outside the door, George the gardener told her, are Death Caps.'

'*Amanita phalloides*,' Dr Andres declared as he stood by his desk in the forensics lab. 'Just one-point-one ounces – half a normal-sized cap – is enough to kill an adult human.'

'How did you figure it out?' Reade asked.

'A few things, but ultimately it was the timeline from your witnesses that made me suspicious, so I took a sample from the victim's bladder. It was positive for alpha-Amanitin, an amatoxin – the toxic compound found in three genera of poisonous mushrooms. Death Cap, of course, being the most common of the three.'

Tish reached into her handbag and extracted a mushroom wrapped in a cloth napkin. It was the one she had found outside Glory's kitchen door. 'Is this a Death Cap?' she asked, passing the parcel to Dr Andres.

Donning a pair of surgical gloves, he took the package and carefully unwrapped it. 'I'd have to send it for analysis, but given the olive color of the cap, the whiteness of the gills, and the presence of a skirt or veil on the stem, it's very likely. Were there pine trees near the spot where you collected this?'

'Yes, there was an older pine within a few feet of where these were growing.'

Dr Andres nodded. 'Death Cap grows on the roots of native pines in this area. The fact there was a pine tree so close to an outcropping makes it more likely they are, indeed, Death Caps.'

Tish glanced at Reade, her eyes full of worry.

'Is there a problem?' Dr Andres asked.

'The owner of the B and B where Mr Randall was found is a friend of mine,' Tish explained. 'Yesterday, after a heated exchange, she served Mr Randall a mushroom omelet for breakfast. That Death Cap mushroom you just examined was growing a few feet from her kitchen.'

'Pardon me, but when did your friend serve the omelet to the deceased?'

'Yesterday morning. Friday.'

'*Madame*, the Death Cap mushrooms may grow on her property, but your friend had no role in the death of the decedent,' Dr Andres assured her in a slight French accent. 'The poisonous mushroom in question was ingested sometime on Wednesday, possibly even late Tuesday.'

'That early in the week?' Reade asked.

'Yes. As I said, it was the witnesses' timeline of events and the fact our victim was a chef that made me suspicious. The Death Cap mushroom causes severe gastrointestinal distress within five to twelve hours of ingestion – sometimes sooner if the patient is compromised or has consumed a large amount of the mushroom. The vomiting, headache, diarrhea, and other symptoms gradually dissipate and the patient feels remarkably better for the next twenty-four to forty-eight hours or so. However, the deadly amatoxins are still hard at work, killing liver cells and passing through the kidneys unfiltered, thus recirculating through the patient's system and causing further damage. Eventually, the patient succumbs to liver, kidney, and other organ failure.'

'So did Randall eat these mushrooms raw?'

'Raw, boiled, baked, sautéed in butter, defrosted from frozen, added to a stew – it doesn't matter. Amatoxins aren't destroyed by conventional cooking or preservation methods. Also, the Death Cap mushroom neither smells nor tastes remotely of death. In fact, the few people who have survived *Amanita* poisoning claimed it was the most delicious mushroom they'd ever eaten.'

'So what are we looking for here?' Reade clarified. 'Someone who fed this to Randall or . . .?'

'. . . or did he accidentally cook them for himself?' Dr Andres filled in the blank. 'According to the itinerary you emailed me, the deceased arrived at Richmond International Airport at five in the morning on Wednesday, meaning he left California at midnight Eastern Daylight Time and was at the airport no later than eleven. Anything he might have cooked for himself at home before leaving for the airport is outside the five- to twelve-hour window from ingestion to the onset of symptoms. No, I'd say the Death Caps were either part of a restaurant meal he ate at the airport prior to boarding, in something he ate on the plane, or in one of the meals he ate here.'

SEVEN

'Accident or murder?' Tish posed when she and Reade were back in the car.

He pulled a face and extracted his phone from his pocket. 'It's hard to see how it could be an accident. Still, I'm going to have Clayton check Gunnar's receipts to see where he might have eaten pre-flight and whether he had an in-flight meal. I'll also have him check to see if any other cases similar to Gunnar's have cropped up in Los Angeles or here in Richmond.'

'Death Caps look an awful lot like straw mushrooms. It would be easy for a forager to confuse the two. But if Gunnar ate at a restaurant before boarding his flight, we're not talking about foraged mushrooms – we're talking about mushrooms that are cultivated specifically for the food market and put through quality-control measures. A Death Cap wouldn't be allowed anywhere near the premises.'

'Could be a disgruntled employee who slipped one – or several – into a batch of wholesale mushrooms,' Reade suggested with a shrug of his shoulders. 'I know it sounds implausible, but we need to rule it out, just in case there's some nut out there on a rampage.'

Tish agreed and waited until he'd disconnected from his call to Clayton to continue. 'We also need to consider that if Gunnar didn't forage and cook the mushrooms for himself – and unless he brought food from home on to the plane, which seems unlikely – then the poisonous mushrooms were prepared by either a chef or a professional cook.'

'Agreed,' Reade concurred.

'Well, even if a poisonous mushroom had somehow managed to make it into a restaurant's food shipment, that mushroom would then have to make it past the cook and, in a larger kitchen, a sous chef, in order to be served to a customer. I find it difficult to believe no one would have questioned it.'

'But you're a professional cook and you didn't immediately recognize the Death Caps at Abbingdon Green.'

'That's right, I didn't recognize them. But that doesn't mean I'd serve them either. Celestine and I operate under a strict "when in doubt, toss it out" policy. If either of us had seen an olive-green mushroom in a sea of white buttons, that mushroom would have gone straight into the compost. Talk to other restaurant owners and they'll tell you the same thing. Between the insurance claims, the fines from the Health Department, and the negative impact on a restaurant's reputation, the worst thing a professional cook can do is make a patron ill.'

'So you're saying that Gunnar was intentionally poisoned,' he surmised.

'I'm saying that given the timeline of the poison, the facts of the case, and my experience in the food industry, it's the only explanation that makes sense to me.'

Reade bit his bottom lip. 'I'm not in the food industry, but I have to admit it's the only solution that makes sense to me as well.'

'So where do we start?'

'I'll call Shae Fisher and have her email me Gunnar Randall's complete itinerary for Wednesday.'

'So we can walk in his gastronomical footsteps?' she asked excitedly.

'Figuratively, not literally. Not only did the man eat poisonous mushrooms, but he ordered fried catfish for breakfast.'

Lou-Lou's Biscuit Palace was housed in a single-story yellow clapboard building at the end of a strip mall and on the corner of a street lined with multi-story brick dwellings. Tish and Reade stepped beneath the wide yellow-and-black awning and through a glass door upon which was posted a sign that read *CASH ONLY*. Inside, they found rows of booths outfitted in dark woodgrain Formica and a long counter lined with tall red stools.

'Grab yourselves some menus and sit wherever you like,' instructed a gravely voice from behind the till.

Tish and Reade grabbed a menu from the caddy by the door and took two seats at the end of the counter. The owner of the gravely voice – a diminutive woman in her mid-sixties with long, yellowish gray hair that had been twisted into a bun and secured in a hairnet – appeared before them. 'What can I get you folks to drink?'

'Tea, please,' Tish requested, prompting the woman to fill a tall glass with ice and sweet tea. That a customer might want hot or unsweetened tea was not a consideration at the Biscuit Palace.

'And you?' she asked Reade.

'Coffee. And to speak with the owner, if possible.' He held his badge aloft.

The woman behind the counter donned a pair of spectacles that hung from a chain around her neck. 'Hobson Glen Sheriff's Department,' she read aloud. 'I'm the owner. Well, one of 'em. I'm Lula Mae – one half of the Lou-Lou on the sign. The other half is Eloise there in the kitchen.' She signaled toward a black woman, also hair-netted and in her mid-sixties, flipping hotcakes on a wide griddle.

At the mention of her name, Eloise wandered to the counter. 'Lou and I met forty years ago at a church biscuit bake-off. When we both tied for first place, we decided to work together and try to corner the biscuit market here in Richmond, so we scraped together all the cash we could find and opened this place.'

'Best decision we ever made,' Lula Mae declared as she presented Reade with a cup of coffee and two tiny plastic pots of non-dairy creamer.

'Congratulations on creating and maintaining a successful business all these years,' he commended.

'It's easy when you love what you do and the person you're doing it with.' Eloise gave Lula Mae a pat on the shoulder before returning to the kitchen to retrieve the hotcakes.

'Very true,' Lula Mae said with a warm smile. 'Very true. Now then, what did y'all want to talk to us about?'

Reade opened a photo of Gunnar Randall on his tablet. 'We believe this gentleman had breakfast here earlier this week.'

As Eloise plated the hotcakes and served them to a man at the other end of the counter, Lula Mae gazed through her spectacles at the image on the tablet. 'That's that TV fella. Yep, he was here Tuesday mornin'.'

'He wasn't here Tuesday,' Eloise corrected, leaning over her friend's shoulder and gazing at Randall's photo. 'I had to start the fryer to cook his catfish and I wasn't here first thing Tuesday morning, remember?'

'Oh, that's right. You were helpin' your daughter get Naomi ready for her last day of camp, weren't you?'

'Yep, didn't get here till nine thirty. That TV fella came here on Thursday, I think.'

'Can't be. Thursday we had those bikers come through. He was here Wednesday.'

'According to Mr Randall's – the TV fella's – assistant, Mr Randall and his crew ate here Wednesday morning,' clarified Reade, fearful the women's debate might last all morning.

Lula Mae wrinkled her nose and glared triumphantly over the top of her glasses at Eloise. 'See?'

'You thought it was Tuesday,' Eloise countered, then addressed the sheriff. 'I remember that group. There were five of them. Our first customers of the day.'

On these two points, Lula Mae and Eloise thankfully agreed. 'Yep, they got here just after we opened and sat at that booth in the corner beside the window.'

'Tell us about their visit,' Reade prompted.

'Well, when I first noticed it was the TV fella, I thought we were done for,' Lula Mae exclaimed.

Eloise placed a hand on her chest. 'Me, too. I thought for sure we were gonna wind up on his show. I don't watch it, mind, but I know what he says and does to the folks who are on it. I've heard some of them even lose their businesses because of it.'

'Our hands were shakin' so,' Lula Mae recalled with a nervous laugh. 'I nearly spilled the coffee once or twice.'

'And when I told him he'd have to wait while the oil heated in the fryer, I thought I was gonna die!' Eloise added.

'But the TV fella – what did you say his name was? Randall? – didn't complain at all. We were in shock! He said he'd eaten at our place with a friend years ago and enjoyed everything he'd tasted – especially the fried catfish – and wanted to taste everything again while he was in town. We sure as heck weren't gonna complain.'

'So Gunnar Randall was mellow?' Tish asked in disbelief.

'Yeah, you could call him that. He didn't say much. Kept himself to himself.'

'How were the people with him?' Reade questioned.

'Miserable,' Eloise replied. 'No one seemed very happy.'

'Looked like a funeral gathering,' Lula Mae seconded. 'But that might have been because we don't serve health food.'

'Health food?' Reade repeated.

'First, one of the fellas with Randall – a tall fella with a turban – anyway, this fella asked for soy milk for his coffee. I explained that we don't keep soy milk on hand because no one ever asks for it. Then the girl with purple hair – I guess Randall's secretary or somethin' – she asked if we had anything gluten-free for another of the fellas and anything vegan for her. I told her we had a veggie omelet, overnight baked steel-cut oatmeal, and individual packets of cereal, but she was none too thrilled.'

'We try to keep up with food trends,' Eloise explained, 'but to be honest, we just don't have a call to carry those things. We make simple food for simple folk. Except for the oatmeal and veggie omelets, we haven't changed our menu since we opened. With just a few years left before we sell this place and retire, we don't see much reason to change it now.'

Tish nodded. Forty years was a long time to be rustling up biscuits, eggs, and corned beef hash for hungry diners. Eloise and Lula Mae had already proven themselves. Despite fads, recessions, inflation, and the anti-fat/anti-cholesterol campaigns of the eighties and nineties, their business didn't just survive – it thrived. Tish couldn't blame them for spending their last bit of time as restaurateurs coasting on their previous success. 'How did everyone react to that?'

'The turban fella just drank his coffee black and ordered the veggies from the veggie omelet made without the eggs – so just the spinach, asparagus, and mushrooms by themselves – and cooked without milk or butter,' Lula Mae described. 'It was an odd request, but he was nice about it. The girl was downright rude, though, until her gluten-free friend told her to order the oatmeal like he did and be quiet. And the last fella at the table ordered a fruit cup and a cup of hot water for his green tea. He didn't seem happy, but he didn't say anything either.'

'And Gunnar Randall?'

'He seemed amused by the whole thing,' Eloise answered. 'It almost looked like he was about to burst out laughing.'

'That's right,' Lula Mae agreed. 'He just smiled and ate his breakfast. And took his time doin' it. That seemed to upset the rest of them, too – him takin' his time when they'd already finished their breakfast – but he just kept on eatin'.'

'He ate everything on his plate,' Eloise continued. 'And then he ate the turban fella's veggie plate, too.'

'The veggie plate?' Reade questioned.

'Yep, turban fella took one bite and didn't like it, I guess.'

'Of course he didn't. It was a plate of cooked vegetables. Can't get more tasteless than that – you need the good stuff like eggs, butter, milk, and cream to start your morning off right,' Lula Mae said with a boisterous laugh.

Eloise fell in with the laughter as Tish and Reade exchanged glances.

'May we see your mushrooms?'

'Sure. Why?'

'We just need to see them,' Tish told the ladies as Eloise waved them behind the counter and into the galley kitchen. Swinging open the stainless steel refrigerator door, she pointed to a basket of slightly brown button mushrooms on the bottom shelf.

Tish picked up the basket and examined them. 'Plain old white mushrooms like you'd find in the supermarket. Turning a little brown due to age, but still good – actually, a bit tastier when cooked. I don't see anything here that resembles a Death Cap.'

'Death Cap?' Lula Mae repeated. 'Of course not! The health inspector was here just last week and he found nothing wrong with that refrigerator. Clean as a whistle and the perfect temperature, so you won't find any sort of black mold or funky fungus or anything like that.'

'The health inspector was very happy with us,' an insistent Eloise echoed. 'He always is.'

'We're not here because of a health inspection,' Reade assured them.

'Then why are you here?'

Lula Mae gasped. 'You're here because of that TV fella, aren't ya? Is he . . . is he sick or something?'

'I'm afraid so, ma'am,' Reade replied. 'He consumed a poisonous mushroom sometime on Wednesday.'

'Well, it wasn't here! We were afraid of that TV fella because we thought he might give our place a bad review, but we'd never—'

'Shh!' Eloise hushed. 'The less we say, the better, Lula Mae. Now, are you finished asking questions, Sheriff, or do we need to call a lawyer?'

'No, we're finished, ma'am. Although I would like to take your mushrooms for analysis.'

The two restaurant owners looked at each other and then replied in unison, 'Take them!'

EIGHT

'I think we can both agree that the Biscuit Palace ladies didn't murder Randall,' Tish asserted as she and Reade headed to the Hampton Inn on Main Street.

'I think we can both agree that the Biscuit Palace ladies are charming. However, I'm not so sure they're innocent. The two of them are planning to retire at the top of their game, sell the business and the building, and turn a good profit—'

'They own the building?' Tish asked, wishing she were somehow in the same situation.

He successfully read her thoughts. 'They do. You will as well, someday.'

She gave a dubious frown and dropped the subject. 'The Biscuit Palace is in a prime location downtown. Sale of the real estate alone would provide them with a healthy windfall. Tack on the sale of a turnkey business, and they'd be looking at a very happy retirement.'

'Exactly. But then who happens to walk through the door but Gunnar Randall? A single negative word from him had the potential to make their business all but worthless to prospective buyers.'

'So they decided to murder Gunnar by serving a poisonous omelet to another person at his table?' Tish argued.

'I hadn't gotten that far yet,' he replied sheepishly.

She laughed and reached for his hand. 'It's actually a very good theory. Except that Lula Mae and Eloise seemed to have no idea what a Death Cap was.'

'If those women are smart enough to have kept a successful business running for this long, they're definitely smart enough to know when and how to try to throw us off the track.'

'You're right, of course. I suppose I feel sympathetic toward them because they're female restaurant owners, but I still don't see how they could have poisoned Randall.'

'I don't either,' Reade confessed.

An idea sparked in Tish's brain. 'Aside from the catfish, what else did Randall order?'

'Umm, fried eggs, biscuits with sausage gravy, and grits.'

'That's it! The sausage gravy. Doctor Andres said less than half a cap could kill a man. The earthiness and texture of the mushroom would have enhanced the meatiness of the sausage, while the spiciness of the sausage and the richness of the cream would have concealed the flavor of the mushroom. Randall would never have guessed there was a mushroom in there.'

'And this is standard chef stuff?'

'Yes. Even a good home cook knows that mushrooms can replicate the flavor of meat.'

'Hmm, the timeline works. All we'd have to do is prove the mushrooms were in the sausage gravy.'

'Yeah, unfortunately, I can't help with that, unless one of Gunnar's tablemates noticed chunks of mushroom in his sausage gravy. Even then, it would be their word against the Lou-Lous. Then, of course, there's the whole veggie omelet thing. Why would turban fella give such explicit instructions on how to prepare his food and then not eat it?'

'Well, you'll soon have a chance to ask him that yourself. By the way, his name is Dalbir Singh. He's the principal camera operator for *Taste of America* and his turban isn't a fashion choice, it's a religious one. He's Sikh.'

'That explains the omelet and the soy milk. Sikhs are strict vegetarians. They won't eat anything derived from animals,' Tish explained.

Upon arriving at the Hampton Inn, Tish and Reade traveled by elevator to the third floor and knocked upon the door of room 323. They were greeted by a tall, elegantly handsome man in his early thirties.

'Sheriff, Ms Tarragon,' he greeted after Reade's introduction. Dalbir held the door open and gestured to an armed wing chair and a desk chair while he perched on the edge of the bed. 'Shae Fisher told me about Randall's death. I'm shocked.'

'There's been a development since we last spoke with Ms Fisher,' Reade announced. 'Gunnar Randall died from mushroom poisoning.'

Dalbir's face registered surprise. 'Mushrooms? That's highly unusual, isn't it?'

'It is. In the United States last year, just thirty-nine people died from mushroom poisoning.'

'Wow. Do you know how it might have happened?'

'No, that's why we're here.'

The young man nodded. 'Tell me how I might help.'

'We suspect that Gunnar ingested the poisonous mushrooms sometime on Wednesday. Can you shed any light on his movements that day?'

'Sure, although Shae would have a better idea of Gunnar's schedule than I would.'

'Ms Fisher gave us the schedule, but we'd like to review it with you, if that's all right.'

Dalbir folded his arms across his chest. 'That's fine.'

'So Randall arrived at Richmond International Airport at approximately five in the morning,' Reade prompted.

'There was a bit of a wait for his luggage, but thereabouts, yeah. Randall hated flying – absolutely terrified by it. He booked all his long flights as red-eyes and Shae would give him a couple of her Xanax, which he'd chase down with Scotch.'

'Ms Fisher gave him the Xanax?'

'Yes, antidepressants, anti-anxiety meds – you name it, Shae has it.'

'That's a lot of pharmaceuticals,' Tish noted.

'That's because Shae is in a race with herself. She wants to be a showrunner by the time she's thirty which, in her mind, means she shouldn't be in a post longer than two years. These past few months, she's been trying to move on to another job. I tell her she might reach her goals faster and with less grief if she meditates rather than medicates. She doesn't believe me. She shakes her head and calls me a crazy Indian dude.' Dalbir smiled.

'So, what happened after Randall's arrival?'

'We all met up at the studio we're renting for the episode to store our gear and review each day's footage. That's when Randall suggested we all go out for breakfast – his treat.'

'Was that usual?' Reade asked.

'No. Randall always wanted breakfast first thing upon arriving on location, but he never invited the crew to join him. It was only when we arrived at the restaurant that I realized why he invited us – because we'd hate it. He said that he'd been there with a friend back in the day, which may or may not have been true. One thing was for certain: Randall selected that particular breakfast place because no one on the crew would have enjoyed eating there.'

'But why?' Tish quizzed.

'Because he enjoyed the power it gave him, the control he had over us. He knew no one would dare refuse his offer of breakfast, nor would they question his choice of restaurant, because it would mean him complaining to the studio heads and, subsequently, one of us losing our job.'

'So, in essence, he took you to breakfast in order to torment you.'

'Yes. Have you seen the show?'

Tish replied that she had.

'When Randall humiliated people on the show, he wasn't acting. He wasn't going from a script. He was a complete narcissist. He never put himself in a situation where he wasn't the center of attention. He had a deep-seated need to be the best, and he fed that need by putting down those around him.'

'Including the crew?'

'Especially the crew. He was always on Shae about her weight, asking her if she was going on a diet. She knew he was trying to get to her and yet . . .'

'It seeded self-doubt.'

'Exactly,' Dalbir confirmed.

'And what did Randall do to you?' Reade asked.

'He made fun of my ethnic background. Randall was a narcissist and a bully, but he wasn't very creative. When I first started the job, he called me Gunga Din and asked who was watching the 7-Eleven while I was working for him. When I naively explained that my mother was German American and my father Punjabi with the hope that doing so might put an end to his behavior, he nicknamed me "CC" – Curry 'n' Kraut. That sauerkraut is spelled with a K is simply evidence that ignorance and illiteracy travel hand in hand.'

'Getting back to breakfast, the owners of the Biscuit Palace told us you ordered the contents of a vegetable omelet, but that you didn't eat it. Is that true?'

'That's correct. The moment I tasted those vegetables, I realized that although the cook may not have added butter while cooking, there was still butter on the griddle where she cooked it.'

'Why didn't you complain or send the plate back?'

'Because I saw the expression on the two ladies' faces when Randall walked through the door. They were already frightened of a bad review. I could see it in their eyes. My complaining would only have put them more on edge. I couldn't do that to them – not having been in their shoes.'

'Whose idea was it for Randall to finish your vegetables?'

'His. I was going to have them wrapped in case someone in the crew wanted to heat them up later in the day, but when he saw I wasn't eating, Randall reached over and grabbed them off my plate.'

'Was that typical behavior for him?

'I didn't dine with him often, but Randall was a man with a large appetite. We Sikhs strive to keep the body pure. Randall could never have been Sikh,' he remarked with a smile. 'But why are you so interested in my breakfast? You don't think . . .?'

'We're not sure what to think. We need to examine every possible means by which Gunnar Randall might have ingested those mushrooms. Which reminds me, Randall's breakfast that morning – do you remember it at all?'

'Yes, it was a plate containing practically every fat and animal-derived protein imaginable.'

'Was there anything unusual about it?' Tish asked.

'Unusual how?'

'Well, you've been photographing food for *Taste of America* for how long now?'

'Five years.'

'Five years,' Tish repeated. 'In that time, you must have learned how to shoot food so that it looks appealing. And through that, you must have acquired an understanding of what good food looks like. The bright orange yolks of a free-range egg, the smooth texture of perfectly blended hummus. Did anything on Randall's breakfast plate look not quite as it should have?'

'Hmm, now that you mention it, the gravy for the biscuits was quite a bit browner than it should have been. It was a dark ecru instead of a creamy white.'

At Dalbir's description of the gravy, Tish's eyes slid to Reade. 'Did you notice anything else?' she prompted.

'No, everything else on that plate looked exactly as it should have – unappetizing to one who doesn't eat animal products.'

'Where did you go after breakfast?' Reade inquired.

'A mushroom farm just outside the city, strangely enough.'

'Did Randall sample any of the mushrooms?'

'Of course. The show is called *Taste of America*. He tasted several varieties, although I can't remember them all by name. I can give you the footage from the shoot, if you'd like,' Dalbir offered.

'That would be great. Actually,' Reade said as he passed Dalbir his card, 'if you could give me the footage from the entire day, that might be useful.'

'Sure. I'll upload the files to my Dropbox and email you the link.'

'I'd appreciate it. So, did anything unusual happen at the mushroom farm?'

'Yes. Randall gave one of his exceedingly rare, positive gold-star reviews.'

Tish leaned forward in her seat. 'Really?'

'Indeed. He raved about the mushrooms. Said they were top quality and that restaurants should be clamoring to order them.'

'Wow, that's not just a positive review, that's practically an endorsement.'

'Yes, in the five years I'd been with the show, I can't recall a time when he went on about a food producer the way he raved about that farm. Although you'd never guess it from the farm's owner – from the look on her face in the footage, you'd have thought Randall gave her a negative rating.'

'You mean she wasn't happy with the review?'

'I'm sure she was, eventually,' Dalbir asserted. 'At the time, she was still miffed at Randall for taking the interview in a direction she didn't like and for snooping around the farm while she wasn't looking.'

'Snooping?'

'Randall was like a child at times. If he got bored between shots, he'd wander around – that's what happened at the farm. We were filming a segment with the farm owner where she tells the audience her story – what she does and how she got her start. Randall wasn't the type to wait patiently, so he took a stroll. The farm owner found him in a section of woods that's off limits to visitors. It really upset her, and understandably so. If anything had happened to Randall, the studio would have blamed her, not Randall.'

Tish had a hunch. 'Did Randall sample the mushrooms before or after wandering into the woods?'

'He ate them after wandering off.'

'Where did you go after the mushroom farm?' Reade asked.

'A winery with a restaurant. They served Randall a flight of wine and dishes that complemented them. I can't remember every-thing served – between the food and the wine, there were six different items – but a thorough description should be in the footage. It was an ordinary visit but an unusually nasty one, even for Randall. I'm pretty sure the owners of the place thought wine would smooth Randall's rough edges, but the alcohol made him even bolder and less inhibited.'

'After that?'

'We broke for lunch. Randall was gone for nearly two hours. It was a nice break, since we'd been with him since early in the morning. When he returned, we shot at a vegan restaurant.' Dalbir added with a smirk, 'You can imagine how that review went. Then we closed the day at a gastropub here in the city. It was a standard Randall encounter, extremely negative but not overly venomous. He was feeling tired by then and not altogether well.'

'Stomach upset?' Reade guessed.

'No, he said had a headache.'

'You're positive?'

'Absolutely. His stomach was fine. He sent Shae out to get him dinner before we got to the studio – a mushroom Swiss burger. With extra mushrooms.'

NINE

Tish and Reade stopped at the sheriff's office on their way to the mushroom farm that Gunnar Randall had visited the Wednesday before his death. 'Log these into evidence and give them to Doctor Andres for analysis,' Reade instructed Clayton as he passed the young officer the basket of mushrooms confiscated from Lou-Lou's Biscuit Palace.

'Will do. By the way, I made some inquiries,' Clayton reported. 'Randall visited an airport bar before boarding his flight. The bartender recognized him from TV. He says Randall ordered three Manhattans and no food. Randall's bankcard transactions for that night substantiate the bartender's account. Also, I spoke with the airline. Because Randall's flight was a red-eye, no food was served. I'm waiting to speak to the flight attendants who waited on Randall to see if he brought food with him from home, but as it stands right now, he most likely ate the deadly meal here in Richmond.

'Using that logic,' Clayton continued, 'I called all the Richmond area hospitals. Since Wednesday morning, only a handful of people have visited emergency rooms with stomach pains and vomiting. They've all since been discharged and are doing well.'

'Good work, Clayton,' Reade praised.

'Is it me or is it looking increasingly less likely that Randall's death was an accident?' Tish said as she perched on the edge of Reade's desk.

'I'm with Tish.' Clayton sat down beside her, prompting a raised eyebrow from Reade. The officer immediately stood up again. 'I, um, I still need to hear from the flight attendant, but I doubt a guy who downed three Manhattans did anything other than sleep during the flight. Also, to say that Randall is pretty much hated in the restaurant industry is an understatement. He must have ruined hundreds of cooks' careers through the years. It wouldn't be too shocking if one of them took revenge.'

'The question is who and when?' Reade asked.

'Well, we already have four suspects – Dalbir Singh, Shae Fisher, and the ladies from the Biscuit Palace,' Tish listed.

'So I guess the Biscuit Palace ladies aren't off the hook yet.'

'Technically, their food is off the hook – in the slang sense of the term,' Clayton interrupted. 'The place looks like a hole in the wall, but have you ever tried their ham biscuits? So. Good. Literally food for the gods.'

'Wait. You've been to Lou-Lou's Biscuit Palace?' Tish asked.

'Oh, yeah. Everyone who's grown up in this area has been there at least once. It's been around forever. I've never eaten inside – that's typically for the older crowd – but I've been to the walk-up window they open late at night on weekends and party holidays. They sell ham biscuits, ham and cheese biscuits, and biscuits with gravy, six dollars each. It's the ultimate hangover food, er, um, or so I'm told.'

'At ease, Clayton,' Reade instructed. 'Even the Governor has had a hangover in his lifetime.'

'So the Biscuit Palace is actually a bigger business than we first thought,' Tish noted.

'It's way bigger than just the restaurant. When the bars and clubs close, there's a line down the road waiting for their coffee and biscuits,' Clayton described. 'The place is a goldmine.'

'No wonder they were so frightened when Gunnar Randall walked through their door. Jim, do you happen to recall what the biscuit and gravy looked like when you last ordered it?'

'Yeah, it's perfection. A big, fluffy biscuit,' Clayton indicated the thickness with a thumb and forefinger, 'loaded with meaty chunks of sausage and covered in a thick creamy gravy.'

'And do you remember what color the gravy was?'

'White, of course. With flecks of black and red pepper.'

Tish folded her arms across her chest and stared at Reade. 'Dalbir Singh told us that the gravy served to Gunnar Randall was more brown than white. The only way that could have happened is if they overcooked their roux or . . .'

'. . . added mushrooms to the mixture,' Reade deduced.

'Precisely.'

'All right, the Biscuit Palace ladies are still on the list, but Dalbir Singh? He's a religious man. A vegan.'

'You could be the most religiously devout, most vegan-est

person out there, but after five years of being mocked for your ethnic heritage, it's still possible that you might crack,' Tish argued.

'Vegan-est?' Reade questioned.

'You know what I mean. Randall was a verbally abusive bully. You and I only met him once, and we both wanted to punch him. Imagine dealing with him eight to twelve hours a day, five or six days a week.'

'OK,' Reade conceded. 'So how did Singh do it? How did he get the mushrooms into Randall?'

'On the plate of veg he ordered, of course,' Tish stated. 'Remember, it already contained mushrooms. One more to the mix wouldn't have made a difference.'

'How did he add it without anyone seeing him?'

'He was at a table with a bunch of coworkers focused entirely upon Gunnar Randall and his reactions. Would Randall lose his temper? Would he lash out at the Lou-Lous over the food, the service, or some other perceived deficiency? Why was he treating them to breakfast? Was he going to be in a good mood during the day's shoot? Would they still have a job at the end of the day?' Tish shook her head. 'They were so preoccupied that they'd scarcely have noticed, or even cared about, Dalbir adding something to his own food.'

Reade nodded. 'Seems reasonable. And Shae Fisher? Dalbir said she brought Randall a mushroom Swiss burger with extra mushrooms, so we have the means, but what about the motive? Another disgruntled employee seeking revenge?'

'No, Ms Fisher had slightly more complex reasons for wanting Gunnar Randall dead. Dalbir said she was ambitious.'

'When I interviewed Shae, she told me as much herself.'

'Dalbir also said that Shae was trying to move on to another job. Not that she was *looking* for another job, but that she was *trying to move on.*'

Reade filled in the blanks. 'As if she already had a job in mind.'

'Or had actually been offered one, but someone – most likely Randall – wouldn't let her go.'

'To be fair, if someone brought me cheeseburgers whenever I wanted, I probably wouldn't let them go either,' Clayton quipped.

'I'll put Shae Fisher on the re-interview list,' Reade stated. 'First, though, we'll head out to the mushroom farm and the winery since they're nearby.'

'Sounds good. But after that I need to head to the café and prepare for tomorrow's wedding,' Tish stated. 'That is, of course, if there still is a wedding. Have you given the go-ahead to tomorrow's proceedings?'

'Not yet. Clayton, what's going on over at the B and B?'

'Forensics are still looking over Randall's room, but they should be done by early afternoon. There are uniformed officers outside the driveway and front gate to keep reporters and nosy townspeople at bay, and, inside, there are two plain-clothes officers – one standing guard at Randall's room and the other on hand to serve as liaison between police and guests. The liaison officer is basically there to put minds at ease.'

'Sounds as if everything's secure. If forensics finish as early as you say, I see no reason for the wedding not to proceed as planned.'

'Yay!' Tish cheered. 'When we finish at the winery, you can drop me home so I can get my van. I'll check in on the cats while I'm there.'

'Good idea. I'll bring some dinner home when I've finished for the night. We can go over the case then.'

'Home? Dinner? Cats?' Clayton repeated, agog. 'Are you guys living together?'

'Yes,' Tish confirmed. 'As of yesterday.'

'That's awesome! That's really awesome! Now, whenever we need help on the case, Sheriff Reade can pick your brain because you'll be right there.'

Once again, Reade lifted a questioning eyebrow.

'I mean congratulations,' Clayton amended. 'I'm happy for you both. Really happy.'

'Thanks, Jim,' Tish acknowledged.

'Thanks, Clayton,' Reade echoed. 'By the way, I've sent you a Dropbox link containing all the footage Randall and his crew shot on Wednesday. Go through it and document everything Randall ate that day. Also, take note of the attitudes of the food providers and the crew as well as anything that seems suspicious to you.'

'Will do,' Clayton replied with a nod. 'How many hours of footage is there?'

'About an entire day's worth.'

'Ah. I'd better go nuke some popcorn.'

TEN

'Mushroom poisoning?' Karma Frumm, owner of Frumm's Fungi Farm, asked Reade when he announced the purpose of his and Tish's visit. 'And you say he died this morning?'

'That's right,' the sheriff confirmed.

'So you beat a path directly to my door because, as a mushroom farmer, I must have poisoned him – is that it?' she asked as she shoveled rich, black compost into a wheelbarrow with a spade.

'No, ma'am. We're interviewing everyone Randall had contact with on Wednesday – his crew, food producers, even the owner of the B and B where he was staying.'

Karma appeared satisfied with Reade's explanation. 'What would you like to know?'

'How was Gunnar Randall the day he visited you here at the farm?'

'About how you'd expect. Loud, brash, egotistical.'

'So you had words with him?' Tish asked.

'No, he had words with me. He waltzed across the parking lot and into my front office as if he owned the place, demanding his French roast coffee with half and half and two sugars and a bottle of Evian water. When I informed his assistant that I didn't have those things, Randall overheard and started screaming, "Didn't you read your instructions? How can I be expected to do this show when you people can't be bothered to read your Goddamn instructions." Well, I nearly burst into tears.' Karma turned to Tish. 'I turn fifty next week; the tears and hot flashes come fast and easy these days.'

Tish nodded in empathy. 'What happened next?'

'Randall's assistant got snippy with me. Insisted she'd emailed the instructions, and obviously I hadn't read them. I understand she was covering her own behind, but I seriously didn't need her piling on top of me as well, especially since she should have known I wasn't the recipient of her email. My brother was.'

'Your brother? Why?'

'Because Everest is the one who applied for me to be on the show. I muck out horse stalls and chicken coops to make growing compound for mushrooms.' She gestured to the pile of compost beside her and then her frizzy blonde ponytail. 'I'm not exactly the type who wants to be on camera, but Everest . . . well, Everest doesn't think of those things. He's developmentally challenged, you see. He lives with me in the house we grew up in – our parents left it to us when they passed. Everest works part-time bagging groceries down at Kroger's. The rest of the time, he surfs the web, plays video games, and watches TV – especially TV shows with big, macho, larger-than-life characters. A couple of volunteers check in on him while I'm here at the farm to make sure he's taking care of himself and getting exercise, but they're not big on disciplinary action, and he can be quite charming. Everest does pretty much what he likes. Including writing emails to his favorite TV shows.'

'In this case, his email worked out well. You received a favorable review,' Reade noted.

'I did.' Karma frowned.

'You don't seem very happy about it.'

'I am. When – if – that episode airs, business will increase exponentially.' The furrow in her brow grew deeper.

'But?' Tish prompted.

'But I didn't like the way Randall went about the whole thing. He made a big deal about my brother's "condition," played up the fact that I was Everest's sole caregiver, and made Everest sound completely helpless and housebound – like he's a burden to me, which he isn't. I didn't want that interview to be broadcast all over the country. I wanted my brother to be treated like a human being – not some charity case, but a caring human being who applied to the show because he thought he was doing something nice to help his sister.' Karma wiped tears from her eyes with the back of a gloved hand. 'During my time in the makeup chair, I made that very clear to Randall's assistant. I told her that although mentioning Everest as the person who applied on my behalf was more than fine – my brother would have been over the moon to hear his name mentioned on TV – anything beyond that was completely off limits.'

'And Ms Fisher – Randall's assistant – agreed?'

'Yes, she said she understood and would share my concerns with Randall. That's why I was completely blindsided when the interview started with talk of my brother's "mental state" and how I should be applauded for not "putting him in a group home." I don't even possess the words to describe how angry I was.'

'What did you do?' Reade asked.

'I threw possibly the biggest tantrum I've ever thrown in my life. I would never have made a scene twenty years ago, but now . . .' She shrugged. 'Randall walked off in a huff and his assistant followed him. The cameraman, however, was very understanding and sweet. He apologized for the incident and then had me watch as he edited the segment on his camera before it even made it to final processing. I was still angry for having been put in that situation, but at least my fears that Everest might see the footage were assuaged.'

'I was told that you were angry with Randall for more than just his insensitivity during your interview. Is that correct?'

Karma looked startled. 'Well . . . I . . . yes. While I was having my makeup done and shooting the segment where I gave the history of Frumm's, Randall decided to snoop around my farm. When we were ready to shoot that infamous interview, we went looking for Randall and found him coming out of an area that's off limits to visitors.'

'I agree that was unacceptably rude behavior, but was it a big deal otherwise?'

The color rose in her cheeks. 'Of course it was a big deal!' she sputtered. 'The development shed is out there – the place where I experiment with different composts and spores. All the heavy farm equipment and compost pasteurizers are there as well. If Randall had fallen and injured himself – or, God forbid, handled the pasteurizer – I could have been destroyed financially. My insurance company wouldn't have paid a claim because Gunnar Randall wasn't supposed to be there!'

'Ah, yes. That makes sense. Um, would you mind showing us around the farm?' Reade asked in a clear attempt to calm the woman.

His idea worked, for Karma Frumm not only relaxed but broke into a broad grin. 'I'd love to. Giving tours is actually one of my favorite things to do here at the farm.'

She led Tish and Reade past the wood-shingled office building to a series of long hooped buildings clad in thick white plastic sheeting. 'When my parents started this place in the sixties, they had just one mushroom tunnel. Then, in the seventies, as fresh mushrooms started to become available in supermarkets, that number grew to three. They'd always hoped to expand even further, but what with the watering and air conditioning mushrooms require, the energy bills made expansion cost-prohibitive.

'We're growing food here, so if you don't mind,' Karma explained as she distributed a pair of blue disposable facemasks and nitrile gloves to each of her guests. 'When I took over the farm after my parents died, I secured a loan that enabled me to install solar panels on one of our fields. Those panels saved enough on energy that I expanded the farm to five tunnels. They've almost paid for themselves in the seven years since installation.'

Karma swung open the door to one of the tunnels and allowed Tish and Reade admittance. The cool, dank space was lined, from floor to ceiling, with shelves of growing substrate upon which grew thousands of brilliantly white mushrooms.

'White buttons, Crimini, and Portobellos are the most popular mushrooms here in the States, so they occupy three of the five tunnels. The other two tunnels contain the exotics like Shiitake, Oyster, and Enoki, which grow on a variety of things: bottles, wood logs, and containers filled with sawdust,' Karma explained. 'There's been a jump in demand for specialty mushrooms as of late, which translates to a jump in price. If the trend continues, I may look into adding another tunnel.'

'Ms Frumm,' Tish addressed the farmer, 'which varieties of mushrooms did Gunnar Randall sample while he was here?'

'All of them,' Karma answered with a chortle. 'And multiple times. It was like he was trying to eat his weight in them.'

'And were any of the mushrooms cooked?'

'Yes. I did a campfire fry-up of mushrooms with fresh thyme and butter which I served on bruschetta. Why?'

'We're simply documenting everything Randall ate that day,' Tish explained.

Reade gave one of the shelving racks of perfectly formed button mushrooms a careful examination.

'You won't find anything strange there, Sheriff. There's not a mushroom farmer on this planet who would allow any intruding species – let alone a poisonous one – to get near their food crop. It just wouldn't happen. If word of it ever got out, they'd be ruined.'

He nodded. 'Can we see the area where Randall trespassed?'

'Sure can. Follow me.'

Karma led them out of the mushroom tunnel, back toward the office, and along a narrow footpath that led through the woods and into a clearing. There, in the clearing, stood a tin-roofed building with a smoke stack and, beside it, a straw walker combine harvester. 'This building houses our compost pasteurizers as well as our rakes, shears, and garden hand tools.' She opened the door to reveal an enormous stainless steel tank operated by a digital control panel. 'And that harvester gathers the straw for the compost.'

'Where's the development shed you mentioned?'

'Um, well, it's a little ways from here,' Karma sputtered as her anxiety level visibly increased. 'Y–you won't see very much. I harvested everything the day before yesterday.'

'That's OK,' a sanguine Reade replied. 'We just want a quick look around.'

Karma reluctantly escorted them farther down the path to another clearing, the centerpiece of which was a run-down, wood-shingled barn with a tin roof. 'Well, here it is,' she announced upon arrival. 'Not much to see.'

'I wouldn't say that. It's quite a sizable building to be referred to as a "shed." Mind if we take a look inside?'

'No.' With trembling hands, Karma took a key ring from the belt loop of her cargo shorts and unlocked the brand-new padlock that secured the sliding barn door to its frame. 'But, like I said, there's nothing in there since this week's harvest.'

Tish took note of the lock and surveyed the surrounding woods. From their vantage point on the side of a hill, she could see that there wasn't another farm or house for miles. 'Do you have many employees here at the farm?'

Karma shook her head as she opened the barn door and switched on the inside light. 'Nope. I've managed to expand the business, but not to that level. Everest lends a hand with the larger harvests, a friend's daughter pitches in giving tours during the busy summer season, and I pay a local man to use the harvester to reap the straw from our fields, but everything else is on me.'

'That's a lot of work for one person,' Tish remarked as she led the way through the barn doors.

'You have no idea. I didn't even want to be a mushroom farmer. I took over when my parents became ill. By the time they passed away, I couldn't get work doing much of anything else. Employers prefer your most recent experience to actually be in the field in which they're hiring. They're funny that way.'

Whereas the mushroom tunnel contained shelves of loose compost, the barn shelves held growing matter in clear bags, the tops of which were open, but bore no evidence of having ever grown a mushroom.

'I told you there wasn't anything to see,' Karma boasted and turned on one heel as if to depart.

Before she could reach the barn door, Reade spoke. 'Ms Frumm, where are the mushrooms that you harvested?'

Karma spun around, her mouth the shape of an 'O.' 'The what?'

'The mushrooms that were growing in this barn – the mushrooms you harvested – where are they?'

'W–well, they were no good. Th–the stalks were tough and woody, and the caps had flecks of mold, so I threw them into the compost.'

'Is it possible to retrieve them from the compost?'

'Er, um, no. I threw them and the rest of the batch into the pasteurizer last night.'

Reade paused and extracted a small manila envelope from the front pocket of his shirt and held it aloft. 'Then I'll have to be satisfied with a sample of the growing compound. With your permission, of course.'

Karma blanched and then rallied. 'Sure. Go ahead. If you're looking for traces of poisonous mushrooms, you won't find any in there.'

'I sincerely hope I don't.' Reade promptly sunk the envelope into the opening of one of the bags of substrate. 'One last question. How did you leave things with Mr Randall?'

Karma was evasive. 'I'm not sure I understand the question.'

'The cameraman resolved your issues with the interview, and Randall gave you a rave review. Those two things must have gone a long way toward making your television experience less miserable.'

'An apology would have gone further, but men like that don't apologize.' With a grimace, Karma looked downward and to her left, as if recalling a painful memory. 'They never apologize. As for the review, Randall did that for his own benefit, not mine.'

'How so?' Tish inquired.

Karma became flustered. 'B–b–because men like Randall don't do anything unless it somehow benefits them,' she explained while waving her arms in the air. 'That man came here with an agenda – to play up the whole helpless female narrative so that he would come off as the savior. The middle-aged white man coming to the rescue of an overwhelmed female farmer and her special needs brother. That's not to say that my mushrooms don't deserve praise – I raise a premium product, but none of that mattered to Randall. His reviews were all about control, and I wasn't about to allow any man to control me. I've worked too hard for that. Too long and too hard.'

ELEVEN

'Karma Frumm certainly had the motive and the means,' Tish stated as Reade pulled his police-issued SUV out of the farm parking area.

'And the temperament,' he added.

'I'm not about to judge her for that. She gave up her chosen profession and whatever life she'd built for herself to become a full-time caregiver, first to her parents and now to her brother and the family farm. It would be difficult for anyone to remain chipper under those circumstances.'

'She maintains that Everest isn't a burden,' Reade was quick to point out.

'Because he isn't. He's her brother and she loves him, so she'd never think of him that way. But that doesn't mean she doesn't occasionally find herself longing for her old life and perhaps feeling angry that things didn't turn out differently.'

'Hmm, that development barn of hers was interesting, wasn't it?'

'Yes, particularly the brand-new lock on the door. The barn is in the middle of nowhere, and she has no other employees who might go snooping around, so what made her decide the barn needed a lock? And when?'

'Randall's visit, most likely. That's probably why she got rid of the development shed's harvest. I'm willing to bet she was growing poisonous mushrooms in there,' Reade asserted.

'If Karma was knowingly cultivating them, that's where she'd do it – as far away from the edible mushrooms as possible. Her story about why she destroyed the development shed harvest didn't sound very convincing to me either, but why would she be growing poisonous mushrooms in the first place? It would imply premeditation and, as far as we know, Karma had no reason to kill Gunnar Randall until she met him.'

'You make an excellent point.'

'Frumm's Fungi Farm is surrounded by acres of natural wood-lands consisting of native pine and oak,' Tish continued. 'It's the perfect growing environment for Death Caps. Karma could have been out by the development barn, spotted a bunch, and harvested them – maybe even to prevent a dog from eating them – only to put them to use on Gunnar.'

'Then what was being grown in the development shed?'

She shook her head. 'Your guess is as good as mine. Hopefully, that compost sample you took will clarify matters.'

Reade nodded. 'Honey, why did you ask Karma whether she served Randall cooked mushrooms?'

'Honey?' It was the first time Clemson had used a term of endearment while working a case together, and she rather enjoyed the sound of it. 'Because, *my dear*, Gunnar Randall was a chef. He would have recognized all the mushrooms grown at the farm in their raw form. If Karma slipped him a poisonous mushroom, it must have been chopped and cooked; otherwise, Randall might have questioned its appearance.'

'You know, having a cook on this case might prove valuable.'

'Just this case?' Tish challenged with a cheeky grin.

'I texted the Señors Betancourt. They will be with you shortly,' the older, dark-haired woman at the hostess booth informed Reade and Tish. 'In the meantime, may I get you something to drink? We offer many beautiful wines.'

The sheriff declined. 'None for me. I'm on duty, I'm afraid.'

Tish also refused the offer. 'It's a little too early in the day for me.'

'Ah, what is the saying, "It is always five o'clock somewhere"? Still, we also have soft drinks, water, tea, and coffee, if you'd like.'

'A glass of water would be lovely, thank you,' Tish accepted.

The woman waved them into the restaurant and instructed them to sit at a small table in front of an expansive stone fireplace. 'The best seat in the house in wintertime. The site of many proposals of marriage.'

'Oh, we're not really—' Tish began to argue, but then realized that what she was about to say wasn't exactly true.

'Aren't you?' the woman replied with a sparkle in her eye, as she set about retrieving them some water.

All the while, Reade watched Tish with amusement.

'I didn't want her to think . . . well, this is a police investigation – we should try to stay professional,' a flustered Tish explained.

'I thought we were,' he replied. 'We're seated at opposite sides of the table.'

'Well, yes, but she obviously got a vibe from us.'

'A vibe which, if presented, I'd neither confirm nor deny.'

'Sometimes I forget that you're an elected official,' she said with a laugh.

The woman had returned with their water. 'Those grandsons of mine are still not here?' she asked, her tone registering annoyance.

'Grandsons?' Tish repeated.

'Yes, Alejandro and Francisco's father was my son, but he wound up being a deadbeat dad who walked out on his family – where he got that from, I do not know; we did not raise him that way! – so my daughter-in-law and the boys moved in with my husband and me here at the winery. My daughter-in-law and my husband are both gone now' – she invoked the sign of the cross – 'and the boys are grown men, of course, so now they run this place . . . with a little help and advice from their *Abuela Pilar*.'

Pilar's smile disappeared as she brought her cellphone to her mouth and shouted into it in Spanish. 'Just hurry up,' she urged the party on the other end of the connection before signing off. 'Sorry, my grandsons get so involved in their sides of the business that they forget it's the people who matter! Can I be of any assistance until they get here?'

'If you were here during the filming of *Taste of America* on Wednesday, you might be,' Reade answered.

'Yes, I was here.' She pulled over a chair from a nearby table. 'I was the one who got the boys on the show. I would not have missed it, though in the end I probably should have. Why? What do you need to know?'

'Gunnar Randall, the host of the show, is dead from mushroom poisoning.'

'No!' Pilar gasped. 'How?'

'That's what we're trying to find out,' Tish explained.

'It was not us. I can tell you that. My boys have issues' – she brought her hands to the sides of her face to emphasize the point – 'many, many issues – but they are not murderers.'

'No one's implying they are. For now, we simply need to document what Randall ate before he died and track down any and all food suppliers in order to prevent any other possible deaths.'

She nodded. 'I can give you the names and numbers of our suppliers. I handle all the books for the restaurant and winery.'

'So, tell us about the shoot on Wednesday,' Reade prompted.

'It was all very exciting! The minute I heard Alejandro and Francisco would be on *Taste of America*, I told all my friends and then went shopping for a new dress and scheduled to have my hair and nails done. My husband and I started this vineyard when we were first married – new immigrants to the country – and now that business was going to be seen by viewers across the country. My husband would have been so happy and proud – until our grandsons goofed everything up.'

'Start from the beginning and tell me what happened.'

'The beginning? You mean the application for the show?'

'The beginning of the shoot,' Reade clarified.

'It was very exciting – fixing up the winery, getting things ready – but when it finally happened, there was a lot of waiting around. Señor Randall and the crew got here late morning, and nothing started until he had his coffee and his mineral water.'

'How was Randall?'

'About what you'd expect. Loud, bossy, like you see on TV. Not much different.'

'Did that surprise you?'

'No. He's just that kind of guy, you know? Hot-blooded.'

'Did that bother you at all?'

'No, not until he told his makeup person to redo my hair. Me! After I paid good money to have it washed and set by the best stylist in town, Randall said I had the "helmet of the hair." *El idiota!*'

Tish eyed Pilar's hair. It was soft, wavy, and dark, with long streaks of silver, but most of all it was absolutely lovely. That Gunnar Randall should insult an elderly woman about her appearance was despicable, but not surprising. 'Did you have your makeup redone, too?'

'Yes,' Pilar replied, a look of surprise on her face. 'Not right away, but a little while after my hair was done, Señor Randall said the way I did makeup was all wrong for someone my age.'

'That's rather harsh, especially as I think your makeup right now looks wonderful. Very tastefully done.'

'*Gracias*,' Pilar replied with a gracious smile. 'I am an old lady, but I do take pride in my appearance. I drink plenty of water, moisturize, eat well, and I belong to a nature hiking group.'

'All the more reason for Randall's comments to really hurt.'

'Meh.' Pilar dismissed the idea with a wave of her hand, but the hint of a tear in her eye showed her true feelings. 'Men like that never mean what they say.'

'So after your makeup and hair were redone, what happened?' Reade prompted.

'I gave a history of the winery for the camera and said why I wanted the boys to be on the show. All that fuss over my hair and makeup, and I only talked for about five minutes. Then Alejandro and Francisco served Randall his food and wine.'

'Do you remember what was on the menu?'

'No, I can name a few of the wines, but the food is Alejandro's end of things. When my husband died and I signed the winery over to the boys, the first thing Alejandro did was to add the restaurant. He has no interest in the wines except to pair them with his food. Francisco is in charge of the winery,' she explained with a proud smile. 'He took after his *abuelo*. He loves the outdoors and super-vising the growing of the grapes. He has my late husband's flair for wine, too. Alejandro is like his mother – quiet, likes being in the kitchen, keeping things organized. The boys are so different. I think it's why they fight so much.'

'How did the food tasting go?'

Pilar pulled a face. 'Not good. The boys fought about which of them would serve Gunnar first. Not just loud words, but a fight with the fists – all for the camera, you see. Then, once he was served, Señor Randall seemed more interested in the wine than the food.'

'That's not necessarily a bad thing. Betancourt is primarily a winery,' Tish said.

'Yes, but Señor Randall wasn't really tasting the wine. He was gulping down each glass, and he was gulping them out of order and by themselves, instead of drinking them with the food Alejandro matched with them.'

'He drank a flight of wine out of order? Ouch.'

'It got worse. The more Señor Randall drank, the more he would talk bad about the food – how bad it looked on the plate, how bad it smelled.' The hint of tears that flashed in Pilar Betancourt's dark gray eyes unleashed in a torrent. 'Then, after he said bad things about the food, he said bad things about the wine. Even while he was still drinking it.'

Reade pushed his untouched glass of water toward the elderly woman.

'Thank you, señor,' she said after taking a sip and collecting herself. 'I know my boys did a bad thing by fighting. Señor Randall used that as a reason to give them a bad review, but in my opinion, he was worse behaved than they were. Oh, how it hurt to see my boys treated that way! If I had it all to do over again, I never would have signed them up for that show. *¡Yo era estúpida!*'

As Pilar blew her nose loudly, two men in their mid-thirties entered the restaurant. They both were tall, slim, and darkly handsome with well-defined cheekbones and a firm jawline. The slightly taller of the two – dressed in a button-down, long-sleeved, striped dress shirt and khakis – strode confidently into the dining room, his almond-shaped eyes looking ahead, defiantly. He approached his grandmother and, placing a hand on her shoulder, leaned down to kiss her on the cheek. '*Buenos días, abuelita.*'

She reached up to pat his hand affectionately. 'Francisco, where were you?'

'The vineyard, preparing for this week's harvest. The Viognier and Merlot are ready.'

'So soon?'

'*Abuelita*, they're always ready in August. Cabernet Sauvignon, Petit Verdot, and Cabernet Franc are harvested in September and October.'

'Ah, yes. I get confused at times.'

Francisco's brother, dressed in chef's whites, followed some distance behind, his head lowered. '*Abue*,' he greeted, choosing the shortened version of his grandmother's title and bestowing a kiss on the top of her head.

Tish marveled, not at the affection displayed between Pilar and her grandsons, but at the fountain of youth from which the woman had apparently drunk. Either she had become a grandmother at a very young age or Betancourt wines had a reversing effect upon aging.

'Alejandro. Where have you been?' the older woman chided. 'I thought at least I could count on you to be nearby. If this restaurant is to be a success, you cannot keep people waiting!'

'*Lo siento*, I was receiving a shipment from the butcher for the weekend. You know I like our ingredients to be the freshest possible, *abue.*'

'I do, but sometimes people are more important than ingredients. Like when those people are from the sheriff's department,' she warned as her eyes slid toward their guests.

'Sheriff's department?' Francisco questioned. 'What's going on here?'

'Yes, what's going on?' Alejandro echoed. 'We've passed all our recent health inspections.'

'Quiet, Alex.' Francisco hushed his brother. 'I'm handling this.'

'We both own this business, Frank,' Alejandro argued. 'We both have a right to speak.'

'You speak all the time in your restaurant. This is a matter that concerns the entire winery—'

'*Silencio,*' Pilar demanded. 'Always arguing and never listening. You don't even know why the sheriff is here.'

The brothers fell silent and gazed at Reade in anticipation.

'Gunnar Randall died from mushroom poisoning early this morning,' Reade explained.

'What does that have to do with us?' Francisco asked.

'Yeah,' Alejandro rejoined. 'He was here on Wednesday.'

'Which happens to be the same day Randall consumed the poisonous mushroom,' Reade informed them.

'We had nothing to do with it,' the brothers cried in near-unison.

'No one is suggesting you did. My associate, Ms Tarragon, and I are simply creating an account of everything Mr Randall ate on Wednesday so we can pinpoint when and how the poisoning occurred.'

'Well, it didn't occur here,' the chef maintained.

'Alejandro, relax,' Pilar cajoled. 'Just sit down and answer the sheriff's questions.'

'You've been talking to them?' Francisco asked.

'*Sí*, they need to make sure none of our suppliers are responsible for Señor Randall's death.'

'I don't like them asking you questions, *abuelita.*'

'I don't either,' Alejandro seconded.

'You're both highly protective of your grandmother. I understand completely. My grandmother raised me as a boy.' Reade passed his card to Pilar. 'Ma'am, you're free to go. Thank you for your time. If you think of anything else that might be of importance, just give me a call.'

Pilar acquiesced with a nod of the head before departing for the restaurant lobby.

'Gentlemen,' Reade greeted when Pilar had gone. 'Please have a seat.'

The brothers pulled over an additional chair and sat down simultaneously.

'What do you want from us?' Francisco asked.

'A timeline and a menu from Wednesday, as well as anything interesting you might have noticed during the shoot.'

'Interesting? You mean like Gunnar Randall verbally abusing our *abuela*?' Alejandro asked angrily.

'Your grandmother told us that Mr Randall had her hair and makeup redone,' Tish replied.

'It was more than that. It was the things he said to her – the remarks on her appearance. Saying that her hair was a helmet, her makeup made her look like Elvira, and that she was "mutton dressed like lamb." I wanted to punch him in the face.'

'We both did,' Francisco agreed. 'Alex and I may argue, but when it comes to taking care of our *abuela*, we are always on the same side.'

'Although our tactics might differ,' Alex qualified. 'Frank's the older brother, so he always thinks he has the right answer.'

'Because I usually do,' Frank answered with a smirk.

'So which one of you came up with the menu for Wednesday?' Tish asked, hoping to capitalize on a moment of camaraderie between the brothers.

'It was a rare moment of harmony. Alex created and selected restaurant dishes that use our wines, and I paired those dishes with the Betancourt wine that best suited the flavors of the dish, which wasn't always necessarily the wine Alex used in the cooking.'

'Sounds like a labor of love,' Tish remarked.

'Yes, for our *abuelita*,' Alex clarified. 'Neither of us had much respect for Gunnar Randall or his show, but *abuelita* wanted us to do the show so badly that we did our best to make her proud. I started the menu with mussels steamed in white wine—'

'Which I paired with an un-oaked, steel-barrel-aged Chardonnay,' Frank added.

'Then we moved on to chicken Madeira with wild mushrooms.'

'Served with an oak-aged Petit Verdot with hints of vanilla, hazelnut, and mocha to play off the dark, rich sauce.'

'And, to finish, a lemon and wine syllabub.'

'Paired with a rich, creamy Viognier with notes of apricot that played nicely with the lemon.'

'Sounds fabulous,' Tish praised, making a mental note of the mushroom dish that was served.

'I thought it was a solid menu,' Alex stated. 'Gourmet enough to earn a foodie's respect, yet accessible enough that TV audiences wouldn't feel alienated by some strange, unknown ingredient. The wine was a little different, but not overly expensive.'

'Yes, I purposely selected bottles that retail for under fifteen dollars, so that the folks at home might go out and buy some. I know the Petit Verdot and the Viognier were probably outside a lot of viewers' experience,' Frank elaborated, 'but I planned on going out of the way to describe their flavors in order to provide them with a frame of reference, as well some background on which grapes grow well here in Virginia.'

'So, what happened?' Tish asked.

'Gunnar Randall happened.'

'He called my menu pedestrian and uninspired,' Alex complained. 'Before he even tasted it.'

'Then, by the aroma alone, he went on to compare our family wine with something he drank in high school to get buzzed,' Frank added with a slight cry in his voice. 'To illustrate the point, he began guzzling the wine, starting with the Viognier, the showpiece of our collection and the wine that was supposed to cap off the menu, not start it. He did it all just to be hurtful – to get a reaction from us. And I'm sorry to say it worked. Our grandfather built this winery, and our grandmother was right there by his side, working hard and making sacrifices. For Gunnar Randall to have done what he did was like a slap in the face to my grandparents and their accomplishments.'

'It was also exactly what we expected the moment *abuelita* told us she'd arranged for us to be on the show,' Alex inserted. 'We tried to be optimistic – for her sake.'

'*Abuelita* always had a way of understanding people,' Frank rejoined. 'She understood them far better than we ever could, so as she had such a great feeling about the show . . .'

'We told ourselves that Gunnar Randall couldn't possibly be as horrible off camera as he was on – that it was all an act and that he wouldn't have a job otherwise,' Frank completed the sentence. 'But it didn't take long until we understood that we were, in fact, dealing with someone who would happily ruin a family food legacy simply for ratings.'

'*Taste of America* has always been described as a show that shines a spotlight on up-and-coming chefs, unique food producers, and family-run restaurants,' Alex further elaborated. 'But it isn't. The only purpose that show serves is to feed Gunnar Randall's massive ego by giving him a platform to put down the people actually trying to make a difference in the food business.'

'What happened after Randall drank all the wine?' Reade asked.

'He asked to sample some of our other varieties to see if those vintages were as "inferior" as the ones he'd just tasted.' Frank flashed a sardonic smile. 'Naturally, they were.'

'When he got through with that, he finally tasted my food,' Alex continued. 'I'm a CIA-trained chef—'

'CIA?' Reade questioned.

'The Culinary Institute of America,' Tish clarified.

'That's right,' Alex replied. 'You must be a foodie.'

'Something like that,' she demurred. 'So, about the food tasting . . .'

'As a professional chef, I'm accustomed to receiving the occasional bad review, but what Randall gave wasn't a critique. It was more like a drunken uncle's opinion of your mother's cooking during a family dinner. It's one thing to find something slightly overcooked or say that a sauce is bland – that I can accept – but what happened that day was Gunnar Randall spewing bile. No serious chef would ever tell you that your mussels cooked in white wine smell like dirty feet. They'd tell you to ditch your seafood supplier. It was all juvenile nonsense intended to endear Randall to a fan base who thinks that fine dining is for erudite elites who need to be taken down a peg.'

'How did the visit from Randall end?' Reade asked.

'His crew gathered up their things, escorted Randall back to their van, and left.'

'And we told them to never come back,' Frank stated.

'After his assessment of your food and drink, that seems a reasonable reaction,' Reade said.

'It wasn't due to his review,' Alex clarified. 'It was because of his treatment of our *abuelita*.'

'Like I said, my brother and I don't always agree,' Frank restated. 'But when it comes to protecting our *abuelita*, we are always on the same team.'

TWELVE

'Two brothers, two motives,' Reade observed as he drove his police-issued SUV back to Hobson Glen. 'Gunnar Randall's review of the winery and his treatment of their grandmother makes both the Betancourts major suspects.'

'All *three* of the Betancourts are major suspects,' Tish corrected. 'Remember, Randall verbally attacked the family business, Pilar, *and* Pilar's grandsons. The only thing I can't work out is how any of them might have done it.'

'I just assumed it was through the chicken Madeira.'

'Well, yes, naturally. But the problem is that would have required premeditation. Not only was the chicken prepared well before Randall's arrival, but the mushrooms in the Madeira sauce would have been sautéed until golden and then cooked down until their juices melded into the sauce. Unlike the case with a quick-cooked omelet, it's not as if one of the Betancourts could simply toss a raw death cap into the dish in a fit of rage – its texture would have been far too noticeable.'

'To a sober person, maybe, but Randall must have been pretty hammered after all that wine he drank,' Reade stated.

Tish pulled a face.

'Maybe the Betancourts knew how intoxicated Randall might get,' he continued. 'Alex Betancourt graduated from the CIA. He could have phoned his chef friends before the show and gotten the LD on Randall and his habits.'

'LD?'

'It's short for low-down.'

'Short? It's just as fast to say "low-down" as it is to say "LD,"' Tish reasoned.

'But it's not as fun,' he countered, prompting her to laugh.

'OK,' she sang as she played along, 'Alex might have gotten the "LD" from his chef friends, but whether Randall was drunk or not, the killer would still be taking a huge chance by plunking a raw bit of mushroom in the middle of a plate of brown gravy.

I don't care if Randall was cross-eyed – it would have been noticed straight away.'

'Even as a garnish?'

Tish tossed her head from side to side. 'Raw mushrooms aren't typically used as a garnish unless they're fluted – which is a high-end chef's technique, so it's not entirely impossible given Alex's training. However, if Randall sampled the dish for the show, I doubt he would have eaten the garnish. He would have gone directly for the meat and the sauce so he could critique the flavor, texture, etcetera. The garnish would have been for aesthetics – to let the eater know what, precisely, they were eating. Also, Gunnar Randall most likely would have noticed if the mushroom garnishing the plate was olive green rather than white or brown. Again, it wasn't a very professional tasting and Randall was most likely intoxicated, but still . . .'

'Randall wasn't a complete idiot,' Reade surmised.

'I wouldn't go quite that far. Let's just say his training would have precluded him from being poisoned by a Death Cap in its raw state in that particular dish.'

'Clayton is sifting through all of Dalbir's footage from Wednesday. That should tell us how and when Alex Betancourt's food was presented, as well as answer any other questions we might have about Frank's wine, Randall's behavior, and the sequence of events that day. It will also either corroborate or contradict our witnesses' statements.'

Reade pulled into the driveway of the house he now shared with Tish. 'I wish you could join me for the rest of today's interviews.'

'I wish I could, too,' she answered in earnest. She was finding the case highly engrossing. 'But you'll do fine without me, and Sunday's wedding isn't going to cater itself.'

'I know.' He leaned forward and gave her a kiss. 'I'll check in with you later.'

'Sounds good. Take good notes so you can fill me in on all the details.'

'I will,' he promised. 'I love you.'

'I love you, too,' Tish replied before exiting the SUV with a wave. After sneaking a quick peek at a sleeping Tuna and Marlowe and refilling their water bowls, she bundled into the van and headed to the café where she set about mixing the pastry for her individual oyster and lobster pies.

She had just finished enrobing the buttery pâte brisée in cling wrap when a familiar face entered through the back door of the café.

'Hey, darlin',' Celestine Rufus greeted as she balanced a nine-by-thirteen-inch Tupperware container and a bright green oversized handbag on one arm while shutting the door behind her with the other. 'Three dozen of my famous buttermilk biscuits and, in the car, the weddin' cake, featuring seven layers of vanilla chiffon filled with luscious chocolate ganache. Girl, it smells so good, I was droolin' while puttin' it together.'

'Ooh, I can't wait to see it.'

'Well, it ain't much to look at right now. I'm gonna finish assembling it at the bed and breakfast tomorrow; otherwise, the text on the decorative white chocolate collars might melt into the frostin'. But I am pretty impressed with myself.' Celestine raised a hand and primped her cherry-red close-cropped hair. 'I tried callin' you earlier to tell you I'd be here around noon, but your phone must have been off.'

'Yes, I switched it off while I was at Abbingdon Green this morning,' Tish explained. 'The food critic, Gunnar Randall, was staying there. He was found dead in his bed by one of the house-keepers. Mushroom poisoning.'

'Are you and Clem on the case?'

Tish nodded. 'We got the call first thing. The sheriff's office notified Clemson, and Glory Bishop contacted me.'

'"We" got the call?' Celestine questioned.

She felt her face color slightly. 'I, um, I decided to move in with Clemson.'

'That's great news!' The senior baker rushed forward, her shoulder-length earrings jangling, and captured her friend in a bear hug. 'I'm so happy for you two.'

'Yeah, I came back here from Jules's place last night and realized this is no longer my home – it's my past. Clemson, however, is my future.'

Celestine took a step back. 'Sounds kinda bittersweet.'

'It is,' Tish acknowledged. 'I'm excited about what's in store for Clemson and me, yet I can't help but wonder what's going to happen to Cookin' the Books.'

'What about the old Bar and Grill building? I heard the seller cut the price in half.'

'She did, but it's still beyond my budget. Opening a business and purchasing a new van over the course of less than a year has pretty much maxed out my line of credit. I sent an email to my former boss at the bank yesterday to see if there are other financing options, but I haven't heard back from her yet.'

'Well, I'm sure there must be somethin' you can do.'

'If there is, I'm not sure what it could be,' Tish sighed as she went to her purse and switched on her phone. 'I'm thinking I'd better rent something – anything – quickly. Otherwise, with the café closed and no imminent plan for reopening, I won't even have an income to report.'

Celestine frowned. 'I'll follow you anywhere, Tish; you know that. If we wind up workin' in that tiny storefront in the Coleton Creek strip mall, I guarantee we won't be there for long. People will line up outside the door, and before you know it, we'll have enough money for a bigger place. It'll all turn out OK, honey. Folks love your food too much for it not to!'

Tish stared at her phone, crestfallen.

'What's wrong?' her friend asked.

'My former boss sent a text. In order to buy the old Bar and Grill property, I'd need to put down an even bigger deposit to offset my lack of credit. The bank was already looking for thirty percent – I'd need to put down close to fifty. I don't have that kind of money, Celestine,' Tish explained with a cry in her voice.

'The check from Lloyd's life insurance arrived last week. How much money do you need?'

Lloyd Rufus, Celestine's husband, had passed away earlier that year. 'Celestine, I'm not going to take Lloyd's life insurance check.'

'Why not? I was partners with Cynthia Thompson back in the day. Ain't no reason I can't partner with you – if you'll have me. Now, how much do you need?'

'Nothing. You need that money to live,' Tish argued.

'Honey, if I ain't bakin' at your café, I ain't livin'. I learned that the hard way when Cynthia passed. Without that job, I didn't even see the point of gettin' up in the mornin', but when you hired me, all that changed. Things have been hard lately, what with Lloyd passin' away, but comin' here and talkin' to you and bakin' bread and waitin' tables and workin' these big parties has kept me goin'.' She crossed her arms over her ample bosom. 'Now, I need about five thousand of the insurance check for bills and expenses, but the rest is yours. That means you have an extra twenty thousand dollars to put down on the Bar and Grill. How does that sound?'

Tish blinked back the tears in her eyes. 'I can't believe you'd do that for me.'

'Of course, darlin'. You're more than a friend – you're like family to me. Same goes for Clem, Mary Jo, and Jules. I'd do anything to help y'all, but there's more to it than that. This café is good for the town. Senior citizens meet here on Sundays, Girl Scouts on Saturday mornin's, and old friends and family at just about any time of day. Then there's all the things you do for the library and the Rotary Club. It would be a shame to take all that away from Hobson Glen. What would happen if Cookin' the Books wasn't here? What if it was at the strip mall with no seatin' – where would all those people go?'

'I'm afraid we're about to find out.' Tish sighed. 'I only have ten thousand to put down on the Bar and Grill building. Even with your help and the lower asking price, we're nowhere close to the fifty percent deposit required for a loan.'

'How much do we need?'

'In total? One hundred and fifty thousand.'

Celestine whistled. 'You tellin' me the Bar and Grill is sellin' for three hundred thousand? I thought it had been discounted.'

'It has been. Three hundred thousand dollars for a turnkey operation isn't much at all . . . to those with more cash and better credit.'

'Well, what are you goin' to do?'

Tish threw her hands up in the air. 'Cry, eventually. But right now I have to start the filling for the lobster and oyster pies and then get to work on the vegan Brunswick stew.'

'Need a hand? After that kinda news, I feel like I need somethin' to do.'

'You can clean some okra for roasting and maybe chop some garlic,' Tish suggested.

'I'll get right on it after I put my cake in the refrigerator,' Celestine confirmed before returning to the parking lot.

The two women worked in silent harmony, Tish combining flour and butter for a roux and then adding milk, vermouth, and the seafood poaching liquid to create a savory béchamel sauce for the seafood pies, and Celestine, after placing the okra in the oven for roasting, rolled the chilled, buttery pie crust and cut it to fit the individual ramekins.

Once the sauce and seafood had cooled, Celestine filled the ramekins, topped them with the crust, and baked them so that they only needed a quick reheat prior to serving. As the pies baked, Celestine whipped up a rich and creamy ambrosia salad – that fruity staple of southern gatherings, chocked full of oranges, pineapple, maraschino cherries, and coconut. Meanwhile, Tish sautéed chopped onion and minced garlic in a combination of butter and oil before adding diced carrots, cubed potatoes, diced tomatoes, fresh herbs, and vegetable stock to form a flavorful and hearty soup. She then covered the mixture and lowered the heat, allowing the stock to simmer and the vegetables to cook thoroughly before the addition of vinegar, fresh corn kernels, lima beans, and a thickening agent.

With only the chutney salad dressing left to make, Tish wiped her hands on her apron and placed them on her hips. Thanks to Celestine's help, she'd finished the cooking in half the time antici-pated. 'We do make a great team, don't we?'

'We sure do. I can't believe some of the parties we managed to pull off,' the baker said with a chuckle.

'I can. We pulled them off because of your hard work and commitment, Celestine – especially those events that we catered while I was simultaneously working on a case with Clemson. Just like today, your help has made running this business a whole lot easier. Your money might not be enough to help with a down payment on the Bar and Grill, and the future of the café is still up in the air, but if and when I can get things sorted, I would very much like to make you a partner.'

Celestine's brown eyes grew wide. 'You're not puttin' me on, are you?'

'I would never do that to you. As I said, I'm not sure what that partnership might look like right now, but . . .'

'You don't have to talk it down, honey. I understand we have a battle in front of us, but for right now, I accept.' She embraced Tish in another of her customary bear hugs. 'We're gonna keep

Cookin' the Books alive and we're gonna make it even better than ever. I just know it.'

A voice came from the front door of the café. 'Hey, what do you think you're doing having a group hug without me?'

Tish looked up to see a dark-haired woman in her early forties standing in the frame of the open screen door. 'Mary Jo! You're back early.'

'Not according to the traffic reports, I'm not. I left just in time.' She joined the other women in a hug. 'I also couldn't stand watching Gregory no longer need me. I mean, I love that he's got into his first-choice university and that he's already made friends, but I can't believe my eldest child is an adult.'

'Just wait until he has his first kid,' Celestine remarked. 'Nothin' made me feel as old as bein' told I was going to be a grandma. Few things have made me happier, mind you, but boy howdy did I feel like I was ready for the nursin' home.'

'Yeah, well, hopefully I have some time to go before I need to worry about grandkids,' MJ replied as she stepped back from the group embrace. 'So what's up with you two? It looked like you were celebrating. Oh! Did you find a new location for the café?'

'No, we're still looking at the strip mall.' Tish brought MJ up to speed.

'That's great news about Celestine becoming a partner, but a real bummer about the Bar and Grill,' MJ stated when Tish had finished. 'It's such an ideal spot for the new café. There must be *something* we can do to help you get the place.'

'Apart from robbing a bank, I can't think of anything.'

'I don't need to rob a bank,' MJ announced with a broad grin. 'My divorce from Glen settles next week. In addition to clarifying child support issues, the settlement should drop a nice chunk of change in my lap in exchange for my share of the house. How much of a deposit do you need?'

'MJ-a-a-a-a-ay,' Tish sang out in warning.

'Oh, come on. It's my money. I can do what I like with it.'

'That money is supposed to provide housing for you and the kids.'

'It will do, once you and Celestine earn it back.' MJ folded her arms across her chest and grinned.

'No pressure there,' a sardonic Celestine remarked.

'So how much do you need?' MJ pressed.

'One hundred and fifty thousand,' Tish replied.

'Tish and I can come up with thirty,' Celestine elucidated.

'After paying off the mortgage and the property taxes, I'm due fifty thousand,' MJ said with a frown. 'I'm sorry it's not enough.'

'You shouldn't be. That's terrific news,' Tish reacted with excitement.

'Well, for me, maybe. But it doesn't help you much.'

Tish waved a dismissive hand. 'That doesn't matter. We'll figure out something, but fifty grand in your bank account gives you and the kids an amazing fresh start.'

'Yeah, I just wish I could buy a place instead of rent, but without a full-time job . . .' MJ said wistfully.

'It's a downright shame how tough banks make it on workin' folks these days,' Celestine opined, but then swiftly caught herself. 'Sorry, Tish. I forgot you used to work in finance before openin' the café.'

'That's OK,' Tish excused. 'Why do you think I was so eager to leave my job and start this place? Not only did banking lack the creativity I craved, but I was tired of seeing decent people get turned down for mortgages, loans, and other programs while the wealthy kept reaping rewards.'

MJ shook her head. 'I understand banks trying to minimize risk, but I feel like I'm being punished for leaving the job market to raise my kids. It's beyond deflating.'

'I know the feeling. If I could hire you full-time, MJ, you know I would.'

'I know, I know. This isn't your fault at all. It's no one's. And I don't mean to complain – I'm still better off with the settlement money than I was before. I just wish it were easier.'

'I know I just became a partner,' Celestine ventured, 'but what if we made Mary Jo a partner, too?'

'I'd love to make MJ a partner in Cookin' the Books but I'm not sure how that would help,' Tish questioned. 'The café is currently closed and there's no reopening scheduled due to a lack of both cash and credit. Making MJ partner at this point might be more of a hindrance to her than a help.'

MJ nodded. 'I agree. As much as I'd love to be a partner once this place reopens – and it will reopen, because it has to! – what I really need is a full-time job. "Under-employed" is how the bank classified me when I applied for mortgage pre-qualification. Funny, between parenting, waiting tables at the café, working as an assistant for Augusta Mae and the library board, and helping with marketing for the Virginia Commonwealth Bake-Off, I don't feel "under-employed" – I feel exhausted.'

'It's simply ridiculous that you two girls are having the troubles you are,' Celestine lamented. 'I wish I could wave a magic wand and make everything better.'

'I wish you could, too. In the meantime, you're doing more than enough by letting Kayla and me stay at your place.'

'Are you kiddin'? I love havin' you two around. The big ol' house gets kinda lonely with just me in it. Where is Kayla, by the way?'

'At a friend's house. I dropped her off on the way here.'

'Well, why don't you get back home and fix yourself a nice, hot bath to relax the muscles you used movin' Gregory into his dorm?'

MJ stretched. 'Mmm . . . that doesn't sound like a bad idea.'

'Course not! Before you go, though, Tish has some big news,' Celestine announced with a wide grin. 'Good news, this time.'

'Really?' MJ said excitedly.

'I wouldn't call it *big* news.' Tish downplayed the situation. 'I just – well, I decided to move in with Clemson.'

'That's terrific! When's the happy day?'

'Last night, actually. I still have to gather up the rest of my things from the bedroom and kitchen – which I'll do when this wedding is over – but, yeah, Tuna and I stayed at Clemson's last night. We'll be living there from now on.'

'Wow! I know that's a pretty fast move for you, but I really think you made the right decision.'

'I do, too,' Tish confirmed. 'I had my reservations about rushing in at first, but being there with him last night and then again this morning really felt like home. I know it's a bit cliché, but I feel as though Clemson and I have known each other forever.'

'It's not cliché at all, honey,' Celestine assured. 'It's wonderful.'

'Agreed,' Mary Jo chimed in. 'I'm so very happy for you both.'

The trio repeated their group hug.

'Now if only MJ and I could get our financial life in order,' Tish lamented.

'All in good time, my sweeties,' Celestine soothed. 'All in good time.'

THIRTEEN

After dropping Tish at home, Reade drove into downtown Richmond, arriving at The Eager Vegan just before the lunch crowd had begun to descend.

Preferring not to call attention to his presence, he waited in the takeout order queue until the woman at the till called him to the counter. 'Next!'

Reade gave a quick and covert flash of his badge. 'Sheriff Clemson Reade. Hobson Glen Sheriff's Office. I'm looking for Tiffany Harlow.'

A youthful face peeked through the serving window that connected the counter with the kitchen. 'I'm Tiffany Harlow. Is there a problem?'

'I'd prefer to speak with you in private.'

With a nod, Harlow pointed him toward a small and sparsely populated dining area lined with potted plants where, upon emerging from the kitchen, she plopped down at a reclaimed oak table and invited Reade to join her. 'What's this all about?'

Reade eased into the chair opposite hers. 'Gunnar Randall.'

'Gunnar Randall? That misogynist pig,' she hissed, prompting her nose ring to shake violently. 'What about him?'

'He's dead.'

'So?'

'You don't seem particularly surprised or upset.'

Tiffany Harlow adjusted the headscarf that kept her light brown dreadlocks away from her face. 'Middle-aged, animal-eating stress-bucket dies from a heart attack. It's happened to a few of my friends' dads. Only, when it happened to them, it was sad.'

'What if I were to tell you that Randall didn't die of a heart attack?'

'I don't know.' She shrugged. 'I guess I might be surprised, but then again the police – although guilty of many things – don't usually get involved in heart attack cases.'

Reade raised an eyebrow. He understood many people's mistrust of the police and had, earlier that summer, taken a knee to show his solidarity and commitment to fair policing practices, but interviewing a somewhat belligerent suspect might prove to be tricky. 'No, we don't. I'm here because Mr Randall was killed by mushroom poisoning.'

The color temporarily drained from Tiffany's face, but she swiftly rallied. 'And, *of course*, the vegan chick with the rainbow and BLM flags outside her restaurant must have been the one to feed it to him.'

'I never said that. Nor did I think it. In fact, I'd already spoken with the owners of three other restaurants before coming to see you.'

'Why? Do you think one of us fed him the mushrooms?'

'Not necessarily. It's also possible that the poisonous mushroom was accidentally delivered to your restaurant or one of the others Randall reviewed.'

The young bistro owner seemed appeased by this explanation. 'Finding a good supplier is a *total* pain these days. Every place in town has followed the vegan "trend,"' she whined as she drew quotes in the air. 'The prices of tofu, jackfruit, and meat substitutes are absolutely *in*sane. *Real* vegan places like mine are having *such* a tough time getting what we need at a decent price . . .' Her voice trailed off.

'That must be rough,' Reade sympathized even though he found Ms Harlow's overly dramatic speaking manner a bit irritating.

'It's ex*cru*ciating.'

'I bet. So, Gunnar Randall,' Reade prompted. 'If you disliked him so much, why did you agree to appear on his show?'

'I *to*tally thought I could change his mind about vegan food. I'd heard a lot about how he trashed vegans and veganism, but one night I was watching his show with some friends and I noticed that *no* one really introduced vegan food to him in a way that made sense, *you know*? Like explaining the health benefits behind certain ingredients and why some non-vegan items should be eliminated instead of substituted. The light suddenly went on.' With both hands, Tiffany gestured to a spot above her head. 'Like, what if I applied to the show and actually took the *time* to explain to Gunnar Randall exactly *why* vegan food is so great? Like, for sure he'd give this place a rave review.'

'So, what happened?'

'What happened is that Gunnar Randall is a dirtbag. Er, *was* a dirtbag. What*ever*.' She sighed. 'You get what I'm trying to say.'

Reade nodded. 'What transpired to help you form that opinion?'

'Just about *every*thing. First, Randall made fun of my dreads and my nose piercings. He wanted to know if my café passed its health inspection – like I was some *dirty* hippie or something. When the makeup person finished pinning back my dreds and doing my makeup, Randall told me I cleaned up nice. *Real* nice. It was super creepy.'

'Did you mention anything to him or anyone else at the shoot?'

'Noooo.' Tiffany drew out her reply. 'We started shooting right away, so I didn't get a chance and I . . . I guess his comments caught me by surprise. I *knew* Randall could be a tough critic but I *didn't* know he was a perv. Though I'm wondering if maybe I should assume *all* men are pervs.'

'I can understand why you might feel that way,' Reade commiserated, 'but not all of us are like Gunnar Randall. Many of us are decent people who are trying to do better by speaking out against the Randalls and other "pervs" of the world.'

Tiffany pulled a face. 'Maybe, but so far all I've ever met are the guys like Randall.'

'I'm sorry,' Reade said with a frown. Had Randall done more than just make suggestive comments to Ms Harlow? Had he touched her? Assaulted her? Having met Gunnar Randall in person, Reade felt he wouldn't be at all surprised if the chef had acted on his urges. However, it was clear, as the youthful cook stared down at the table, that she was saying nothing further on the subject.

Reade made a note on his tablet to ask Randall's crew about their boss's interactions with Tiffany Harlow. And if that came up empty, he'd ask Tish to talk to her. In the meantime, he needed to get Tiffany talking again. 'What did you serve Randall that day?'

The change of tack worked – Tiffany Harlow bolted to life. 'Only my three most popular menu items *ever*,' she said animatedly. 'A lentil burger with avocado, red onion, spring mix, and spicy vegan mayo on an organic spelt bun, sweet potato home fries, and a glass of our best blend of green juice, featuring kale, pear, and late-season asparagus.'

'How did Randall respond?'

'Like an arrogant, know-it-all jerk. When I explained how my lentil burger was held together with silken tofu, which also helped to keep the patty moist, he rolled his eyes and told me I was unoriginal and to shut up and let him eat.'

'Did he at least like the food?'

Tiffany Harlow's face went red with rage. 'Nooooo. He called it – and I *quote* – "uninspired Hipster fare better suited to a shopping-mall food cart than a city-center eatery." Didn't stop him from Hoovering up the whole plate, though.'

Tiffany's story sounded similar to that of the Betancourts. 'What happened then?'

'I don't give up easily. When I saw that Randall had eaten *every*thing on his plate, I thought I could *still* win him over, so I presented him with one of the best and most unusual hand-blended teas. He only took a sip before calling the whole thing – I quote *again* – "holistic hogwash."'

'What type of tea was it?'

'Oh, just an herbal blend,' she answered evasively. 'It was full of prebiotics and adaptogens.'

'Adaptogens?'

'Yes, they help the body adapt during times of stress. They can be found in ginseng, licorice, Thai basil, and—' She stopped abruptly.

'And mushrooms?' Reade guessed.

'Ugh.' Tiffany's eyes rolled into the back of her head. 'Yes. OK, I gave him mushroom tea, but I swear I didn't poison him.'

'Where and how is your mushroom tea made?'

'Right here in my kitchen. It's a proprietary blend. That means I *can't* tell you.'

'If you don't tell me now, I can get a warrant that will force you to tell me.'

Tiffany exuded another loud 'ugh.' 'You know, this *might* be why people want to defund you guys.'

'Because I have reasonable cause to search your kitchen, but I won't violate your Fourth Amendment rights by doing so without a warrant?' he challenged. 'And here I thought the defunding had to do with excessive police violence. Violence that I deplore, by the way.'

Her jaw dropped open. 'Are you sure you're a cop?'

'Positive,' Reade said with a smile as he gently pushed his badge across the table for her to examine.

She stared at it for several seconds before sighing. 'OK. The mushroom tea is made from a blend of dried Lingzhi mushrooms – known as Reishi, the ancient mushroom of immortality – and Chaga mushrooms. I get the mushrooms from an Asian herbalist here in town, grind them down, and spoon them into teabags.'

'Then the teabag you served Gunnar Randall was part of a batch,' Reade presumed.

'That's right.'

'May I see the other bags in the batch?'

'Sure,' she said reluctantly before leading him to the front counter where she bent down and retrieved three bags from a hidden location.

'Thanks. And how do you prepare the tea?'

'Like any *other* tea,' she answered in a tone that suggested Reade was stupid. 'I steep the bag in boiling water, then I add lemon juice and a slice of fresh ginger.'

Reade made notes of the preparation on his tablet.

'I don't know what you expect to find,' Tiffany Harlow sneered. 'The idea of *me* giving Gunnar Randall a poisonous mushroom in a teabag is ridiculous. Abso*lute*ly ridiculous.'

'Ridiculous as it might seem, I still need to have the bags analyzed.'

She sighed yet again, but her voice gradually grew more fraught. '*Fine*, but if you find anything strange in those bags, I didn't put it there. I don't know *any*thing about poisonous mushrooms. Not a thing! If there's even a trace of poisonous mushrooms in those teabags, it's because the herbalist made a mistake. It *has* to be! These suppliers are *such* a pain . . .'

FOURTEEN

Clemson Reade stepped from the bright, sun-filled sidewalks of Richmond's Carytown to the dark wood and corrugated steel interior of Honor Amongst Thieves Gastropub.

'We're not open yet,' advised a man's voice from the distance.

When Reade's eyes had adjusted to the dim light, he was able to pick out the figure of a man seated at the bar. He was dark-haired, in his early thirties, and appeared to be in the process of matching paper receipts to files on his laptop.

'That's fine. I'm not here for food or drink. I'm here to see Zach Farraday, the owner,' Reade explained.

'Is he expecting you?'

'No.' Reade displayed his badge. 'Hobson Glen Sheriff's Office. I need to speak with him about Gunnar Randall.'

'Gunnar Randall? What about him?'

'I'd prefer to discuss that with Mr Farraday, if he's around.'

'He is,' the man vaguely replied. 'If you haven't already guessed from the stacks of receipts, I'm Zach Farraday. Why do you want to talk to me about Gunnar Randall?'

'Because Mr Randall is dead.'

'And?' a nonchalant Farraday questioned. His voice and demeanor made it abundantly clear that Randall's demise had absolutely no impact whatsoever on either his personal or professional life. But Reade wondered if he was trying just a little too hard to appear casual.

'Randall died of mushroom poisoning. The mushroom that killed him was consumed Wednesday – the day he came here to record your segment for his television show.'

'And, of course, you thought it must have something to do with the guy with the police record.'

'Actually, I figured it had something to do with the food Randall sampled for his show that day, but this record of yours intrigues me,' Reade added with a smile.

'It was a long time ago. Kid stuff.'

'If you fulfilled your obligation to the court, your juvie files would have been expunged from your record when you turned nineteen, meaning I wouldn't have seen them. Unless, of course, we're not really talking about "kid stuff."'

'You know what, Sheriff?' Farraday proposed with a smirk. 'I'll save you the hassle of pressing the keys on your laptop. My last conviction occurred when I was twenty-two. Car theft. But I finished my sentence and have since amended my ways.'

'Church?' Reade presumed.

'No, not church, Sheriff. Unless Julia Child was named a saint – and she probably should have been. No, I didn't find Jesus, Sheriff – I found cooking. Jackson Payne, the world-famous chef, offered classes to those of us who were to be released on parole. If we excelled at those classes and entered his program, we stood a better chance of having our sentences reduced. If we graduated from his program and found work in the restaurant industry, our sentences were commuted.'

'So you graduated, entered the food industry, and now you have your own restaurant,' Reade said, filling in the blanks. 'That's quite commendable.'

'Commendable?' he sneered. 'I should have guessed that a cop would be impressed by a story that reinforces the old trope that hard work and clean living will get you "back on track." In reality, the justice system is broken, and if it weren't for good people like Jackson Payne, I'd still be bouncing back and forth between parole and a prison cell like every other juvenile offender with no obvious shot at a new life.'

'I agree – to a point. The justice system has obvious flaws in the disparity of its treatment of the rich and the poor, but I don't think it's completely broken. The prison system, on the other hand, is. Private enterprise has taken over, and it's more about keeping bodies in cells – often in deplorable conditions – than rehabilitating souls.'

'A lawman who talks about souls? Which Clint Eastwood movie did you step out of?'

Reade ignored the obvious jab at his age. 'So, why does a guy who's sensitive about his criminal record apply to be on *Taste of America*?'

'New restaurants need publicity,' he answered with a shrug.

'From a guy like Gunnar Randall? That's quite a switch from the benevolent Jackson Payne.'

'Jackson Payne's foundation gave me the grant to start this place.' Farraday looked around the room appreciatively. 'But that's not enough to keep it afloat. A great menu, reasonable prices, and excellent service help to generate word-of-mouth, but if you're gonna stay in the game for longer than the average four years, you need to raise the stakes.'

'So you applied for the show, despite knowing what Gunnar Randall was like, just to raise the stakes?'

'Mostly. If I'm perfectly honest, there was also a competitive element to it. I wanted to beat Randall. I wanted to be the cook who got the gold-star review. I wanted it to come out that the kid from the wrong side of the tracks defeated the chef from Beverly Hills, so I put together a plan to win. I polled my most loyal customers and asked them which menu items were their favorites. Then I rented a booth at the Saturday farmers' market and served the items my local customers enjoyed to see how they played out to a crowd that was unfamiliar with the pub. The items that repeatedly sold out were the ones I served for *Taste of America*.'

'Which were?'

'Arancini for a starter, followed by steak frites – a boneless rib-eye steak with Roquefort butter and duck tallow fries. And, to wash it all down, the Scarlett Pimpernel, my pub-brewed red IPA.'

'Arancini?' Reade questioned.

'Deep-fried balls of risotto. In this case, mushroom risotto . . . *wild* mushroom risotto,' Farraday elaborated in a gloating tone. 'Are you going to bring me in for questioning?'

The sheriff shrugged. 'Because you made mushroom risotto?'

'And because I have a record.'

'I'd prefer to learn what happened during the shoot first.'

'Not much. As expected, Randall showed up like he owned the place – he made his assistant request his coffee and water the moment they entered. The makeup person did my hair and smeared some cream on my face, and the camera and sound guys went over what they wanted from me for the intro, then we shot it. When that was finished, we shot the scenes of Randall tasting my food.'

'How did that go?'

Farraday shook his head and flashed a sardonic grin. 'About as well as anyone with a brain would have expected. I should have realized Randall was never going to give me a positive recommendation. He'd already decided against me when he arrived for the shoot. It didn't matter what I did or what food I turned out, I was never going to win.'

'So you believe the outcome was predetermined,' Reade presumed.

'Definitely. Randall's assistant, the makeup person, the crew – everyone who came here that day was operating under the impression that I would get a bad review. Whether that was an individual decision or whether Randall was expected to unilaterally dis everyone, I don't know, but the outcome was clear before we even started.'

'Did you say anything about your suspicions?'

'What and be accused of being a paranoid conspiracy theorist? Or worse – of being a sore loser even though I hadn't lost yet? Yeah . . . nah. I know when to keep my mouth shut.'

'When Randall criticized your cooking, what did he say?'

'He referred to Honor Amongst Thieves as a "gast-bro pub" because I serve "unenlightened bar food for dudes." More proof that my defeat was prearranged – Randall wasn't smart enough to come up with a line like that. Someone wrote it for him.'

Having met Gunnar Randall, Clemson Reade was inclined to agree with Farraday's assessment, but then how and why had Karma Frumm received a coveted excellent review? Had that been prearranged as well? 'How did you react to Randall's assessment?' Reade asked while typing a note about Karma into his tablet.

'Well, it was ridiculous, wasn't it?' Farraday laughed. 'I mean the guy wanted to sound cool and go for a laugh, but to pull the bro card was embarrassing.'

'So you weren't angry?'

'No,' Farraday denied with a sanguine smile. 'Not at all.'

'Really? Because I would have been pretty upset if I were you.'

'Baiting, Sheriff? Really?' the restaurant owner teased as he shook his head. 'No, I wasn't upset. When you've done time, you get used to being treated like a second-class citizen.'

'Are you saying that Gunnar Randall knew about your criminal record?'

'No, I'm saying that Gunnar Randall looked at everyone as if they were second-class citizens.' Farraday's eyes grew cold. 'Every. Single. One.'

FIFTEEN

Reade returned home just as Tish had finished sifting Marlowe and Tuna's litter boxes. 'Your timing is uncanny,' she remarked as she washed her hands in the kitchen sink. 'That's because I waited outside in the car until you were finished,' he wisecracked before planting a kiss on her lips.

'Who said that the romance dies once you move in together?' she quipped before returning the kiss. 'How was your afternoon?'

'Busy. Informative. Interesting. Lonely.'

'Ah . . . well, I can help with the last one.' She kissed him again. 'If you tell me about the first three.'

'Deal. And how was your afternoon?'

'Busy. Enjoyable.' She stared off into the distance. 'And yet . . . somewhat depressing.'

Reade's brow furrowed. 'This about the new place?'

'Yes.' She sighed. 'I have a riddle for you. How many women does it take to put a down payment on a new café building? Answer – a lot more than three.'

He gave her a puzzled look.

'MJ and Celestine both offered to front money for me to purchase the Bar and Grill building,' Tish explained. 'But even with their help, I still don't have enough for a down payment.'

'How shy are you?'

'Too much to mention.'

'You know, I have some money saved . . .' he started as he slid his arms around her waist and pulled her closer.

'I don't want to take money from everyone I know just to make this happen, Clemson.' She placed her head on his shoulder and held him tight. 'Especially MJ and Celestine – they need that money more than I do. I have no issue in bringing them in as partners in the business, but I can't allow them to invest every cent of their settlements into the café. And then there's you . . .'

'What about me?'

'I've only just moved in, and now you're offering to invest in a building for my business as well. It's too much. Too much, too soon.'

'I wouldn't be investing in your business,' he clarified. 'I'd be investing in you. Which, by the way, is all I want out of this: you and nothing else. We're a team, Tish – partners for the long haul. There may come a time when I'm not able to work. If and when that were to happen, I know you'd do whatever you could to take care of finances and help me through those difficulties, because that's what loving partners do for each other.'

Tish pulled back and gazed at Reade, tears welling in her blue eyes. 'I'm so thankful to have you. But what if I'm never able to recover from this? What if this is the end of my business? How am I supposed to help you through those difficulties should they arise, if I, myself, am a liability?'

'You're not a liability, Tish. You'll never be a liability. Least of all to me.' He stroked her hair with his right hand and smoothed it behind her ear. 'You'll make it through this, and I'll be by your side every step of the way, in whatever capacity you need – friend, significant other, business partner, carpenter . . .'

She smiled despite the tears that had begun streaming down her face. 'Carpenter? Are you going to build me a café?'

'Hey, if we can find a reasonable plot of land you like, I'd give it go,' he pledged.

'You would, wouldn't you?' She burrowed her face in his shoulder once again. 'And until we find that plot of land?'

'You're the Hobson Glen Sheriff Department's lead consultant. You won't be bored.'

She gave a soft laugh. 'No, I won't, will I? Ever since I first arrived here, cases have followed me. I kinda feel like Angela Lansbury.'

'Minus the sweater vests and sensible shoes.'

'I dunno, a nice little Fair Isle knit might be nice for winter,' she teased.

Reade raised a questioning eyebrow.

'Or maybe a blazer with shoulder pads,' she continued. 'Those should be making a comeback soon, shouldn't they?'

'I'd love you even if you wore a burlap sack, but Jules might have something to say about your fashion choices.'

'Ugh, that's right. He still hasn't forgiven me for wearing a scrunchie in my hair during one of those one-hundred-degree days we had this summer. The café was closed and I was standing over a stove, cooking a vat of barbecue sauce for an American Legion pig roast, but I still committed a crime against fashion – even though Jules was the only one who saw me commit it.'

'I'm surprised Jules doesn't make citizen's arrests,' Reade joked.

'From a patrol car with a glitter ball instead of flashing lights? Yeah, let's not give him any ideas,' she laughed, this time more heartily. 'So, what's new with the Gunnar Randall case?'

They flopped on to the living-room sofa, and Reade recounted his interviews with Tiffany Harlow and Zach Farraday.

'So Tiffany Harlow served Randall mushroom tea, and Zach Farraday served mushroom risotto arancini? Hmm . . .' Tish mused aloud when Reade had finished.

'What does "Hmm" mean?'

'"Hmm" means that we should probably consult with Doctor Andres regarding both menu items. In Harlow's case, the mushrooms are dried, chopped, and then steeped in boiling water. We know that cooking or freezing a Death Cap doesn't diminish its lethality, but what does drying do? Likewise, during the steeping process, precisely how much poison would seep into the tea and how much would be retained by the mushroom? Would the steeping liquid from the mushroom be sufficient to kill a man or would someone need to actually eat the mushroom itself?'

'Hmm, indeed,' Reade remarked as he made notes to himself on his phone. 'I'll shoot Doctor Andres an email.'

Tish nodded. 'You also need to ask about Zach Farraday's arancini. We already know that cooking a Death Cap has no effect on its toxicity, but what about cooking a Death Cap twice? The mushrooms in the arancini were cooked once in the risotto and then a second time during the frying process. Would that have any effect on the levels of amatoxins?'

Once again, Reade made notes.

'Of course, the real problem here,' she added with a frown, 'is that both delivery methods require meticulous planning.'

'Otherwise, Harlow and Farraday would have poisoned a bunch of other people in the process.'

'Exactly. In order to avoid compromising an entire batch of tea – which few restaurant owners can afford to do – Tiffany would have needed to dry the Death Cap, grind it up, and place it in a separate teabag just for Randall. Same goes for Farraday. The Death Cap couldn't have been cooked with the rest of the wild mushroom risotto. It must have been cooked separately and inserted into a ball of arancini prior to it being breaded, fried, and served to Randall.'

'So the crime would have been premeditated.'

'Yes, but why go to all that trouble if you're not sure whether you're receiving a bad review or not?'

'You wouldn't, unless you already knew that Randall was going to lambaste you.'

Tish's face was a question. 'Farraday said he suspected the show was rigged, but he only came to that conclusion after the filming.'

'We only have his word for that. What if he suspected the show was fixed all along? What if that's the real reason he applied to be on it?'

She tossed her head from side to side as she contemplated the scenario. 'It's possible, I suppose. It's also possible that one of the show's guests had a different axe to grind.'

'Such as?'

'Well, these are all people in the food industry. Maybe one of them crossed paths with Randall at an earlier date.'

'I wondered about that,' he stated. 'That's why, in addition to reviewing the video footage, I have Clayton looking into the featured food providers' backgrounds.'

At the mention of Clayton's name, the doorbell rang.

'I wonder who that could be on a Saturday night,' Tish stated as Reade rose from his spot.

'Me, too. I thought I'd made it clear to my other girlfriend that you'd be living here from now on and that she'd have to call before dropping by,' Reade joked, prompting Tish to send a fringed scatter pillow sailing past his head.

Still grinning from ear to ear, Reade opened the heavy door of the Cape Cod to reveal Officer James Clayton standing behind the thick glass of the storm door.

'I have some news on the Randall case,' Clayton announced and then held a brown paper bag aloft. 'And some Thai food – if you haven't already eaten.'

Reade held the storm door open to allow Clayton admittance.

'We haven't, actually. I was supposed to pick up Thai on the way home, but somehow I forgot. This is, um, this is new for you, though, isn't it? Typically, we say goodnight and, as long as nothing new crops up, we don't see each other again until the next morning.'

'Yes, sir. I know, but during your absence a few months back, me, Tish, and a couple of her friends would meet for dinner every night in order to review the notes on the bake-off case. I thought maybe a dinner meeting might help shed some light on this case.'

'That's an excellent idea!' Tish exclaimed as she bounded to the door and took the bag from Clayton's hands. 'I'll get the table set. I can't wait to hear about your findings.'

As Tish bounded off for the kitchen, Reade looked at Clayton dubiously. 'You really want to spend your Saturday evening with us?'

'I thought with Tish living here now, we could get some good work done.'

'Uh-huh.' Reade frowned. 'So, what happened to your date?'

Clayton feigned innocence. 'What date?'

'The one that fell through and prompted you to come here rather than go home to your parents or meet up with your buddies.'

The young officer sighed. 'OK, she stood me up.'

'I'm sorry.' Reade's sympathy was genuine. 'If it helps, it's happened to most of us at one time or another.'

'Yeah, that doesn't really help, but thanks anyway.'

'Sorry,' Reade replied awkwardly. 'I have some beer in the fridge.'

Clayton nodded. 'That would help.'

'Sure.' Reade led the officer to the kitchen, where Tish was in the process of arranging plates, napkins, and utensils on the square drop-leaf table. 'How much do I owe you for the takeout?'

'Nothing. I got it. Although . . .' Clayton paused. 'I am due for review soon and a raise would come in handy.'

Reade said nothing about the forthcoming review, but instead extracted two twenty-dollar bills from his wallet. 'Will this do for now?'

A flushed Clayton took the bills from the sheriff's hand. 'Yes, sir,' he mumbled.

'What did you find out, Jim?' Tish addressed the officer by his first name.

'How unbelievable it is that no one tried to kill Gunnar Randall before now.'

'We've yet to find hard evidence that Randall was murdered,' Reade cautioned.

'I know, and I'm keeping an open mind, but look at the odds, sir. I mean, everyone Randall knew – *everyone* – had a reason to want the guy out of the way.'

'Jim's right,' Tish agreed as she spooned a portion of chicken pad Thai on to her plate. 'It's unlikely Randall's death was an accident.'

'I admit that accidental poisoning is looking far less probable,' Reade relented as he took the container of pad Thai from Tish and added a helping on to his plate, alongside a vegetable spring roll. 'But we need to rule out every possibility. Now, apart from Gunnar Randall being universally disliked, what else did you unearth today?'

'For starters, I found Randall's journal among the belongings in his room. I only leafed through it, but it looks like he talks a lot about food and the show,' Clayton replied, scooping some crab fried rice and a tangle of pad kee mao on to his plate.

'Would it help if I take a look at it?' Tish offered. 'There could be some sort of clue in his food notes that you might not catch.'

'You read my mind. As one who can scarcely cook spaghetti, I thank you.' Clayton reached into his messenger bag and passed the leather-bound book across the table. 'Although I didn't have a chance to read the journal, I did go through most of the video footage from Wednesday, and everything seems to line up with the stories given to you, except for a couple of things . . . Mmm.' He slurped some of the drunken noodles into his mouth before referring to his phone. 'First, the Betancourts.'

'Really?' an intrigued Reade questioned.

Clayton took a sip of beer and helped himself to one of the veggie spring rolls. 'Yeah, according to your notes, the Betancourts claim that they let Randall leave without a fuss, but that wasn't the case at all. After the shoot, the grandmother confronted Randall and proceeded to strike him repeatedly with her handbag. The grandsons came along and pulled her away, but then they started shouting at Randall. The one in the suit poked him in the chest several times with his finger, while the one in the chef's outfit hit him with a tea towel.'

Clayton played the clip on his phone for Reade and Tish to view.

'It's like a sketch from *Monty Python's Flying Circus*,' she observed in disbelief.

'Well, it certainly reinforces the Betancourts' motives,' Reade noted.

'But there's still the question of premeditation.'

Reade nodded. 'Go on, Clayton.'

The officer took a sip of beer and continued, 'Since we're on the topic of video, there's Dalbir Singh. I'm not sure if he intended to capture it or if he just happened to have his camera on at the time, but there's a clip of Randall reaming the guy out, and it's brutal. Like, I don't know how the guy kept from socking Randall in the mouth, let alone how he kept from quitting his job.'

'Brutal how?'

Clayton tapped the screen of his phone twice and then presented it to his hosts. A video-player app launched a clip of Gunnar Randall standing outside a white panel van. He was staring at a spot directly above the camera and shouting. 'I'm the boss here, not you. You're just the cameraman. When I say I want something reshot, you reshoot it. Got that, towel-head? This is my show. My show, not yours! Hell, this isn't even your damn country. Are your relatives even here legally?'

As the clip ended, Tish and Reade stared at the blank screen of the phone, a look of contempt on their faces. 'Is it wrong to be happy that this man can't hurt anyone any longer?' Tish asked.

'If it is, then I'm wrong, too,' Clayton replied.

'I don't blame either of you for feeling that way,' Reade stated. 'But it's still our job to find out what happened to him.'

'And we *will* find out what happened to him,' Tish assured them. 'In the meantime, we can privately commiserate about what a terrible person he was.'

'The worst,' Clayton remarked before taking a hostile bite of spring roll.

'So,' Reade segued after a few seconds has elapsed, 'Singh has a strong motive for poisoning Randall, plus he had sufficient time and opportunity to plan the crime.'

'Same goes for Shae Fisher,' Clayton indicated. 'She mentioned acing an interview with the Cooking Network last month on her Facebook page.'

'She had an interview with a rival network and she made a public announcement on social media?'

'Um, it wasn't really a public announcement, no. Shae shared the post with just her friends. I only saw it because I, um, I asked my brother-in-law, the tech guy, to check into her account.'

'You mean *hack* into her account,' Reade corrected.

'Um, no, my brother-in-law swore to me it wasn't a hack, just a security loophole that allowed us to view her posts as a friend. Not comment on them – just view them.'

'Sounds suspiciously like a hack to me, but go ahead.'

'Shae raved about the interview and then, a week later, posted a rant about someone who was keeping her from following her dream because of his own mean-spiritedness and self-centeredness.'

'Gunnar Randall?'

'She didn't mention his name, but more than a few friends commented that they were sorry to hear that Shae's boss was being more of a jerk than usual. Shae didn't correct them. In fact, she thanked them for their sympathy.'

'She could have been talking about another boss at the Food Channel,' Reade suggested, playing devil's advocate.

'I doubt it,' Tish replied after slurping a forkful of pad Thai. 'Shae answered directly to Randall, didn't she? Also, the Food Channel bosses had no reason to keep her where she was. There are plenty of young graduates out there who'd be thrilled to take Shae's place for less money than she was probably earning after two years. No, the only person with a vested interest in ensuring that young woman remained an assistant was Randall.'

'You say that post appeared approximately three weeks ago, Clayton?' Reade verified.

'Yep,' he replied. 'Last week of July.'

Tish's eyes narrowed. 'That's certainly enough time to plan a murder. Shae knew Randall's order of choice in Virginia was a mushroom Swiss burger. She also brought him food frequently enough that he wouldn't question what she gave him. Also, the bun and the other burger condiments would have concealed the look of an odd mushroom.'

The sheriff helped himself to a second helping of drunken noodles and nodded. 'That burger was one of the last things Randall ate that day. Does it mesh with Doctor Andres's timeline?'

'If Randall consumed a large portion of mushroom, it does,' Tish noted.

'Hmm, what else do you have, Clayton?'

'Oh, this is a good one,' Clayton exclaimed. 'Around the same time Shae aced her interview, the Lou-Lous received an offer from none other than the Food Channel for a one-off documentary.'

'Gunnar Randall's network,' Tish confirmed as she got up and poured both herself and Reade a glass of white wine.

'That's right. Food Channel execs are currently in negotiations with the Lou-Lous' attorneys for the purchase of the Lou-Lous' story and all their recipes. The goal is to produce a network special and corresponding cookbook that would be available to the public sometime next year.'

'And the property and business?'

'No record of either being on the market. Not yet. Once the Food Channel special comes out, they'll probably be able to sell both for double what they're worth now.'

'Unless the deal with the Food Channel doesn't go through,' Reade proposed.

'Which might have been the case if they happened to get on the wrong side of the Food Channel's biggest star,' Tish speculated.

'Although, according to Shae Fisher, Gunnar's star was beginning to wane.'

'Eloise and Lula Mae didn't know that. They only knew Randall as a big TV star. Can you imagine how they must have felt when he walked through the door?'

'Terrified,' Clayton chimed in, 'but terrified enough to kill?'

'They had a lot to lose,' Tish reasoned. 'Just a little bit of sautéed mushroom in Randall's sausage and gravy would ensure their sudden windfall wasn't lost.'

'But where did they get the Death Cap mushroom from and why did they have it in the first place?' Reade argued. 'They didn't know Randall was going there for breakfast.'

'That's true. But then again, why would anyone have a Death Cap mushroom lying around the kitchen? Glory Bishop has them growing outside her kitchen door, but as for the other parties in this case . . .'

'As you mentioned earlier, it would indicate premeditation,' he stated before eating a bite of pad Thai.

'Well, if you're talking about premeditation, Zach Farraday is right up there with Fisher and Singh,' Clayton announced. 'I sifted through past records and, as far as I can find, he's the only member of this group who actually met Randall before this week.'

'Farraday and Randall knew each other?'

'I wouldn't go that far, but they did cross paths. Six years ago, Randall gave a cooking demonstration at the prison where Farraday was serving time for car theft. It was part of some inmate enrichment program. According to prison records, Farraday was in attendance. I have no other details on the demonstration or whether Farraday and Randall even came in contact with each other that day, but I have a call to the records office to see if there's a transcript or video recording of the event.'

'It's already been established that Farraday knew who Randall was, but if the two men connected during the demonstration at the prison that day, then there's a chance that Randall might also have recognized Farraday.'

'Which might explain why Farraday appeared to be predestined for a bad review,' Tish theorized. 'It could have been Randall's way of getting even for some perceived slight.'

Reade nodded. 'If they didn't interact, then it's fair to say that Randall probably wouldn't have remembered Farraday as being at that presentation.'

'Farraday would have been just another face in the crowd,' Clayton noted.

'Thus allowing Farraday to serve the poisonous mushroom on Wednesday without Randall suspecting anything,' Tish remarked. 'The only question is, what's Farraday's motive for murder?'

'Same as we discussed before – Randall's attitude toward ex-cons and other supposed failures in society,' Reade asserted.

'And the fact they were at the same presentation?'

'Doesn't change the motive one bit. Randall gave a presentation, but that doesn't mean he liked or was even pleasant to his audience.'

'So Farraday plotted to kill Randall after all these years just because of his attitude?' Tish questioned.

'It's thoroughly plausible. Farraday has a chip on his shoulder the size of Plymouth Rock. Although I agree that something else could have transpired at that demonstration,' Reade allowed. 'Clayton's going to get the transcripts and, I hope, talk to some of the guards who were there at the time.'

'Of course,' the young officer confirmed and, viewing Reade's statement as his cue to move forward, announced, 'Last but definitely not least, there's Karma Frumm. I received a message from the lab on my way here. That soil sample you brought back contained mycelium,' he read from his phone, 'which, I'm told, are kind of like the roots of a mushroom. Upon analysis of the mycelium, the lab determined that the mushrooms in the development shed weren't Death Caps. They were psilocybin mushrooms.'

'Magic mushrooms? No wonder Karma destroyed them before we got there – psilocybin mushrooms are a Schedule I drug. Trafficking in them carries fines up to half a million dollars and a felony charge of up to twenty years.'

'Should I file for an arrest warrant?' Clayton offered.

'Not yet. Let's get a warrant to search the rest of the farm and then bring Ms Frumm in for questioning.'

'Hoping she might tell you whether Randall found those mushrooms when he was poking around the development shed?' Tish surmised.

'The thought crossed my mind. How about you?'

'If he did, it gives Karma an extremely strong motive for wanting him dead. Her dish, if I'm not mistaken, was the only one that was actually cooked on camera.'

Clayton validated Tish's statement. 'All the mushrooms, garlic, and butter were chopped and portioned out in advance, but you're right, the cooking itself was done in real time.'

'The mushrooms were chopped, you say?'

'Yeah, they were like tiny little squares of mushrooms. I saw them in the footage.'

'In that case, it would have been extremely easy for Karma to slip in a Death Cap. She might have seen some growing on the property and maybe even gathered them up to prevent them from spreading elsewhere. After Randall went wandering around into the development shed, she could have grabbed the Death Cap, diced it up with a pocket knife or something similar that she probably carries with her for chores, and added the pieces to the other prepped mushrooms before cooking the whole thing in a skillet over the fire. The only thing that it doesn't explain is Randall's behavior.'

'How so?' Reade asked.

'Well, why didn't Randall report Karma to the police?'

'Because he wouldn't have a segment for the show if he had,' Reade reasoned.

'Given the way he abused some of these cooks, do you really think Gunnar Randall was concerned about getting a good cooking segment? No, Randall was all about creating drama. After calling the police, Randall would have instructed Dalbir to film Karma being taken away in handcuffs, and he would have enjoyed every single moment of her distress as she was taken away. It would have been a ratings buster.'

'What about the favorable review?'

'I don't know. It doesn't jive at all with Randall finding the magic mushrooms in the development shed. If Zach Farraday is correct and the *Taste of America* reviews are determined prior to filming, then I'd say Randall and his bosses wanted to exploit Karma's caregiving situation in order to make Randall look like a hero. However, if Zach is wrong and Randall made his decision by tasting the food provided during filming – as the show would have us all believe – then Karma's mushrooms must have been truly excellent.'

'According to Doctor Andres, the few people who have eaten a Death Cap and survived said it was the most delicious mushroom they'd ever tasted,' Reade recalled.

'Meaning Karma might have received her favorable review *because* she included the Death Cap,' Tish exclaimed with a gasp.

'Talk about irony,' Clayton commented.

'Not exactly irony – more like unfortunate coincidence. It's kind of like that Alanis Morrissette song. Nothing in it is actually ironic. That line about being surrounded by thousands of spoons when you need a knife? That's just a sad coincidence. Revise it to say that you're surrounded by thousands of spoons in the break room of a Ginsu knife factory – now that's ironic.'

Clayton's face went blank. 'That Morris-what song?'

'I knew what you meant,' Reade said as rubbed her shoulder. 'Although I'd argue that Morrissette's lack of actual irony in the song could, in itself, be considered ironic.'

'Oooh, I never thought of that. What if you're right?'

'It would be a little too ironic. Dontcha think?'

'Nerd alert,' Clayton said under his breath.

'What was that?' Reade demanded, although it was clear from his smirk that he had heard his officer's words clearly enough.

'Um, nothing, sir . . . j–just channeling something Mr Davis would say if he were here.'

'We don't need another Jules, Clayton.'

'That's for sure,' Tish reiterated. 'I have a hard enough time keeping up with the one we have.' With that, the doorbell rang. 'Why did you have to mention Jules's name, Clayton? That's probably him now.'

'Don't be ridiculous,' Reade questioned as he stood up and moved toward the door that connected the kitchen with the hallway. 'Why would Jules come here tonight?'

'Because I told Celestine and Mary Jo that I moved in with you, but I didn't tell him.'

'Come on. Even for Jules, that's crazy.'

'You haven't known him as long as I have,' she called after him.

Within seconds, Jules's voice came roaring from the foyer. 'Why was I the last to know?' He marched into the kitchen and draped himself in the doorway, still dressed in his work attire of well-tailored gray pinstriped suit and purple tie. In one hand, he held Biscuit's leash, in the other, a brown shopping bag. 'How could you do this to me? *Me?*' he asked dramatically. 'Just last night, I was trying to convince you to move in with Sheriff Reade, but you played it cool, only to come running here directly from my apartment! No text, no call. I had to get the news from Mary Jo.'

'I'm sorry, Jules. Between tomorrow's wedding, Gunnar Randall's death, and looking for finance options for the Bar and Grill building, it's been a busy day.'

'OK. I can accept that, but why did *he*' – Jules pointed an index finger at Clayton – 'know before I did?'

'I only found out because we're on a case,' Clayton said defensively.

'A case? Did you even consider that Tish and Sheriff Reade should be spending their first night in their mutual home—'

'Second night,' Tish corrected.

'First full day as a cohabitating couple,' Jules revised with the clearing of his throat, 'alone and without discussions of death and murder?'

Tish rose from her seat and poured Jules a glass of wine. 'Is that why you're here? So Clemson and I can have "alone time"?'

'Of course! I brought Thai food, didn't I?' Jules held the brown bag aloft while eyeing the wine glass eagerly.

Tish grabbed the bag from Jules's hand and replaced it with the wine glass. 'Delivering dinner for two, huh?' she questioned after a quick rummage through the bag. 'Is that why there are three shrimp summer rolls in here?'

Jules took a sip of wine. 'Naturally,' he answered with a chuckle. 'That man of yours has a healthy appetite.'

'Uh-huh, I suppose that's why in addition to my favorite basil chicken and Reade's pad Thai, there's a serving of Panang prawn curry – your favorite dish – in here as well?'

'There is? Oh, my! I order from that restaurant so often, I guess they just added it automatically!'

'Yes, and I know what you're like. You came here because you were afraid of missing out on the party.'

'All right, guilty as charged.' He passed Biscuit's leash to Reade, who, in turn, tied it to the base of the kitchen table. 'But you can't be angry with a friend who wants to congratulate you! Especially after you made him uncover the news on his own.'

'Well, you are a journalist, aren't you?' she teased, her arms wide open.

Jules flew into them and embraced her tightly. 'I am, but you shouldn't make me work, honey. Congratulations!'

'Thanks, Jules. I'm sorry again for not telling you.'

'All is forgiven.' He extended his hand to Sheriff Reade. 'Congratulations. I'm so excited for you two.'

'Too excited to eat?' Tish asked with a laugh.

Jules sat down at the table while Tish grabbed a plate and a fork. 'Are you kidding? I'm never too excited for that. Now, tell me, what case are y'all working on when you should be dancing and drinking champagne?'

'Off the record?' Reade asked.

'Clemson – and I am going to call you Clemson rather than Sheriff now that you and Tish have made things more official – when have I ever quoted you without your permission?'

'You haven't.'

'That's right. And I'm certainly not going to start now, so spill it.'

'Gunnar Randall was found dead at Abbingdon Green Bed and Breakfast this morning.'

'Yes, I got a whisper of that at the station. I didn't believe it! Gunnar Randall dying at a quaint little country inn just doesn't seem to fit his personality, does it? Oh . . . what about the wedding? It's still on, I hope.'

'Clemson cleared us to go ahead,' Tish explained as she took her seat.

'Excellent.' Visibly relieved that the weekend's festivities were still on schedule, Jules extracted his dinner from the bag that Tish had placed on the table and dished some food on to his plate. 'Sooooo . . . what about Gunnar Randall? What happened to him? Did he finally choke on his own bile?'

'Close. He died from mushroom poisoning.'

'Mushroom poisoning?' He wrinkled his nose. 'Accidental or intentional?'

'Off the record?' Reade reiterated.

'Seriously, Clemson, you're asking me again? Show me some love, will you?'

The sheriff relented. 'We're not sure yet, but it seems most likely that someone fed the mushroom in question to Randall while he was filming for his show.'

'The list of people wanting to bump off Gunnar Randall has to be a long one.'

'It is,' Clayton confirmed.

'Glory Bishop isn't on it, is she?'

'No,' Tish replied before opening the container of basil chicken and stabbing a piece with her fork. 'There are poisonous mushrooms growing in her yard, but the mushroom omelet she cooked for Randall was ingested far too late to be considered suspicious.'

'But you're forgetting that Glory does a welcome tray for her guests,' Jules reminded her. 'My mama stays at Abbingdon Green whenever she visits, and she raves about it.'

'A welcome tray,' Tish repeated, her voice a near whisper. 'You're right. I'd completely forgotten.'

'What's on this welcome tray?' Reade asked.

'Depends on the time of year. But it's mostly refreshments and snacks – a large bottle of water, some canapés, maybe some cheese, crackers, and fruit, and some wrapped items like cookies and chips to enjoy during the stay.'

'And when does a guest receive a welcome tray?'

'Upon arrival, of course.' Jules answered matter-of-factly while spooning a helping of sticky rice on to his plate. 'That's why it's called a welcome tray. However, if you don't finish it right away, the staff will wrap it for you. My mama always saves hers and brings it to my apartment – plate and all – covered in plastic wrap. We always enjoy it with some tiny bottles of airline wine she stashes in her purse during her flight. That's my mama for you! Waste not, want not.'

Tish smiled, but she was lost in thought. 'The welcome tray puts Glory back in the spotlight, doesn't it?'

'With what motive?' Reade challenged. 'Glory says she had no idea Gunnar Randall was booked into the Turret Suite until Shae checked him in.'

'That's not exactly true. When I spoke with Glory, she stated that she had no idea the booking was being made on Randall's behalf, but she never told me precisely *when* she learned the identity of her mystery guest – only that had she known from the beginning it was Randall, she'd never have accepted the reservation. I just assumed she found out when Shae checked him in, but that's not necessarily the case.'

Clayton scrolled through the files on his phone. 'Tish is right. Ms Bishop's statement from this morning says the exact same thing – when the reservation was made one year ago, she had no idea it was for Gunnar Randall. If she had it to do all over again, knowing what she does now, she would have told Shae Fisher the B and B was completely booked. There's no mention of when she learned the room was for Gunnar Randall.'

'If Glory knew in advance that Randall was coming, that gives her opportunity, but we still need a motive.'

'I didn't see any previous connections between Bishop and Randall.'

'You probably won't find any, either. Randall was trash and Glory Bishop is a lady,' Jules pronounced as he beat Clayton to the last of the spring rolls. 'But if you want a motive, Glory Bishop was terrified of being on Randall's show. Period. Exclamation mark.'

'Well, yes, she told us she didn't want to be on the show, but I wouldn't say she was terrified.'

'She was,' Jules asserted.

Tish folded her arms across her chest. 'And you know this how?'

'Our makeup artist, Destiny, was giving Ms Enid Kemper's parrot, Langhorne, his weekly wash and blow dry – Enid used to do it herself, but the poor dear's arthritis has been acting up lately, so Destiny volunteers to do it for free – and Enid told her that she had just spoken to Opal Schaeffer, who had just spoken to Glory Bishop, who was a right mess because Gunnar Randall was spending a few nights at her bed and breakfast. Glory said she was absolutely petrified about the possibility of her place being critiqued on his show.'

'When was this?' Reade asked.

'Let's see . . . Destiny was in the studio Tuesday, so she must have spoken to Enid either Monday or sometime over the weekend.'

'Meaning Glory knew Randall was arriving as early as Monday.'

'And Destiny found all this out while blow-drying Langhorne's feathers?' Tish questioned.

'Yes. You know how Enid is.'

'And yet I knew nothing about it?'

'Well, you would have, honey, but since the café is closed and Opal doesn't bring you veggies from her garden, and Enid doesn't stop by for her Sunday pimento cheese sandwich with a side of Langhorne's pasta with seeds, you're a bit out of touch with local gossip. But don't worry – once you find a new café, you'll be back in the loop.'

'I don't care that I'm not in touch with local gossip, Jules, but why didn't you tell me Gunnar Randall was going to be at Abbingdon Green this weekend? You knew we were catering a wedding there,' Tish complained.

'Well, I didn't think much of it at the time. I mean who cared if Gunnar Randall was there? It wasn't like I knew he was as mean in real life as he was on his show. Besides, Destiny and I spilled the tea about a good number of things. She was in the studio doing hair and makeup for our segment with Jackson Payne and was killing time at my desk between shots.'

'Wait one minute! You said Jackson Payne was in your studio,' Tish nearly shrieked.

Jules dropped his fork and blushed bright crimson. 'Um, yes, um, no, um, uh-oh . . .'

'Jackson Payne? You were angry with me for not telling you that I moved in with Clemson; meanwhile, Jackson Payne was in your studio and you didn't say a word?'

It might have been the first time Tish had ever seen Jules speechless. 'I–I–I couldn't tell you,' Jules explained after several seconds elapsed. 'The studio made me swear not to tell *anyone*! Jackson Payne hasn't granted an interview to anyone since his wife died last year. He's been up north with friends in Boston, but now he's back home in Richmond, and the city is throwing a party this weekend to celebrate his eighty-fifth birthday. Every restaurant in the city limits will be contributing to the dinner. We only just got the scoop now because Mr Payne's people didn't want him to be swarmed with fans and other reporters.'

Tish still fumed. 'I'm not just anyone, Jules. I'm your best friend. You know how I love Jackson Payne. I grew up watching his cooking shows on TV.'

'Yes, I know, honey. You still watch those old episodes whenever you're sick or in a funk,' Jules replied. 'I binge-watched three different Jackson Payne series with you after you and Mitch broke up.'

'Then you know how much it would have meant to me to have met him.'

'I do and I'm sorry I didn't tell you, but I couldn't. Even though you're my best friend and I love you to death, to the station, you're still "anyone."'

'Jackson Payne,' Reade repeated. 'That's the second time today I've heard that name.'

'You're about to hear the name for a third time. Jackson Payne was Gunnar Randall's lunch date on Wednesday,' Clayton announced.

The news was bizarre enough to make Tish completely forget any perceived slight on the part of Jules. 'Lunch date? I can't believe those two knew each other, let alone spoke to each other.'

Clayton shrugged. 'They were both chefs. Doesn't seem too unusual to me.'

'It does from the perspective of temperament,' Reade explained. 'Jackson Payne's inmate education program gave Zach Farraday the incentive he needed to get out of the system. Then, once Farraday had the cooking chops, Payne's foundation provided Farraday the seed money to start his business.'

'Meanwhile, Gunnar Randall degraded up-and-coming food producers and made Farraday feel like a loser,' Tish said as she assessed the two chefs. 'My only question is, if Randall truly felt that people in the criminal justice system were second-class citizens, why did he do a cooking demonstration at a prison? It doesn't really fit, does it?'

'I'll see if I can find out the circumstances behind his presentation when I speak to the prison officials,' Clayton promised.

'And I'll contact Jackson Payne's staff to find out the details of his lunch with Randall and possibly schedule a visit,' Reade added.

'Oh, I know exactly who you should speak with,' Jules said excitedly. 'His name is Nick Latanzza. He's Jackson Payne's right-hand man and, I think, a cook in his own right since he tests Mr Payne's recipes before they go into his cookbooks.'

'For someone who just hung out and gossiped with Destiny during Jackson Payne's interview, you seem to know a lot about his writing process,' Tish sniffed, prompting Jules to roll his eyes.

'I saw him discuss Latanzza's role in one of the preview clips we're airing this coming week,' an exasperated Jules explained.

'A preview clip? And you didn't even think to send me a link?'

'I didn't have a link to send,' Jules replied with a sigh. 'Because it's an exclusive interview, the station manager aired the preview in the conference room as a celebratory event. Unless I held my phone in the air and recorded it, there was no way to share anything with you.'

Tish pulled a face as she mulled over the feasibility of Jules performing such a maneuver without being caught by his coworkers. 'OK,' she relented and then, turning to Clemson, stipulated, 'but if you think I'm staying home while you visit Jackson Payne at his home, think again.'

'Honey, I wouldn't dream of leaving you behind,' Clemson assured her as he wrapped an arm around her shoulders and grinned. 'Not after seeing how you treated poor Jules.'

She pushed his arm away and pretended to slap his hand. 'I'm sorry for reacting so badly, but Jackson Payne is an idol of mine. When I was home sick as a kid, I learned how to make myself an omelet by watching his show. Later on, it was to freeze onion skins, carrot peels, and other bits and bobs of vegetables that otherwise might go to waste and then, when the freezer bag was full, simmer them into a rich stock. Jackson Payne is a teacher – an artist who shares his gift with the world. Gunnar Randall wasn't fit to lick his boots, let alone dine with him.'

Jules reached across the table and gave Tish a fist bump. 'After watching him with you while we were in college, all I can say is amen, sister.'

Tish reciprocated.

'Am I forgiven?' Jules asked.

'You know you are,' she replied. 'Am I forgiven for not telling you about Clemson and me?'

'Sweetie, it was a non-starter,' Jules responded. 'All I wanted was to be part of things. Look, I came here with food.'

'The true Southern white flag!'

'Don't you know it! So, how can I help?'

'Help?'

'Between the wedding tomorrow and you needing to pack up the old café and find a new one, you have a lot on your plate. What can I do?'

'Nothing that I can think of,' Tish replied.

'Nothing? I can collect your things and bring them here. I can scope out potential new places. I can help with the investigation. Let me do something. Put me to use!'

'I honestly can't think of anything, Jules. Everything is pretty much packed up. We'll take care of the rest of it – including my personal belongings – during the week. As for new places, I've already set an alert on the real estate websites.'

'As for the investigation, we're going to follow up with everyone tomorrow,' Reade explained. 'But if we can't get anywhere with the Lou-Lous, they might be ripe for an interview with everyone's favorite newsman: what they're doing now, how much their business brings to the community.'

'Ooh! Everyone loves Lou-Lou's. That's a great public interest story.'

'I think we'd need a little more than a public interest story. It seems the Lou-Lous have struck a deal with the Food Channel,' Tish informed him.

'The Lou-Lous on the Food Channel? OMG, are you giving me a scoop? You are! You're giving me a scoop. Darling, I'm your man.' He straightened the lapels on his dress shirt, and then cleared his throat. 'Well, Clemson is your man, specifically, but you knew—'

'What you meant? Yes. Yes, I did. You know, it might be helpful to have you speak with Randall's assistant, Shae Fisher, as well.'

Reade was skeptical. 'A local television personality speaking with a woman who worked for a national television personality? I doubt she'd give Jules the time of day.'

'She might if I told her I was working on an investigative report about the *real* Gunnar Randall,' Jules replied with a sly grin.

Tish nodded. 'At best, she'll tell you everything. At worst, she'll throw her credentials at you and tell you to get lost.'

'But if she throws her credentials, we'll learn more about her offer from the Cooking Network – the offer she's now free to take,' Reade surmised.

'Just give me the word and I'll be on it faster than I can un-tag myself from an unflattering Facebook photo,' Jules bragged. 'But are y'all going to have the time to question everyone? I mean, together?'

'Tomorrow's wedding puts me in a crunch for the rest of the weekend, but once that's over . . .' Tish's voice trailed off.

Reade reached beside him and squeezed her hand. 'Once that's over, it's on to new adventures.'

'Hear, hear,' Jules seconded.

'And meeting Jackson Payne,' Clayton added.

At the mention of Jackson Payne, Tish's spirits rose. 'Did you know that Jackson Payne had to close down two of his restaurants back in the day? It was after the market crash in the late eighties. The two upscale restaurants – one in New York City and the other in Boston – both Michelin-starred, exclusive, and quite expensive. When the bottom dropped out of the market, the restaurants lost the majority of their clientele, so he shut them down and opened a soup restaurant on Fifth Avenue in New York, just down the block from the library.'

'A soup restaurant?' Jules repeated between bites of curry.

'Yes, three different kinds of soup each day, all served with bread and salad. There was also an array of classic French pastries available for dessert. I ate there once when I was a teenager visiting the city – it was fabulous. That's a strange thing to say about soup and bread, but it was absolutely delicious. So fresh and simple. The restaurant targeted area workers as well as budget-minded tourists, but I'm pretty sure it attracted its fair share of foodies who might otherwise not be able to afford a Jackson Payne meal.'

'Great marketing angle,' Clayton noted.

'Yeah, although I'm not sure it was necessarily an "angle." Jackson Payne never returned to the upscale restaurant scene. Instead, he focused on his TV shows, cookbooks, and teaching. Hmph,' she thought out loud, 'maybe I need to follow Jackson Payne's lead and reinvent myself and the café.'

'Not if it means losing the *Portrait of the Artist as a Young Ham* breakfast sandwich,' Reade warned.

'Or the *Zelda Fitzgerald*,' Jules rejoined. 'There are days when knowing that I'm having that fried chicken and pimento cheese sandwich for lunch is the only thing that gets me through the morning.'

'Same here,' Clayton chimed in, 'except it's the *Fromage to Catalonia*. Ever since you introduced us to bocadillos during the Honeycutt case, Tish, they've been my go-to lunch order.'

'In other words, it's a no for reinvention,' Tish summarized.

'I think your concept is perfect the way it is,' Reade said. 'That's why you were doing a booming business before you closed. The problem is with the real estate market – not you.'

'Clemson's right,' Jules agreed. 'Everyone loved your menu and its punny names. But maybe you can ask Jackson Payne what he thinks. You and Clemson are going to speak with him, right? Maybe just put a little word in his ear about your café.'

'It's not a social visit,' Tish argued. 'We're speaking with Payne to find out what happened to Gunnar Randall.'

'Maybe it's not the best timing, but it's worth a shot. I heard in Payne's interview that he's all about mentoring other chefs these days.'

'That's right, Jules. He mentors chefs, not cooks who moonlight with the sheriff's department,' Tish clarified as both Reade and Clayton's phone chimed in unison.

'I'd hold off on that conversation for now,' Reade advised.

'See?' Tish taunted. 'Clemson's on my side.'

'Well, of course he is,' Jules cried. 'He doesn't want to live with an angry woman. No one does!'

'It's not that,' Reade denied. 'It's Jackson Payne. He's just been rushed from his birthday party at The Jefferson to the Virginia Commonwealth Hospital. He's in extreme gastrointestinal distress.'

SIXTEEN

'I know I wanted to meet Jackson Payne, but a hospital room chat wasn't exactly what I had in mind,' Tish remarked as Reade pulled the SUV into the parking lot of Virginia Commonwealth University Medical Center.

'Doctors finding traces of amatoxins in his urine probably wasn't what Jackson Payne had in mind for tonight either,' Reade stated before exiting the car and escorting Tish through the sliding glass doors of the hospital.

Jackson Payne was located on the fifth floor of the hospital, in a private room in a wing reserved for high-profile patients. The nurse outside his room apprised Tish and Reade of his condition: 'His kidney and liver levels are good . . . blood pressure low but steady . . . Doctors caught the poison early enough . . . He's been given activated charcoal and will receive a course of acetyl-cysteine . . . fluids by IV . . . lots of rest. Only a doctor can give a prognosis, but for now he's stable and responding well.'

'Any timeframe on when Mr Payne consumed the Death Cap?'

'Because of the patient's advanced age and various health issues, the effects of the poison would have struck earlier than in a healthy person. The doctor expects the mushroom was consumed approximately three to four hours prior to arrival here.'

They thanked the nurse and she led them into Payne's room, where a tall, bearded man in a black tuxedo stood vigil. Reade displayed his badge and introduced both himself and Tish.

'Nicolas Latanzza,' the tall man replied with a slight Italian accent. He was just shy of fifty, with brilliant blue eyes that made his dark hair appear even blacker. 'I am Chef Payne's assistant.'

'He is more than that,' spoke the figure in the bed. 'He's one of the most talented chefs I know and the driving force behind my foundation. Without him, it would never have gotten off the ground.'

'As always, Chef Payne is too modest. He is the inspiration for my career, the reason I chose my life's work. He is who I want to be when I grow up.'

A smile spread across Jackson Payne's pallid face. He looked far grayer and frailer than Tish recalled him being – clearly the loss of his beloved wife had taken a physical toll. 'You are too kind, Nick, too kind. But who are our guests?'

'Sheriff Clemson Reade,' the lawman flashed his badge. 'And my associate Tish Tarragon.'

'The health problems of an old man are worthy of calling the police?' he asked with a chuckle.

'When those health problems involve the consumption of a Death Cap mushroom, they are.'

Payne's mood became solemn. 'A Death Cap? Someone clearly made a mistake. A cook's assistant perhaps? I remember when I was a young apprentice, a knowledge of mushrooms was mandatory, but now . . .'

'Sir,' Reade gently interjected, 'your poisoning isn't an isolated incident. Gunnar Randall was found dead from Death Cap poisoning just this morning.'

'Then there must be a bad shipment of mushrooms in town,' Payne insisted. 'There are only a handful of suppliers in this city. Tell restaurants and supermarkets to pull mushrooms from their shelves and then start making phone calls. You should be able to track down the bad shipment fairly quickly.'

'I'm sure Sheriff Reade will do exactly as you recommend, Chef,' Tish addressed the man in a tender voice. 'However, we also need to address the possibility that Gunnar Randall was murdered and that your illness might be the result of an attempt on your life.'

Jackson Payne's heretofore pale complexion turned scarlet. 'An attempt? Are you suggesting that someone at my party intentionally fed me a poisonous mushroom?'

'What time did the party begin?' Reade asked.

'What does that have to do with anything?' Latanzza volleyed.

'Mr Payne asked whether someone at the party fed him the mushroom. In order to answer that question, I need to know when the party started.'

'Five o'clock,' Payne replied, much to Latanzza's discomfort.

Reade and Tish both glanced up at the clock on the wall. It was just shy of nine thirty. 'Then, yes, Mr Payne, I'm afraid someone at the party did feed you the poisonous mushroom,' Tish told the older man.

'I can't believe it. I won't believe that someone from the food community is responsible for . . . for murder. Or attempted murder. Food is love. Food is nurturing. After birth, a mother suckles her young. As the child grows, they are introduced to different flavors, different tastes, different textures, but also different food experiences: birthday cake, Mother's Day chicken dinner, peppermint canes at Christmas, the first spring vegetables from the garden. Even in adulthood, the importance of food remains – the meal you choose to impress that special person in your life,' he explained as his eyes slid between Tish and Reade. 'Then the wedding cake, the anniversary dinners, the new holiday food traditions you create in your own home. And then, of course, the cycle begins again with your children. Food gives life to the soul as well as the body. Food, as I said, is love. Those who dedicate themselves to the creation of food also have to be dedicated to the well-being of other beings. If they are not, then they should not be in the food industry.'

Nick Latanzza nodded. 'No one whose heart and soul are grounded in cooking should ever use food as a weapon.'

'You're right,' Tish agreed. 'Food bridges the space between individuals and allows them to become acquainted with each other in a way that words can't always achieve.'

Payne's face broke into a broad smile. 'Your words . . . you're a cook, too, aren't you?'

Tish longed to answer and yet she didn't want to sideline the investigation. 'Um, I, um . . .'

'Ms Tarragon runs a fantastic little café just outside the city. It has a literary theme and serves up the best breakfast and lunch items I've ever tasted. She might moonlight with the sheriff's office, but her heart is one-hundred-percent chef.'

It was Tish's turn to blush.

'A literary theme? Intriguing. Once I am free from my intravenous shackles, I'll have to visit this café,' Payne responded.

'Oh, that's nice of you, but . . . um, well, you can't,' Tish informed the elderly chef. 'My café is closed and I'm not sure when or where it will reopen.'

'Why? What has happened?'

'Oh, it's a long story and we're here to ask you questions, not to talk about my business.'

'I was the one whose life was threatened this evening; therefore, I think I should decide what we discuss. As for time' – Payne smirked as he held both arms aloft to display the myriad of tubes and wires to which he was connected – 'you have a captive audience.'

'I'll make this brief. I was evicted from the building I was renting by my former boyfriend and now, what with this being a seller's market, I'm having difficulty locating a new site for my restaurant.'

'It's tragic, is it not? To be a chef, one needs to have the heart and soul of an artist. But to be a chef who is also a successful entrepreneur, one also needs the brain of a businessperson and the riches of Croesus. How many people did your café seat?'

The question caught Tish off guard. 'Um, about thirty.'

'Good for a start, but too small. Your business must be exceedingly busy on weekends.'

'It was.' She made certain to emphasize the past tense.

'That is why you need a space that seats between seventy-five and one hundred people. Families having a big breakfast, millennials meeting for brunch, girlfriends getting together for lunch while the children are at school – these all require larger tables and, therefore, larger seating capacity.'

'Yes, I suppose they do.'

'We agree. Good! Then, as soon as you can, start looking for a larger place.'

Tish frowned. She couldn't even afford a new space that seated fifty. How was she to afford a space that accommodated double that number?

'I see the doubt in your eyes, but it's true,' Payne continued. 'My wife, Jeannette, was from France – a descendant of one of the legendary *Mères Lyonnaises*, the female chefs who drove the restaurant industry prior to the World Wars. Jeanette inherited a sensitive palate and a keen business sense, and she taught me to see stumbling blocks as an opportunity to expand. I was reluctant to follow her advice at first, but she was right, and I was foolish in my reluctance, but, of course, I never had the business sense – only the passion for cooking.'

Payne fell silent and stared off into the distance, his face full of grief. His companions allowed him to remain in his fugue state for several seconds before speaking.

'Thank you, Chef,' Tish said quietly. 'I appreciate your advice.'

Payne did not reply but instead closed his eyes.

Again, the room was swathed in silence. After a few more somber moments had elapsed, Payne opened his eyes, but still he said nothing.

'Mr Payne,' Reade addressed the man. 'Mr Payne?'

The chef blinked slowly and turned his head to look at the sheriff. 'Yes?' he asked groggily.

'Are you OK to answer some questions?'

'Yes. Yes, I'm sorry. I was lost in the past there for a moment. It seems to happen more and more – me finding myself wandering among the shades of what were. I suppose that's what happens when you realize that the road ahead of you is far shorter than the road you've traveled. I suppose I knew that years ago, but it was easy to ignore with someone at my side. Now that I'm alone . . .' Payne drew a heavy breath and smiled wearily. 'What would you like to know, Sheriff?'

'Tonight's party – can you think of anyone in attendance who might be holding a grudge against you?'

'Oh, there's one chef who might be upset that I won thirty dollars from him in poker last night, even though he took me for fifty last time we saw each other. And there's another chef who would love to have created my ricotta quenelle recipe, but she knows that I'm secretly envious of the brilliance behind her recipe for quick brioche. I think we might be even.'

'You can't think of anyone else?'

'No. No one.'

'And nothing out of the ordinary occurred tonight?'

'Apart from me dressing up in a tuxedo for the first time in twenty years, no.'

'You and Gunnar Randall met with each other this past Wednesday. What did you meet about?'

Payne shrugged. 'Nothing. Since I returned to Richmond, I've received dozens of visitors. Chef Randall happened to be one of them.'

'So there was no agenda on either of your parts?'

'I cannot speak for Chef Randall, but I certainly did not have one.'

'So what did you discuss?'

'What chefs typically discuss when they're together – food trends, techniques, new ingredients, favorite meals, new tools.'

'Had Chef Randall ever visited you before?'

'No, but I knew who he was, just as he knew who I was.'

'You're a fan of his show?'

Payne suppressed a laugh. 'No. No, I am not. Chef Randall is – er, was – an example of a new breed of chefs. This new breed sees cooking as a competition rather than art.'

'But there have always been cooking competitions,' Tish noted.

'Yes, Ms Tarragon, there have been, but not the kind of competition that Randall and his ilk promote – a competition that touts strength and superiority rather than beauty, art, and skill. A competition that does not provide careful and helpful criticism to those who fall short of expectations, but humiliates them and categorizes them as "losers." Food, as I said, is love, and the creators of food should treat each other with courtesy and respect. They should offer help and advice to each other rather than kick each other when they're down. So, no, I am not a fan of the show.'

'And your thoughts on Chef Randall himself?' Reade asked.

Nick Latanzza leaped forward. 'Chef Payne has already provided you with his opinion of Chef Randall. What's the point of asking him again?'

'Chef Payne has told me his opinion of Randall's show, not Randall himself,' Reade clarified.

'It's all right, Nick.' Payne urged his assistant to back down. 'I respected Gunnar Randall as a chef. He was actually quite talented, but he also had a reputation for being arrogant. He worked in, and was let go from, several restaurants before taking the television job.'

Latanzza huffed. 'You could have found out about Randall's work history on your own, Sheriff. You didn't need to bother Chef Payne.'

'Sometimes it's good to have your findings verified by other sources. What about you, Mr Latanzza? Were you present at Chef Payne's meeting with Gunnar Randall?'

'Yes, I was,' the assistant confirmed.

'Nick was there for only part of the meeting,' Payne elaborated. 'After serving us coffee, he left Chef Randall and me alone to chat.'

'Chef—' Nick began to argue.

'It's true. You were out of the room for most of the visit.'

'Chef, this isn't—' Nick started in a stern tone but then apparently thought better of it.

Reade glanced at Tish, his face a question. She nodded her reply.

'Mr Latanzza, why don't you and I continue our conversation outside?' The sheriff escorted him out of the room, leaving Tish to continue questioning Jackson Payne.

'You're quite protective of Chef Latanzza,' she stated when the assistant had left the room.

'He's quite protective of me,' Payne replied.

'How and when did he become your assistant?'

'Ten years ago, I shot a series that featured younger chefs I admired. I was turning seventy-five and figured since that would be one of the last television series I'd film, it would be nice to pass the baton to the next generation.'

'I binge-watched that series not too long ago. It was called *Jackson Payne and Friends*. It was an entertaining show – an informative one, too. I picked up several useful hacks that came in handy while running the café.'

'I'm glad you found it helpful. Since you watched it, then you probably know that Nick was one of the fifteen chefs to make a guest appearance on the show.'

'Really? I don't remember seeing him.' Tish gave her head a vigorous shake as if to loosen the cobwebs clouding her memory. 'I must have been watching while I was tired or sick or something.'

'Nick was one of the first chefs to appear. He was in the second episode – maybe the third. My memory isn't what it used to be.' He paused and drew the blankets up to his chin. 'What I do remember is that Nick and I had so much fun on the set that we decided then and there that we had to work together again, so when the show was finished, we set a date for him to come to my house and brainstorm. We decided to work on a cookbook together – hints from the chefs, kitchen tricks both old and new – which would also feature some of our favorite recipes and each of our variations on them.'

'I own most of your books and I don't think I've ever heard of that one.'

'That's because it was never published. I called my agent, who called my publisher, who shot down the idea. The reason? Nicolas Latanzza was an unknown. My agent then contacted the company that produced my television shows and pitched the idea to them. They rejected it on the same ground my publisher cited – had I decided to do a series with Julia Child, they'd have supported it, but Nicolas Latanzza was an unknown quantity. No one wants to see a celebrity chef and an unknown, they said.'

'So what happened?'

'We decided to do a different book – one of holiday food and traditions from around the world. We combined our travel and eating experiences and met with home cooks from different cultures. It was quite the undertaking.'

'Yes, I own that book and use it for celebrations for family and friends. It's fabulous! However, if I recall correctly, only your name is on it. I don't believe there's a co-author listed.'

'There isn't. My publisher, again, refused to do the project with an unknown chef. By this time, Nick was so engaged in the project, he urged me to go ahead and publish it under my name, with him listed in the credits as my assistant and chief creative consultant. Every book I've written since has been credited the same way, even though Nick helps to devise and choose the recipes. I split all advances and royalties with him – he just isn't credited in the books.'

'Why would he agree to such an arrangement?'

'Nick was tired of the restaurant business – the late nights, the days off that are spent ordering supplies. He was in his forties when we met and wanted more time to spend with his children.'

'So Chef Latanzza isn't really your assistant, is he?'

'He wasn't at first, no. And I still don't consider him an assistant, as much as I consider him a business partner and friend, but when Jeanette fell ill two years ago, I found it difficult to keep up with all the engagements, emails, and the foundation. Nick stepped in and kept me on track. Sometimes, he'd even answer emails and reader questions for me. He was indispensable. When

Jeanette died . . .' Payne took a lengthy pause. 'It's no exaggeration to say that without Nick's assistance, my business, my legacy, my foundation would have withered while I locked myself away from the world and hid. He's kept everything going. Even now, as I lie here in a hospital bed, I know that everything I've built during my life will be fine because Nick will take care of it.'

'What happens to your book rights and other interests should you pass away?' Tish asked.

'Jeanette and I never had children, so they would go to Chef Latanzza. As I said, he may act as my assistant, but he is a dear, dear friend.'

Tish refrained from comment. Standing to inherit Chef Payne's vast empire, Chef Latanzza was also a dear, dear friend with a strong motive for murder.

'Did Chef Latanzza know Gunnar Randall?'

'Now, now, Ms Tarragon. It's quite clear what you're doing. You're suggesting that Nick might have fed both me and Chef Randall poisonous mushrooms.'

'I'm not suggesting. I'm simply exploring the possibility.'

'Well, stop exploring. Nick Latanzza is a loyal and faithful friend. He wouldn't hurt me any more than he'd hurt his own children.'

Seeing that Payne was agitated, she decided to change the subject. Perhaps Clemson would get further with his questioning of Latanzza. 'I hear that practically all of Richmond's restaurants turned out for your birthday party tonight.'

'Yes, that is what they tell me.' He pulled the covers to his chin – a gesture indicating to Tish that he felt he needed to protect himself from her questions.

'Were there any chefs or restaurant owners you were particularly happy to see?'

At the mention of food and restaurants, Payne's attitude softened. 'Ah, there was the owner of that new pie restaurant I've been wanting to try. She brought a smoked salmon, leek, and potato pie that was truly inspired. Then there's Jean-Claude, the owner of La Maison du Chocolat. He's been a friend for years, but I haven't seen him for a long time. And then there's Zachary Farraday, one of the most successful graduates of my foundation's education initiative. Zachary was in prison when he joined my rehabilitation program. He went on not only to secure a job within the food industry, but to train as a chef. He opened a pub near the river not too long ago. Being away, I haven't had a chance to visit it, but this evening, I had the opportunity to taste one of his signature dishes.'

'Really? What did he serve?'

'French onion soup. He must have remembered, during one of my lessons at the foundation, that it's been a lifelong favorite of mine.'

'How was it?'

'Possibly the best onion soup I've ever eaten. I know that might sound silly, but it's an easy dish to get wrong – too much salt, onions burned rather than caramelized, a flavorless stock. Caviar and champagne have their place, but there's no comparison to simple food prepared well. So many restaurants these days give you microscopic portions of unrecognizable foods accented with dribbles of sauce. I like food to look like food and not a science experiment. I want the braised lamb shanks on my plate to look like lamb shanks and the gravy on my plate to be drizzled and pooled artistically on the plate, not splashed like an apostrophe. And although a Portobello mushroom might be grilled like a steak, I still want to see its beautiful dark gills. On the opposite side of the coin, chefs should maintain some sense of romance when creating a menu. Too many restaurants can't even be bothered to give their dishes a name. Instead, they give us a grocery list of ingredients and how the dish is prepared – with a demi-glace, with a balsamic reduction, with umami mushroom powder. Bah!' Payne briefly cast his eyes heavenward. 'Diners need to know what they're eating, yes, but that description should be a subheading – an explanation displayed beneath an alluring and intriguing title, like Chicken Marbella or Charlotte Russe. But, of course, I am an old man. My ideas are mostly outdated.'

'I don't think so,' Tish stated. 'I rather enjoy giving my menu items names that are riffs on books and authors. Not only does it feed into the literary theme of the café, but it sets the mood for the customer. My place is – well, was – relaxed and playful. I think the names of the dishes I serve help to establish that.'

'Yes, that's precisely right. They establish a mood. Zachary Farraday's menu items keep the names of the original dish, but with a modern descriptor to add an edge. It tells the diner that this is not the onion soup your grandma made.'

'You must feel very proud of Mr Farraday. How long had it been since you'd seen him?'

'Oh, not since his graduation, maybe four or five years ago.'

'Wow. He must have been happy to see you, too.'

The smile ran away from Payne's face. 'Yes. Yes . . . He was extremely busy, though. Too busy to talk for very long. He had a lot of soup to serve.'

Tish sensed trouble between the chef and his protégé. 'Yes, I imagine there were a lot of mouths to feed at your party.'

'Too many. When I was younger, such a turnout for my birthday would have been a boost to my ego. Today, it means more hands I have to shake.'

'Did you know that Gunnar Randall was in town shooting his television show?'

'I knew Chef Randall was in town, so it stood to reason that he was filming.'

'Did you know that Farraday was one of the chefs being featured on Gunnar's show?'

'Zachary may have mentioned it in passing,' Payne answered somewhat evasively. 'It was a crowded room, and my hearing is not what it once was, but I do remember him saying something about television.'

'Other chefs being featured in the episode were also at your party.'

He shrugged. 'This is not surprising. Many restaurant owners think an appearance on *Taste of America* is good publicity for their business.'

'Maybe you know some of the other guests,' she suggested. 'Karma Frumm, owner of Frumm's Mushroom Farm?'

'Yes, I know of Frumm's Mushrooms. I ordered them many times for dinner parties before Jeanette fell ill. They are some of the best mushrooms in the area, but I do not know Ms Frumm. I've never met her.'

'Not even tonight?'

'No. Her mushroom vol-au-vents were here, but she was not.'

'Pilar, Alex, and Frank Betancourt?'

'Yes, Señora Betancourt actually sent me a flight of wines a couple of years ago. She wanted me to taste them and determine if Betancourt Winery could sponsor my next PBS cooking show. Signora misunderstood the meaning of sponsor, because when I called to find out how much money her winery wished to contribute, she went completely silent,' he said with a laugh. 'I explained that what she wanted was product placement, not sponsorship. *Señora* was not pleased.'

'She was angry?'

'Umm, a bit. But not one to be discouraged, she then asked if I'd visit the restaurant at the winery. Dinner would be on the house, but I didn't need to eat it if I didn't want to. It was enough that I was seen there.'

'What did you say?'

'I explained that there were not enough hours in my day to visit every restaurant to which I receive an invitation. Again, *Señora* was not pleased. She wanted to help her grandsons in any way she could – which I appreciate, of course – but there wasn't anything else I could do. Still, *Señora* was definitely not pleased with me.'

'What about Tiffany Harlow? She owns a vegan eatery here in town.'

'Harlow . . . Harlow . . .' Payne repeated as if it were a magical incantation. 'We had a Harlow in the program, but her first name was Thelma, not Tiffany. Thelma came from a background of trauma. She was abused by her father and uncle, and had been bounced around the foster care system before the court remanded her to a residence for survivors of abuse. When she showed a predilection for cooking, one of her counselors contacted my foundation. Thelma wasn't a gifted chef – it did not come naturally to her – but she was passionate and unique in her style. Because of the abuse in her past, Thelma would never cook meat or anything that might someday become a creature with a face, so she created vegan specialties and studied how to eliminate animal products from traditional recipes. She also believed in the medicinal quality of tea.'

'Sounds suspiciously like the same woman,' Tish thought aloud. 'Did you meet a Tiffany Harlow tonight? Her restaurant is The Eager Vegan.'

'I recall eating food from The Eager Vegan. A lovely soup and a vegan puff-pastry appetizer – well, everything was presented as a taster so that I could sample a wide array of foods – but I do not remember the owner of the restaurant being present. If I recall correctly, the dishes weren't even served to me by a woman, but by a male server. Likewise, if the owner had been Thelma Harlow, I certainly would have recognized her. She graduated from my program just a few years ago.'

Tish sat silently and pondered Payne's last statement. *Is that why Tiffany Harlow wasn't present at the dinner? Was she afraid Jackson Payne might recognize her and mention her abusive past? Had Gunnar Randall dug into Tiffany's background and discovered she had been a graduate of Payne's program? Had she poisoned both men because of what they knew? But if she wasn't present at Payne's party, how could she have administered the poisonous mushroom?* 'What about Gunnar Randall's crew?'

'What about them?'

'You met Chef Randall on Wednesday. Did any of his crew tag along?'

'No. Our meeting wasn't to air on his show, so there was no need for a camera or sound person. Also, Chef Randall wasn't the type to mingle with staff. He was above that sort of thing. Although I did meet two members of his crew at the party tonight.'

Tish leaned forward in her seat. 'You did?'

'*Certainement*,' he replied in the native tongue of his late wife. 'Chef Randall's cameraman . . . Darryl . . . Dannil . . .?'

'Dalbir. Dalbir Singh.'

'That's it, Dalbir. Dalbir was at the party shooting footage for the Food Channel. They had the exclusive for the party, and since he was in town, he apparently got the job.'

'You spoke to him?'

'Briefly, yes. He was quite amiable, quite personable. He introduced himself as Gunnar Randall's cameraman, wished me a happy birthday, and thanked me for my contributions to vegetarian cuisine. That surprised me – I never set out to be a vegetarian cook. I simply included recipes from my childhood in my books, which just happened to exclude meat – which we could not purchase with our ration cards – and highlighted eggs, beans, peanut butter, and victory garden vegetables. Apart from the eggs, our generation might have been the test group for the vegan diet.' Payne laughed.

'We also ate bread. Lots of bread. It filled the stomachs of three growing boys at minimal expense.'

Tish couldn't help but laugh with Payne. 'Good old carbs. I remember my mother adding an extra potato to the baking tray or an extra portion of pasta to the pot to stretch our meals for the friends I'd always invite for supper. I had no idea back then the burden I was placing on her, but now—'

'No, my dear. Your mother was happy to do it. As was mine during wartime. They'd go without a meal before they'd let you or your friends go hungry. Or let anyone think you had no food.'

She nodded solemnly. Payne's words were incredibly accurate. 'Going back to Dalbir, did you know he was Randall's cameraman when he introduced himself, or did he tell you?'

'Oh, he told me. He apologized for helping to put Chef Randall on American television screens. He wasn't joking, either. He seemed to feel genuinely guilty about it.'

'Did he say anything more?'

'No. He thanked me for my time and went about his business.'

'And the other member of Randall's crew at the party?' Tish prompted.

'That would be Ms Fisher.'

She raised an eyebrow.

'This surprises you?' he asked.

'Perhaps a little.'

'It would probably shock you even more to learn that she was on the arm of Chef William Lee.'

Payne was right – it was surprising news. 'Chef William Lee? The superstar chef from the Cooking Network?'

'Yes, that's him. He approached me soon after arriving at the party to wish me a happy birthday. That's when he introduced Ms Fisher. It was nice to finally put a face to the voice and name.'

'Put a face to the voice? Are you saying you spoke to Shae Fisher prior to this evening?

'Oh yes, she was the one who arranged my meeting with Chef Randall.'

'What was that all about?' Reade questioned once he had led Chef Latanzza down a dimmed hallway devoid of people.

'I don't understand what you mean.'

'I asked a simple question back there – were you present during Payne's meeting with Randall? – and you and Chef Payne gave me two completely different answers.'

'Chef Payne is protective of me,' the tall Italian explained.

'Why?'

He shrugged. 'Because we are like family.'

'OK, so I'll ask again now that "Dad" is not around. Were you present during Chef Payne's meeting with Gunnar Randall?'

'I was.'

'Were you there for the entire meeting?'

'Yes, except for the short time I was in the kitchen preparing the tea and cookies. They met at Chef Payne's home here in Richmond.'

'Tea and cookies? There were three chefs in the house and you didn't cook with each other?'

Latanzza smirked. 'Everyone who visits, chef or not, asks Chef Payne to cook with them. It is not possible for him to meet all those requests. Even as a young man, it would have been too demanding on him. After a visit to England, Chef Payne and his wife adopted the habit of drinking tea in the afternoon. He serves it with those Pepperidge Farm cookies with the chocolate in the middle. They are a guilty pleasure of his, even though he tells everyone there is no reason to feel guilty over pleasure. His fellow chefs might disagree with that statement and his choice in cookies.'

'So you were out of the room just long enough to brew a pot of tea and put store-bought cookies on a plate, and yet Chef Payne insisted you were out of the room for most of Randall's visit. Why? What was he protecting you from?'

Latanzza drew a hand threw his thick, wavy hair and paced back and forth. 'Because I attended the Culinary Institute of America with Chef Randall – just Gunnar Randall back then. He and I were in the same graduating class.'

'I thought you might have attended cooking school in Italy.'

'I did – the school of Nonna and Mamma,' he recalled, his eyes softening. 'But when the time came to arrange my formal education, I chose America. I always dreamed of coming to America. Broke my mamma's heart, but in the end she understood. America has been good to me. I graduated second in my class at the CIA, met my beautiful wife, Marci, and saw the birth of three strong and handsome sons.'

'Congratulations.'

'Thank you.'

'And Randall? How did he fare at the CIA?'

The gentleness in Latanzza's eyes vaporized. 'He graduated first in our class, but only by – how do you say? – the skin of his teeth. He partied, he was loud, he was rude. He was a jerk. Even then, he was a jerk.'

'Yet he was still number one in your class,' Reade reminded the chef in an attempt to bait him. It worked.

'Ack! He did not deserve to be number one. The way he treated people – chefs, junior chefs, fellow students. He had no respect for anyone. And the women? *Mio Dio*, the women. He treated all the females on that campus like they were his personal harem. He didn't get better with age. He and I attended a gala dinner for CIA alumni two years ago, and what he did to the women at the CIA, he did to my wife.'

'And that was?'

'He put his hands on her,' Latanzza shouted.

'And yet you still helped to welcome him into Chef Payne's home.'

'Because Chef Payne insisted that I do so.'

'Is that the only reason?'

'*Certo.* Yes. I wanted to – I tried – to keep Chef Payne away from that *mostro*, that monster, but Chef Payne, he has his own ideas.'

'My grandmother was the same way when she got older. She didn't want to hear from anyone who disagreed with her outlook on the world.'

This comment gave Latanzza pause. '*Sì*,' he responded reluctantly. '*Sì*. Chef Payne was stubborn about meeting Chef Randall, and now his own life is in jeopardy.'

'Can you think of anything – apart from their occupation and the meeting – that might link Payne and Randall?'

'No. They are opposites. More different from each other than the night is from the day.'

SEVENTEEN

'Chef Latanzza is a shoo-in for Payne's poisoning,' Tish opined as Reade steered the SUV past the state capitol building and turned on to the road that led to the historic Jefferson Hotel. 'He's set to inherit the entirety of Jack Payne's estate, which is sizable in itself, but when you add the possibility of licensing kitchenware, books, and cooking classes, that estate could double or triple. My only question is why would Latanzza murder Gunnar Randall? I mean, we *are* definitely looking at a homicide now, don't you think?'

'That's the only thing Payne's poisoning has done to simplify the case. It's helped to classify Gunnar Randall's death as murder. And – I agree with you – it's also put Latanzza front and center as a suspect.'

'Oh?' She looked at him eagerly. 'What did you find out?'

'That Latanzza hated Randall.'

Tish rolled her eyes. 'And so did hundreds of other people. That's hardly a case breaker, honey.'

'I mean Latanzza *hate-hated* Randall. Like with the heat of a thousand suns. They were in the same class at the CIA and were in fierce competition with each other. Also, Randall put the moves on Latanzza's wife at a dinner for CIA alumni a couple years back.'

'Put the moves on or assaulted?'

'Randall put his hands on her.'

'Assault. Well, that's certainly a motive, isn't it?'

'If someone did that to you, they wouldn't leave the dinner alive.'

'Aww,' she cooed. 'Same here. Is it strange that I find it romantic that we'd perform violent acts for each other?'

'Maybe a little.'

'Hmph. Latanzza does seem to be our guy, but how did he murder Randall? Payne said he wasn't there.'

'And Latanzza said he was.'

'Yeah, I gather that's why you took Latanzza out of the room.'

Reade nodded. 'He still maintains he was present at Payne and Randall's meeting. With the exception of a few minutes when he got some tea and cookies from the kitchen.'

'So he served the food?'

'Yep, but before you get too excited, the cookies were store-bought, so we're looking at tea as a vehicle again.'

'What kind of tea?'

'The kind you serve with cookies. Payne gets it from England.'

'The most popular tea in England is black tea.'

'How do you know that?'

'Because it's the most popular tea in the US, too. I run – *ran* – a café. It's my business to know what people eat and drink.'

'OK, so Payne most likely served black tea. What about it?'

'Even though black tea has a stronger, earthier flavor than other teas, it's still not quite strong enough to camouflage the taste of a mushroom. Remember, those who have tasted the Death Cap – and survived – described it as the most delicious mushroom they've ever tasted. In mushroom terms, that means it's earthy, meaty, and full of umami. No matter how strong you brew it, I'm just not sure black tea could conceal that flavor.'

'There goes Latanzza as our suspect.'

'I wouldn't rule him out just yet. We need to run some tests first. With edible mushrooms, of course.'

'Of course.' Reade nodded.

'Also, he's not the only one with a motive for wanting Jackson Payne out of the way.' Tish told him what she'd learned about Tiffany Harlow.

'So, Harlow was an alumna of Payne's institute as well?'

'Yes, a more recent graduate than Farraday, which means that his presence at the party wouldn't have been an issue for her.'

'But Payne's was and possibly Randall's,' Reade guessed.

'Exactly. The only problem is Payne says Harlow wasn't at the dinner. Her dish was presented by a male server. We'll have to ask about the serving protocols, but unless Payne was fed a plate explicitly designated for him, it would have been exceedingly difficult, if not impossible, for Harlow to poison him.'

'Of course. Why should anything in this case be straightforward?'

'Yes, well, if you want straightforward, you're going to hate this next bit of news. Shae Fisher made the appointment for Gunnar Randall's meeting with Payne.'

'Shae did?'

'That's what Payne said.'

'And yet Shae said Gunnar made the appointment himself. I can't see a reason for Payne to lie about the situation.'

'Nor can I,' Tish concurred.

'So why did Shae Fisher lie about such an inconsequential detail?'

'I don't know. But it may have had something to do with the fact that she arrived at the party on the arm of Chef William Lee, the Cooking Network's biggest celebrity.'

'Girlfriend or employee?'

'Payne was confident that it was a professional relationship.'

'Leaving the star of the Food Channel—'

'A waning star according to most sources,' Tish rejoined.

'—for a job with the star of the Cooking Network.'

'Whose star is still on the rise,' she noted.

'That's definitely something worth killing for.'

'Agreed. But why would she attempt to murder Jackson Payne?'

'Perhaps for the same reason she lied about arranging the meeting.'

'OK, but how would she have done it? She's not in the food industry.'

'I don't know, but I intend to find out.'

'Maybe Dalbir Singh captured something while he was filming.'

'Singh was here tonight, too?'

'Yes, he introduced himself to Payne and wished him a happy birthday.'

'Was everyone we questioned at this party?'

'Pretty much. Even Pilar Betancourt made an appearance. Her grandsons dropped her off with their contributions to the food and drink.'

'What's wrong with these people?' Reade asked in exasperation as he pulled the SUV on to the cobblestone-lined entrance of The Jefferson Hotel. 'A man is dead. Why don't they just stay home?'

Tish laughed. 'That would make it easier, wouldn't it? If it helps, I don't think Karma Frumm was present. Although her dish was at the dinner.'

'So she's in the same situation as Tiffany Harlow,' he said, driving past the hotel bell tower that was more than a bit reminiscent of St Mark's Campanile in Venice.

'Exactly the same. Her food was at the dinner, but she wasn't.'

Reade parked the SUV, and the pair walked toward the hotel entrance, which had been cordoned off with yellow tape and was being monitored by two uniformed officers. Stepping into the hotel's famous two-story, marble-lined Beaux-Arts lobby prompted Tish to gasp.

'Wow,' she whispered, her mouth agape.

'You've never been to The Jefferson?'

She shook her head. 'Never had the means. Although I'd heard about it.'

'Yeah, I was here just once for a friend's wedding. A big over-the-top event. I honestly don't get big weddings. I'd go for more of an intimate gathering, myself.'

Tish felt her face grow hot. Listening to Clemson discuss wedding plans was surprisingly unnerving. Thankfully, he veered away from the subject as quickly as he had veered toward it.

'Did you know the pools in this atrium once contained live alligators? That's why there are alligator statues all over the place. The last one died in the nineteen-forties, I think.'

'Right now, wrestling with gators seems safer than questioning the cast of characters waiting for us,' she remarked, scanning the crowd before them for familiar faces.

'No argument here. Poisoning a man on his eighty-fifth birthday is a particularly vicious crime. One I hope to never see repeated.'

The pair approached Clayton, who had sequestered everyone affiliated with the Randall case in an unused dining room. 'Hey, how's Payne?'

'Stable,' Reade replied. 'And the prognosis is good.'

'Cool. I talked to the head of the kitchen. Tasting dishes for Jackson Payne had to be submitted to him by five o'clock. Apart from that, there were no hard and fast rules as to which item was served to Payne. Some cooks marked the specific plate, others told him to serve whichever he thought looked best.'

'Did he have a system for processing those requests?'

'Yeah, he removed the original markers and literally flagged everything to be served to Payne – including the ones he personally selected – with an American flag toothpick. He kept no logs or written record – he simply flagged.'

'Naturally,' Tish said with a sigh.

'Yeah, it doesn't make things easy, does it? Oh, I did receive a text from Doctor Andres, though. He said that Death Cap amatoxins survive both brewing and double-cooking, so tea and arancini are both possible murder weapons.'

'Nice work, Clayton,' Reade praised.

'Thanks, Sheriff. Everyone's inside waiting for you – with the exception of Karla Frumm and Glory Bishop.'

Tish heaved a sigh of relief. 'Thank goodness Glory wasn't here.'

'Well, yes . . . and no. She delivered some sort of canapé earlier in the day to be served tonight.'

'Terrific,' she grumbled. 'Just terrific.'

'Is there anyone else missing?' Reade asked.

'Nope. I even rounded up the Lou-Lous,' he announced proudly. 'There's an empty conference room that connects to this one. I thought you could use that for interviews.'

Reade thanked Clayton again and, opening the door for Tish, followed her into the dining room. Although Clayton's brief roll call had prepared them to anticipate her presence, they were still somewhat surprised to find Tiffany Harlow's girlish countenance amid the group of faces staring back at them.

'Ms Harlow,' Reade greeted. 'May we speak with you in the other room?'

Her eyes turned downward and her arms held stiffly at her sides, Harlow trailed behind Reade and Tish the way a disobedient child might trail behind the parents who were about to reprimand them.

Once in the conference room, he gestured for her to take a seat at one of the several chairs that had been arranged, in rows, to face the dais and podium positioned at the front of the room.

Tiffany Harlow flopped into an end seat and folded her arms across her chest. 'I didn't do *any*thing.'

'No? You were here at the dinner and yet you stayed away from Jackson Payne all evening,' Reade posed, swinging two chairs around to face her. 'Why?'

'I didn't stay away. I was *busy*,' she insisted, although her body language suggested otherwise.

'Too busy to wish a happy birthday to the man whose foundation set you on your chosen career path?' Tish asked before sitting down in one of the chairs Reade had rearranged.

The color drained from Tiffany's face. 'You know?'

'That you graduated from Jackson Payne's institute? Yes, we know. Payne also told us how you got there.'

She attempted to shrug it off. 'Yeah, well, another child of the system. We're *every*where. Kids shoplift every day. I just happened to get caught.'

Tiffany mentioned her crime, but not the abuse that must have played an integral part in shaping her direction in life. 'If it's so commonplace, why did you try to hide it?'

'I didn't try to hide anything. No one *asked* me about my past. They *asked* me about Gunnar Randall.' Her eyes slid toward Reade as he took the seat beside Tish. 'Big, fat, important Gunnar Randall.'

'Did Gunnar know about your past, Tiffany?' Tish asked softly.

Tiffany closed her eyes and began to weep. 'Remember when I said Randall was creepy?' she asked Reade.

'I do,' the sheriff replied.

'Before we started shooting my segment – right after I'd had my hair and makeup done – he leaned in real close and whispered in my ear. He asked me if I still had my uniform from reform school.'

Tish produced a tissue from her handbag and gave it to the young chef. 'I'm sorry, Tiffany. I'm very sorry.'

The young woman accepted it and blew her nose noisily. 'That's what happens to girls who get into trouble, right? It's the story of my life.'

'It shouldn't have been.'

'Yeah, well, tell that to my father. "Bad girls need to be punished," he always said. No one ever punished him, because men can do whatever they want. A guy who goes to juvie is someone who made a little mistake because "boys will be boys." A girl winds up in detention? She's wild and immoral and gets called a whore. A stupid little whore.'

Tish consoled Tiffany as she cried. 'I don't feel that way. Sheriff

Reade doesn't feel that way. I know many other people who would never, ever think that of you.'

'Yeah, but it's the ones who do who can ruin your life. Who *will* ruin it, just because they can.'

'Like Gunnar Randall?'

'No. Gunnar Randall's problem was that he'd seen too many *Girls Gone Wild* videos. He expected me to . . . to . . .' She struggled to explain. 'He was going to tell the whole world about my past if I wasn't "nice" to him.'

'I can't imagine how that must have felt,' Tish sympathized.

'Yeah, well, it's what happens to women like me, right? With a background like mine, I'm apparently asking for it. That's why I've tried my best to keep it secret. I knew the men in our local chamber of commerce would react like Randall while the women tried to force my restaurant out of the neighborhood.' She swallowed hard. 'And so I never mentioned my time with the Jackson Payne Foundation. I omitted every trace of it from my résumé, and instead of looking for a job at a major restaurant after graduating from cooking school, I applied to smaller eateries where my background wouldn't be checked as thoroughly.'

'When I *fin*ally opened my café,' Harlow continued, her voice returning to its normal cadence, 'I thought I was safe. I was my own boss. I put out my *own* publicity for the restaurant, put my *own* bio on my *own* website. I controlled the narrative. And then Randall showed up.'

'But you'd applied to be on his show, hadn't you?' Reade questioned.

'Yes, but I had no idea he or his network would dig as deep as they did. I had to submit my bio in order to apply. I had no clue *whatsoever* that my whole life would be scrutinized. I mean, checking my experience in previous restaurants and my education credentials, sure. But why bother with what I did *prior* to cooking school? What did it matter that I was enrolled in Jackson Payne's program? What did it bring to the show? All the audience *needed* to know was that I owned a restaurant and applied to have Randall judge my food. That's it.'

'Reality television is full of drama. Manufactured or otherwise.'

'This was more than that. It was like Gunnar Randall wanted

control over the people on his show. He enjoyed having something to hold over my head – something more than just the hope
of a good review.'

Harlow's description of Randall aligned with everything Tish
and Reade had uncovered about the man so far. 'I won't even ask
how that made you feel.'

'Everything I've tried to forget came rushing back. I felt like a
child. Not a grown woman with a restaurant, but a helpless child.'
She broke down again.

Reade stuck his head out of the conference room door to request
some water, while Tish did her best to console the sobbing Tiffany.

'Tell us what happened tonight,' Tish urged when the young
chef had regained her composure.

'I'd been so looking forward to the party,' she sniffed. 'I RSVP'd
months ago that I'd be attending – long before I knew I was going
to be on *Taste of America*. I spent *forever* trying to figure out
what to cook that might impress Chef Payne – that might prove
to him that I'd been listening to his lessons and learned from
them.'

'And?'

'And I finally came up with leek and potato soup – a tribute to
Chef Payne's late wife – and vegan puff-pastry pies. Chef used
to tell us about how his English grandmother always made him
little steak and ale pies when he'd visit, so I thought I'd recreate
them without the meat.'

'Using mushrooms?' Tish guessed.

'Yes, Portobello and some dried Porcini.'

Of course, Tish thought to herself as Reade visibly flinched.
What were the odds that all their suspects had presented Payne
with mushroom dishes? 'Sounds delicious. That Porcini would
have added some nice richness.'

'That's what I thought,' Tiffany replied. Her mood had vastly
improved. 'I was excited to present my dishes. Not just because
they were inspired by Chef Payne's past, but because they embodied
one of the most important principles of his teachings: food is love.
I know it *sounds* simple, but when I started training with Chef,
food was about survival. There were days, when I was a kid, when
the only meal I got was at school. Once I was in the program, I
learned that food is also about flavor, but I still didn't fully grasp

Chef Payne's lesson about love until I started working in restaurants. People use food to celebrate a new job, as a way to get to know someone during a first date. They even use it to say goodbye.'

'I'm sure he loved your tribute, even if you didn't present it to him yourself.'

'I wanted to present it. That was the plan at first. I thought I could pop in, present my dish, have a quick – and quiet – conversation with Chef, and then leave before anyone asked any questions.'

'What made you change your plan?'

'Gunnar Randall,' Tiffany snarled. 'I started to wonder who he might have told about my past. Did his crew know? Did he tell the other cooks appearing on the episode we were filming who might be at the party? Did he mention something to the hotel maid? Or the place where he ate breakfast? I grew paranoid, you know? What if there were already whispers about me? What if people were watching to see how Chef Payne and I got along? What if they were listening to what we said? I couldn't take that chance. I just couldn't. I couldn't risk my restaurant – my life. I couldn't go back to being that child again. I *couldn't!*'

EIGHTEEN

'**B**ecause I was already in town, the Food Channel asked me to cover Mr Payne's birthday party,' Dalbir Singh stated while seated in the chair Tiffany Harlow had recently vacated. 'Now that I am without a job for the foreseeable future, I did not refuse, although I wanted to.'

'Refuse?' Tish questioned. 'Why?'

'Because I don't exactly see eye to eye with Mr Payne on certain issues.'

'Care to elaborate?' Reade prompted.

Still impeccably dressed in the black button-down shirt and black trousers of a photographer on a gig, Singh crossed his legs and drew a deep breath. 'Years ago, Mr Payne released a book about Indian cooking. I feel that he appropriated the food of my people.'

'Appropriated?'

'Yes, he used Indian food to line his own pockets and, worse yet, he didn't even follow the traditional recipes. His book boasted that it was a shortcut to Indian cooking.'

Tish spoke up. 'I remember that book. It was one of several books in Chef Payne's "Quick and Easy" series. There was one on French cuisine, Italian, Chinese, Mexican . . .'

'It being part of a series doesn't negate the fact that he appropriated a part of Indian culture for personal gain.'

As a white, non-Indian woman, Tish didn't feel it was her place to comment. 'Did you talk to Chef Payne about it?'

'Not at first. I was taught to respect my elders, so when I approached Mr Payne to arrange for some still shots, I smiled and wished him a happy birthday. He thanked me and began to make small talk. I told him I worked on Gunnar Randall's show for some time. That's when he asked what I thought of chefs. I'm not certain what came over me – anger, frustration, pent-up angst from being with Gunnar Randall on a regular basis – but I told Mr Payne that I didn't think very much of them at all.'

'How did he react?' Reade asked.

'He was not happy, but I don't think he immediately realized he was included in the inference. He asked me how Randall had treated me, so I told him.'

'And?' Tish encouraged.

'He . . . he looked shaken. Not surprised, but shaken. It was all very strange. One would have thought that Randall's abuse had targeted him rather than me.'

'Did he explain why he was so upset?'

'No. He shook his head over and over and muttered something about a code of conduct, but that's all I understood.'

'Did you eventually tell him that he was included in your assessment of chefs?'

'I did, but not in the manner I had initially intended. When I made my remark about chefs, I was prepared to follow it up by shouting and screaming at the top of my lungs, but Mr Payne looked so very weak that I merely referenced the Indian cookbook in question. He apologized profusely. Although I'm not certain he was fully aware of what he was apologizing for.'

Singh's assessment was most likely accurate, for Payne's description of his encounter with Singh lacked any mention of either cultural appropriation or drama. 'How did you end the evening with him?' Reade quizzed.

'I straightened his tie. We shot some great photos, which I agreed I would send to Mr Latanzza, and I went about filming the rest of the party.'

'Did Jackson Payne eat or drink anything during the time of your shoot?' Reade asked.

'No, nothing,' Singh denied, but then quickly amended. 'Except a glass of Scotch. He offered me one, but being a Sikh, I do not drink. So I toasted him with my bottle of water, watched him drink it down, and we continued to shoot. As friends.'

'Was the Scotch given to him while you two were talking? Or did he already have it with him?'

'He had it with him when I approached him.'

'And did he put it down anywhere while you were talking?'

'Yes, twice. When I first approached him about snapping some photos, he put it down on a nearby table in anticipation of me shooting right away. But then, when we started talking instead, he picked it up and took a sip. Later, when I told him about how Gunnar Randall had treated me, Mr Payne put the glass down again. It was almost as if it was too heavy for him.'

'Did you notice anyone lingering near that table during the time the two of you were speaking?'

'Yes, as a matter of fact. Shae Fisher.'

'I didn't lie,' Shae Fisher, dressed in a strapless, form-fitting silver gown, insisted. 'Jackson Payne is ancient. He probably doesn't remember what he ate for lunch this afternoon, let alone who called him last Wednesday.'

'I double-checked with Chef Payne. He was absolutely certain that it was you who made the appointment,' Tish stated. 'He says his assistant, Chef Latanzza, was present when you called. He said you were crying.'

Fisher scowled and threw her hands on to her lap. 'OK, I made the appointment. What's the big deal?'

'You tell us,' Reade demanded. 'You're the one who felt it necessary to lie about it.'

Shae Fisher, visibly defeated, sank into her chair and, with trembling hands, smoothed her dress over her legs. 'It's true. I did call Chef Payne on Wednesday to try to schedule a meeting with Randall that afternoon. I had tried to do it before we left California, but he didn't have an opening in his schedule. I didn't tell Randall – I couldn't tell Randall because he would have flipped. He was already an uber stress-bucket. Getting Randall prepared to travel was always a nightmare, but this time was especially bad. For him, traveling to the East Coast meant New York or Miami. He could maybe deal with Boston or DC, but Richmond? Yeah, Richmond was not his idea of a good time.'

'So why did he choose to shoot here?'

'He didn't. The Food Channel made those decisions. As I told you earlier, Sheriff, they selected locations based on the number of viable participant applications received from a specific area. Once they'd decided on a location, they passed along the applications to Randall so he could decide which candidates he wanted to, erm . . . use? Torture? Have on the show? They all apply, don't they?'

'Did Randall decide ahead of time who was going to get a good review?' Tish ventured.

'No. If anything, he went out with the attitude that everyone was going to get a bad review. He waited for something to change his mind – a really great meal, a really hot female cook . . . you get the idea. Some people, though, would never get a good review – a health food or vegan place, for instance, or someone who, on principle alone, rubbed Randall the wrong way.'

'So, Randall wasn't happy about coming to Richmond.' Reade guided the conversation back to the day in question.

'He was complaining about it before any of us could even book our tickets. I have a three-year-old nephew who behaves better than Randall did. There were temper tantrums, outbursts, things being thrown around his office – it was a mood – until Randall discovered that Chef Payne's birthday was scheduled for the week we were here.'

'Then his attitude improved?' Tish guessed.

'I wouldn't go that far. He was still more difficult to deal with than he'd been before any other trip, but at least I could enter his office without the fear of a cell phone whizzing past my head.' She looked Reade in the eyes. 'And, no, I'm not exaggerating.

'Anyway,' Shae continued, 'when Randall found out about the birthday party, he was thrilled – well, as thrilled as he ever got – at the chance to meet Chef Payne. But, instead of waiting until the night of the party, as a normal human being would, he decided he had to meet Jackson Payne ahead of time. The only open time on Randall's schedule was noon on Wednesday, so he told me to call and make an appointment for that time. You know, as if Jackson Payne had absolutely nothing else on his calendar.'

'But you called anyway,' Tish surmised.

'Of course. If Randall told you to do something, you did it or all hell would break loose. Only, as expected, Jackson Payne was busy at noon on Wednesday. Clearly, he didn't get the memo to drop everything so King Randall could pay a visit.'

'Did you tell Randall that Payne was unavailable?'

Shae's face went ashen. 'No. No, I didn't. I couldn't. I was terrified of what his reaction might be. He was already behaving super extra about having to travel to Richmond. Telling him that Jackson Payne didn't consider him a VIP would have been like detonating a nuclear bomb – and I would have been Hiroshima.'

'You knew you had to tell him eventually,' Tish reasoned.

'I know . . . I know. I kept trying to postpone the inevitable because I knew – I just knew – how bad it would be. It was stupid really – not confronting him with the truth – but I was genuinely terrified of how he'd react. Randall's fragile little ego would have viewed Payne's unavailability as a snub, and as the messenger, I would have taken the brunt of his anger. Even on a good day, Randall could be verbally abusive, so . . .'

'So?'

'So I waited until Wednesday morning and hoped – prayed – that he was too busy to remember the appointment. Again, stupid, I know, but Randall had forgotten appointments before while filming, so there was a chance he'd forget this one.' Shae paused dramatic-ally. 'Naturally, he didn't. That morning, just before we were going to shoot the Betancourts, Randall asked if he was meeting Chef Payne at his home or at a restaurant downtown. I literally don't even remember the exact words I said to him, but I must have told him the truth, because the next thing I knew, Gunnar had me pinned to the ground. He shoved his cell phone in my face and told me to do whatever was necessary to get him in to see Payne.'

'Randall assaulted you?' Reade verified.

Shae nodded as tears stained her pallid cheeks.

'Did anyone see this?'

She shook her head. 'No, Gunnar and I were alone in the winery parking lot. Dalbir and our sound guy had gone back to the ware-house to pick up some additional gear for the shoot. And because it was before lunch, there were no other customers.'

'What did you do?'

'The only thing I could do. I called Jackson Payne. I tried to sound as normal as possible, but I'm no actress. He understood that I was calling him under duress and instructed his assistant to change his schedule for the afternoon.'

'That was very kind of him,' Tish observed.

'It was. He may have saved my life – but he might have ruined my career.'

'What do you mean?'

'Assistants in the food entertainment business are trusted to keep their mouths shut. If it ever came out that I'd even hinted to Jackson Payne that Randall was anything less than a stellar human being, that would be the end of me working in food television.'

'But the guy assaulted you,' Reade reminded.

'Do you think that matters to the network heads? They'd just pay me off and then hire someone else to replace me.'

'But he was a jerk on camera,' Reade continued to argue.

'That was the image Randall cultivated for himself. I was to neither deny nor confirm that he was the same off camera. The network made me sign a nondisclosure agreement. Talking to you guys about the "real" Randall is fine – obstruction of justice charges and all that. But not covering up for Randall when I called Jackson Payne would never be forgiven.'

Tish filled in the blanks. 'And so you lied about who made the appointment.'

'I had to. What else was I supposed to do? I figured Chef Payne was old enough that people would think he was confused and let the issue drop.'

'And tonight?'

'What about tonight?' Shae echoed.

'You met Chef Payne while on the arm of Chef William Lee.'

'I didn't want to. I really didn't want to – for all the obvious reasons. If Payne had said something about my phone call, that would have been it for me. So I tried to squirm my way out of it by saying that Chef Payne was too famous to meet a nobody, but Bill insisted that I join him in saying hello.'

'As his new assistant,' Tish stated.

'Yes, as his new assistant. Is there something wrong with that?'

'No, but you must have interviewed for the position while Randall was still alive.'

'I worked hard for Randall. I deserved better than how he and the Food Channel treated me,' Shae nearly shouted. 'So, yes, I interviewed while I was still working for Randall. Lots of people interview for new jobs while still working their old ones.'

'But not everyone's boss refuses to let them leave,' Reade rejoined.

'You know about that, too? You two have been busy. Look, I'm done with the questions for tonight. From now on, if you want to talk to me, I want my lawyer present.'

NINETEEN

'Tonight, Alejandro and Francisco did me proud,' Pilar Betancourt stated, a satisfied smile on her face. She was dressed in an A-line, cap-sleeved lace chiffon gown in a highly flattering shade of blush pink that played up her dark hair and made her lovely skin look even rosier. 'It's like I always told them, if they work together, they can accomplish anything.'

'Your grandsons aren't here?' Reade asked.

'No, we cannot afford to close down the restaurant on a Saturday night. Francisco packaged up some wine to pair with Alejandro's food and then delivered both of us here.'

'Both of you?'

'*Sí*, me and the food. Then he went back to the winery to help his brother. I pray to the Blessed Mother that they got along as well this evening as they did this afternoon.' She invoked the sign of the cross. 'Otherwise, I have to deal with the Yelp reviews tomorrow: "Great food, but too much shouting in the kitchen" or "Delicious wine and a floor show." It is terrible!'

Tish nodded sympathetically. 'I can't even imagine. What did Frank, er, Francisco cook for this evening?'

'Tapas. *Tapas españolas tradicional – Tortilla de Patatas, Croquetas de Jamon, Espinacas a la Catalanas, y Champinones al Aijilo.*'

Reade slid an eye toward Tish, who immediately translated. 'A baked Spanish potato omelet—'

'Hey, you've made me one of those, haven't you?' Reade responded.

'Yes, potatoes with whatever's left in the refrigerator and what I can scrounge from the freezer.'

'That is what a *tortilla* is for,' Pilar acknowledged. 'Use up leftovers and give the woman of the house a day off from doing dishes, because it's all cooked in one pan.'

'Yes,' Tish confirmed. 'If I'm correct, the rest of your grandson's menu was ham croquettes, spinach with white wine, currants, and pine nuts, and mushrooms marinated with garlic.'

'*Sí*. Your Spanish is very good,' Pilar complimented.

'Not really. I'm just fluent in food.'

'Ah. You are like Alejandro. Always with the food, he is. Even when the restaurant is closed, he's experimenting in the kitchen. But I am very proud of the traditional menu he created for tonight. When I tasted the tapas, it was like I was back in my *abuela*'s kitchen. And when Francisco selected two perfect sherries to serve with it – without an argument – *mi corazón* almost exploded with pride.'

'You'd do just about anything for your grandsons, wouldn't you?' Reade asked.

'Yes, they are my pride and joy.'

'Even beat up Gunnar Randall for them?'

'What? No! No, I—' Her face reddened. 'Who told you?'

'No one. Randall's cameraman caught it all.'

'What? I'm on film?'

'Well, not on film but a memory card. But yes.'

'OK, I hit him with my purse. So what? That doesn't mean that . . . that I did whatever you think I did.'

'You hit him with your purse repeatedly. And your grandsons needed to pull you off him. Then, after they helped you back into the restaurant, they went back and started attacking him, too.'

'They did? Ah, I knew those boys had it in them. They love their *abuela*!'

'Yes, clearly they do. Gunnar Randall could have pressed charges against them – and you – for assault.'

'Assault? After the way that pig acted? No. *Imposible!*'

'It was actually entirely possible, *Señora*,' Reade corrected. 'I understand that he insulted you, but—'

'Insulted me? You think I hit him because of what he said to me? No. It was how he treated the boys. He disrespected them and the food and the wine that they so passionately create. I would have overlooked the mean things he said about my appearance if he had given them a gold-star review. But he didn't. He didn't just give them a bad review, but he ate and drank like a pig while insulting them. He was a disgrace!'

'And so you grabbed your purse and hit him?'

'*Sí*. I was so angry. No one treats my family that way and gets away with it!'

'And tonight? What kind of mood were you in?'

'Excited. Filled with hope. My boys did good. So good they could not be ignored.'

'Ignored by whom?' Tish inquired.

'Chefs. The food industry. Everyone who looks down on us because we're different. When my husband and I first came to this country, we were called Spics and Wetbacks and other ugly names. When the winery became more successful and the locals got used to us, we didn't hear those names as much, but in the past few years, those ugly names have started to come back again. I know they're grown men, but I don't want my boys to have to deal with what their *abuelo* and I did – not just the names, but struggling to make ends meet, sacrificing a new car or even a new pair of shoes to make sure our business stayed alive, and having to be better than the other wineries to overcome the fact we were different.'

'And because of the tasting menu Alejandro and Francisco had created, you were hopeful Chef Payne might provide some sort of endorsement?'

'*Sí*. He had done it for young people who had been in prison – why not Francisco and Alejandro? They're good boys who never got into trouble. Why should some criminal get a pat on the back from Payne and not two young men who have worked hard their whole lives and look after their *abuela*? My grandsons deserve help just as much as some kid who stole a car or got caught up in a gang.'

'You had asked for Chef Payne's help before,' Reade noted.

'Yes, I was stupid and asked to have the restaurant sponsor him. I didn't understand what that meant. I thought sponsoring Chef Payne meant my boys would work with him at cooking events. I thought it would get the word out about the winery and restaurant. I was wrong,' she lamented with a click of her tongue.

'And tonight? Did you approach Chef Payne about helping your grandsons again?'

'I did,' she admitted. 'It still bothers me that he helps criminals but won't lift a finger to help a pair of talented young men.'

'From your attitude, I assume he refused your request,' Reade said with a slight smirk.

'He did,' Pilar said, her nose in the air. 'He said he does not have the time to review the food for our advertising or to visit our restaurant. Time! We made the time to make dishes for his birthday party. If he liked our food, he should have given us a party favor – his recommendation so we could spread it all over town. I tell you what,' she continued angrily. 'If I was young and blonde, he would not have said no. Don't get old, Señorita Tarragon. Once you are over fifty, no one cares what you have to say!'

Dressed in bedazzled vintage waitress uniforms and sequined loafers, and their workaday hairnets replaced with stunning up-dos, dangling rhinestone earrings, acrylic nails, BB cream, and false eyelashes, Lula Mae and Eloise's approach to fashion was distinctly at odds with that of Pilar Betancourt.

'Why are you keeping us here?' Lula Mae demanded.

'My daughter is probably worried sick that I'm not home yet,' Eloise exclaimed. 'Your young man out there wouldn't let me use my phone to call her.'

'I'm sorry, ma'am,' Reade apologized. 'It's standard procedure. I'll let you send her a text right now and then you can call her just as soon as we've finished.'

Eloise nodded and poked at the keys on her mobile phone. 'So, why are you keeping us here?' she asked when she'd finished.

'Yeah, we had nothing to do with that chef fella getting sick,' Lula Mae added. 'Just like we had nothing to do with that Randall fella either.'

'That's right,' Eloise echoed. 'Nothing.'

'And yet you weren't completely open with us when we last spoke with you. You didn't tell us that the two of you had signed a deal with the Food Channel to create a show based on your restaurant and recipes.'

Lula Mae shrugged. 'You didn't ask us about our business. You asked us about the dead chef fella.'

'True, but your deal with the Food Channel made Gunnar Randall a colleague of yours. A colleague who might jeopardize your deal if he wasn't completely satisfied with his experience at the Biscuit Palace.'

The Lou-Lous fell silent. After several seconds wherein they silently shrugged and gestured to each other, Lula Mae finally spoke. 'All right, it's true. When Gunnar Randall walked into the Biscuit Palace that morning, Eloise and I knew there was a lot more at stake than a bad review on his television program. He was the biggest star the Food Channel ever had. If he wasn't completely happy with everything we did that morning, he could make a whole lotta trouble for us.'

'A *whole* lot of trouble,' Eloise repeated.

'So what did you do?' Reade questioned.

'We set about fixin' him the best breakfast he'd ever eaten in his life.'

'With a little help,' Lula Mae added, a smile on her lips.

'Help?'

'I was diagnosed with cataracts a little ways back. Because my blood pressure is high, I'm not a good candidate for surgery, so my doctor prescribed medical marijuana,' Eloise explained.

'Seeing as how wound-up Mr Randall could be, I got to thinkin',' Lula Mae continued.

'My God! You put pot in Gunnar Randall's food,' Tish exclaimed.

'Just a sprinkle of hashish. To mellow him out some.'

'It was in the gravy for the biscuits, wasn't it?'

Lula Mae nodded, a smile on her lips. 'It was the only place I could think of putting it. How did you know?'

'Randall's cameraman noticed that it was a bit browner than usual.'

Eloise brought a hand to her chest. 'We thought that, too, and prayed that Mr Randall didn't notice. I nearly fainted, I was so worried.'

'I was more jittery than a cat in a room full of rocking chairs,' Lula Mae said. 'But we worried for nothin'. He didn't notice a thing except how miserable and uncomfortable everyone was, and I wasn't lying when I told you how much he enjoyed it.'

'And Jackson Payne tonight,' a confounded Reade started, 'did you slip some "hashish" into his food as well?'

'Course not! You think we just go around sprinkling that stuff everywhere?'

'Not at what my insurance company charges me!' Eloise inserted.

'Besides, we had no reason to do anything like that to Chef Payne. He's a nice man.'

'Loved our biscuits and gravy.'

'He posed for a selfie with us, too. You got your phone, Eloise?'

Eloise picked up the mobile phone she'd just used to text her daughter and selected the Gallery app. An image of Jackson Payne, flanked on either side by Lula Mae and Eloise, appeared on the screen. The three of them sported wide smiles and tall glasses of champagne.

'See? Does that look like the sort of man we'd slip a mickey to?' Lula Mae challenged.

'I guess not,' Reade replied.

'That's right,' Eloise answered. 'Mr Payne said he'd traveled through the South and ours were the best biscuits he'd ever tasted.'

'And he wished us luck with our show.'

'And he said he looked forward to reading our cookbook.'

'You can ask anyone there,' Lula Mae added.

Reade drew a deep breath and looked at Tish, who gave him a nod of approval. 'OK, ladies. I believe you.'

Lula Mae and Eloise applauded and hugged each other. 'Now we can go home?' an elated Eloise cried.

Reade spoke up. 'Umm, there's still the matter of the cannabis in Gunnar Randall's breakfast.'

'But cannabis is legal now,' Lula Mae argued.

'Personal possession of less than an ounce is, indeed, legal. Distribution by a non-pharmaceutical business is not, and I'm afraid your "sprinkle" of hashish could qualify as distribution.'

'Oh! But you can just overlook that, can't you?'

'Yes, now that we explained what happened,' Eloise appealed.

'I'd love to, but this isn't my jurisdiction. The Richmond Police Department has allowed me to pursue my investigation here, but I don't have the authority for much else.'

'What does that mean?' Eloise asked.

'Will we go to jail? Will the Biscuit Palace be shut down?' a panicked Lula Mae asked.

Reade patted the air in front of him with both hands in a calming gesture. 'What I *can* do is submit this to the Richmond Police as an individual distribution case, which means you go home tonight, you wake up tomorrow and open the Biscuit Palace like you always do, and life goes on as normal – except that at some point during the next week you'll receive a summons by mail to go down to your local precinct and pay your fines.'

'Fines? We can't afford any fines!'

'Twenty-five dollars for each of you. Unless, of course, this isn't your first offense,' he added with a flash of a grin.

'Twenty-five dollars?' Eloise repeated in disbelief.

'No probation or jail time?' Lula Mae asked.

'Twenty-five dollars per person is the maximum penalty – a civil penalty.'

'And the Food Channel won't get wind of anything?'

'Not a word. Although the offense will be noted on your record, so, um, no more "sprinkles" for difficult customers, ladies. Please?'

TWENTY

'How is Payne?' Zach Farraday asked, dressed in a pair of checkered trousers and chef whites.

'Stable,' Reade replied, reluctant to give away too much about the older chef's condition. 'Seems you weren't completely straightforward with me when I spoke with you yesterday. You led me to believe you hadn't met Gunnar Randall before last Wednesday, but that's not quite the case. Some years ago, Gunnar Randall gave a presentation at the facility in which you were incarcerated. According to records, you attended.'

'Oh, that?'

'Yes, that.'

'Randall did a cooking demonstration. It must have been community service for a DUI or assault charge or something.'

'Do you know that for a fact?'

'No, but Randall wasn't the type to volunteer his time, and his attitude that day was so massive I'm surprised there was still space in the room for an audience. Not to mention, where else would you send Randall to perform community service? Definitely not a school or retirement home. You'd be sued.'

'What happened that day?' Tish asked.

'You mean apart from the disdain and disgust Randall exuded? Nothing really. He just gave an ordinary cooking presentation. He didn't cook anything mind-blowing, but considering he was teaching a bunch of dudes in lockup, I didn't expect it to be.'

'Then why not mention it to me earlier?' Reade remarked.

'Because I forgot. I mean, it wasn't exactly a memorable event.'

'What did he cook?' Tish asked.

The question caught Farraday off guard. 'What?'

'What did Randall cook?' she repeated.

'He showed us how to roast a chicken – a traditional method, nothing revolutionary, kinda boring – and then how to make mashed potatoes and gravy to go with it. His mashed potatoes were more like food glue than mashed potatoes. He used a mixer instead of a ricer. I guess he figured we "guys" wanted to see some power tools involved.'

'Did you say anything to him about his technique?'

'No. The things I'm saying to you now weren't anything I would have thought about back then. It wasn't until I participated in Jackson Payne's introductory course that I became inspired by cooking. I might have commented on Randall's attitude, though,' Farraday confessed with an unpleasant little smirk.

'Might have?' Reade quizzed.

'OK, you win. You've probably already sent for the prison records anyway. That afternoon, Randall was so full of himself, so arrogant, so obviously disgusted with his surroundings that I decided to heckle him within an inch of his life. Whenever I could, I inserted a joke at his expense or mocked his words or made fun of how he pronounced an ingredient or technique.'

'And the guards let you get away with it?'

'Yeah, they could see what a pretentious little toad Randall was. That's why they laughed along with my comments. When they stopped laughing is when Randall came out into the audience to take a poke at me.'

'Randall hit you?'

'No, the guards got to him first. But he was out for blood. I was asked to leave the demonstration after that.'

'Let's fast forward to this past Wednesday. Did Randall remember you?'

'I don't know. I mean, if he did, he didn't say anything – the guards shouted out my last name that day. Maybe he heard it, maybe he didn't. He looked down on all of us, so who knows? But when I met him on Wednesday, I hoped he did remember. It's the primary reason I applied to the show. I know the publicity of getting a positive review would have helped my pub, but all I really wanted was to show Randall up for what he was – a gigantic, thin-skinned, no-talent fraud. A fraud who preyed on little people to make himself feel big.'

Tish allowed several seconds to elapse before questioning Farraday again. 'In contrast, it must have been terrific to see Jackson Payne again this evening?'

Farraday appeared startled by the question. 'Oh, yeah. Yeah, I was looking forward to it all day.'

'Sounds like there's a "but" missing from that statement.'

'No, no "buts." I enjoyed catching up with Chef Payne . . . until he told me he'd had a lunch date with Gunnar Randall on Wednesday. A lunch date! Can you believe it? With that piece of—' Farraday bit his bottom lip. 'I understand the chef code of conduct, but for Payne to actually socialize with a man who was so disrespectful to me and other cooks was an absolute betrayal. I'll always be grateful for what Payne taught me, but any respect or affection I had for him has gone right out the window. In its place, there's only anger.'

Finally back at home, Reade ensured Marlowe and Tuna had sufficient water and kibble for the night while Tish brushed her teeth, donned a pair of boxers and a matching tank top, and crawled into bed. In her hand was Gunnar Randall's leather-bound journal.

Sinking back against the pillows, she paged through the small tome until she reached the Wednesday in question. The early hours had been crossed out in red ink – an indication of the time Randall would be traveling by plane. Beneath the giant 'X,' scrawled in sloppy, left-slanting handwriting, were the words: *BISCUIT PALACE. Old-school food. Tired-looking waitresses and decor. Zero atmosphere. BEST biscuits and catfish for miles!*

Tish frowned. Despite the excellent review of their food, the Lou-Lous would undoubtedly be disappointed at being described as 'tired-looking.'

The next entry was even worse: *FRUMM'S FUNGI FARM. Karma puts the FRUMM in FRUMMPY. If she's Karma, I hate to see what she did in a former life. Maudlin backstory. Mediocre mushrooms. Mud everywhere.*

'A little light reading?' Reade teased as he entered the bedroom.

'Hmph,' Tish grunted in reply. 'Gunnar Randall was truly a disgusting individual.'

He perched on the edge of the bed and removed his boots. 'That was a foregone conclusion, wasn't it?'

'Yes, but every time I think I couldn't dislike the man any more than I already do, I find something that proves me wrong.'

'He was a horse's behind. I'd be more surprised if you learned something positive about him.'

'Mmm, he's also somewhat puzzling.'

Reade took off his jeans and slid into bed. 'Puzzling? I had him down as an open book.'

'So did I, but why would he give one of his coveted gold-star reviews to a woman whose mushrooms were mediocre?'

'That sounds like the opening line to one of Jules's bad jokes,' he quipped as he slid an arm around her shoulders.

'Oh, if it only were.' She pointed to the entry in Randall's journal and read it aloud.

'He wouldn't give her a positive review,' he concluded. 'He'd probably even ridicule her on TV.'

'Exactly. And yet he raved about her mushrooms.'

'She's a caregiver to her younger brother. It's a great backstory.'

'Even though Randall called it "maudlin."'

'The honchos at the Food Channel knew what they had in Karma. They probably demanded Randall go easy on her.'

'I'm not so sure of that. Remember, Shae Fisher said that the Food Channel decided where Randall would travel next. Once that was decided, they let Randall take the reins on which entrants would be selected to be on the show.'

'That's right. It sounded like they took a pretty laissez-faire approach to the show, didn't it? Maybe Randall himself saw the value in making Karma a "winner," so to speak. He had to have realized that doing so would make him look like a hero.'

'Yes, but why didn't he note it in his journal? Why criticize a backstory that could be extremely useful to him? Why not write "interesting opportunity" or "keeper" or something that indicated his intentions? As far as he knew, no one else was going to see this journal but him. He was already candid in his criticism of Karma's looks – why hold back as to his intentions regarding his review?'

'Good point. Anything else in there?'

'Let's see . . . "Betancourt Winery. Lemon-faced grandma at the door. Should be sexy hostess. Food ordinary, wine even more so. Brother owners act like prepubescent boys."'

'Takes one to know one,' Reade wisecracked, much to Tish's amusement.

'Next is the appointment with Jackson Payne,' she continued. '"Can't believe this meeting of geniuses almost didn't happen," he writes.'

'Meeting of geniuses?' Reade reacted with a retching sound.

'And to think you criticized Clayton and me for our derogatory comments earlier this afternoon,' she reminded.

'That's different. We were working then. I'm off duty now, it's late, and I'm not wearing any pants.'

'I'll keep those prerequisites in mind next time I'm tempted to make a remark about the deceased,' she quipped before returning to the journal. '"Can't believe this meeting of geniuses almost didn't happen. I could have murdered that stupid tart for her mistake—"'

'Ouch.'

'"JP was brilliant. His simple approach to food is magnificent. Expectations exceeded."'

'Listening to Randall fanboy is weird, don't you think?'

'You mean because his admiration seems genuine?'

'Yeah – I mean apart from the "two geniuses" bit, Randall's heaping praise on someone other than himself. It seems out of character for him.'

'It does,' she acknowledged. 'Although if anyone on earth were to have garnered Randall's respect – even begrudgingly – it would be Jackson Payne. Not only is he revered for his contributions to the culinary world, but he's one of the nicest people in the business. I don't believe anyone's had a bad word to say about him – ever.'

'If only Randall had learned from him,' Reade said.

'Clearly he didn't. "The only eagerness The Eager Vegan spurs is an eagerness to leave. Garbage hippie joint. Dirty, dreadlocked cow of an owner with an attitude problem. Mushrooms and water make sauce, not tea. Kumbay-nah."'

'That's even more vicious than the first two. You'd have thought his time alone with a "fellow genius" would have smoothed out his rough edges.'

'The only thing that seems to have smoothed out Gunnar Randall's rough edges is death,' Tish observed. '"Honor Amongst Thieves Gast-Bro-Pub."'

'Hey, according to Farraday, he used that line while shooting.'

'"Boring food hidden under guise of comfort. Even Farra-gay's—"'

Reade shook his head. 'The guy calls the Betancourts

prepubescent and then he goes for a juvenile, offensive gay joke.'

'"—former cellmates wouldn't eat this stuff."'

'Randall recognized Farraday,' Tish and Reade exclaimed in unison before falling silent.

'But what does it mean?' she asked.

'I have no idea. All these descriptions do is give everyone a stronger motive.'

'I know,' she acknowledged while carefully thumbing through journal pages. 'As though anyone needed more of a reason to want Gunnar Randall—' She stopped with a gasp.

'What is it?'

'"Abbingdon Green B and B. Granny Palace. Wallpaper and mothballs. Tea served when you're not sick. Breakfast served before anyone under seventy is even hungry. Deviate from rules and wrinkly old shrew berates you. Why would anyone get married here?" Where did Clayton say he found this journal?' she asked when she'd finished reading.

'In Randall's room. It was on his dresser.'

'Where Glory or any one of the housekeepers might have seen it.' Tish closed the journal and leaned her head on Reade's shoulder with a deep, tired breath. 'Yet another motive.'

TWENTY-ONE

'With the café closed, I thought I'd be able to enjoy at least a few late mornings,' Tish stated as she sipped from a stainless steel travel mug. 'But at least this coffee of yours eases the pain.'

'The breakfast queen likes my coffee? That's lofty praise, indeed,' Reade replied as he steered his black SUV toward Frumm's Fungi Farm.

'It's true. I might like your coffee better than mine or even – don't say a word to her – Celestine's. And I could drink hers all day long.'

'Watch it,' he cautioned. 'Keep talking like that and there'll be no living with me.'

'I wouldn't worry about that,' she said with a wink. 'I think you're safe.'

'Good. And thanks for coming out with me this morning. I know you have a wedding to cater this afternoon.'

'I wanted to come. Although I'm in a little bit of a time crunch, I should still be able to make it to Glory's in time to set up for the wedding and, sadly, question her about Randall and the party last night.'

'I can talk to her if you'd like. I know she's your friend.'

'Thanks, but that's precisely why I should talk to her. Although she finds you ridiculously handsome – which you are – she'll be far more open with me.'

'Once again, be careful. Ego inflating in ten . . . nine . . . eight . . .'

'You're probably right. That's enough for one day – otherwise, your head will be so big there won't be room enough in the car for me to ride home with you.'

The pair laughed, but their merriment swiftly evaporated as they neared the gates of the Frumm farm where three marked Sheriff's Office vehicles blocked the entrance. Reade rolled down the window and a uniformed officer allowed him admittance.

Parking outside the farm's office, he and Tish were met by a distraught Karma Frumm. 'What is this all about? What are you looking for? Your officer –what's his name? Claxton? Says he has a warrant, but he won't tell me anything else.'

'Ms Frumm, Officer Clayton is operating on behalf of my office. Samples of soil I took from your shed contained the mycelium of psilocybin mushrooms. My office has a warrant to search the premises for the presence of the mushrooms themselves.'

'You won't find anything,' Karma insisted. 'So why don't you call off your team instead of letting them run loose around my farm? That's my livelihood they're messing around with!'

'I do appreciate the delicate nature of your crops, Ms Frumm. So does my team. I assure you that they'll exercise the utmost caution in the growing areas.'

'They'd better. I don't grow these things for fun. They barely put food on the table and keep a roof over our heads, but they're better than nothing.'

'Psychedelic mushrooms sell well though, don't they? And they fetch a fairly high price if I'm not mistaken,' Reade ventured.

'I wouldn't know,' Karma replied as she stepped forward to oversee the search of her farm.

'Then how did the mycelium wind up in the soil sample?'

'I don't know. It must have been present in the growing substrate I purchased.'

'Do you have a receipt for the substrate so we can track down the seller?'

Karma frowned. 'No. I, um, I'm not sure who I used.'

'You mean to say that you don't keep receipts? That's Business Management 101. I'm just a simple sheriff, but the woman who does my taxes insists I keep receipts for everything I use on the job – shoes, gasoline, jackets, even haircuts. Seeing as you're running an actual business, I can only imagine your accountant must be even more stringent.'

'Yes, he . . . he is.' Karma plastered on a smile. 'Oh, now I remember. I bought that substrate from my usual guy, but I think he used a different supplier. I'll try to get you his number later today.'

'Oh, no,' Reade argued. 'We've troubled you enough already. If you tell us the name of your usual guy, we can take it from there.'

Karma's face fell. 'No, that . . . that won't be necessary. You're even busier than I am.'

'I don't know about that. I have an entire office at my disposal and, quite frankly, the badge tends to get me answers quicker than if I were a civilian. You call that guy of yours and you may not hear from him for days. My office? We typically get a reply within hours, sometimes even minutes. Now,' he started, typing into his tablet, 'what's this gentleman's name?'

'All right, you win, Sheriff,' Karma relented. 'I don't want to get anyone else in trouble, particularly an old friend. I didn't buy that substrate from anyone. I used what I had on hand here at the farm.'

'Thank you for your honesty, Ms Frumm. Now let's see if we can make it two for two. How did the mycelium get into the substrate?'

'I don't know,' she answered abruptly.

'Well, if you don't know, who would?'

'Not funny, Sheriff.'

'I wasn't trying to be. Let me review the situation for you. There's mycelium from a psychedelic mushroom in the substrate found in your development shed, a TV host who was caught sneaking around your development shed and is now dead thanks to a poisonous mushroom, and a legendary chef who's been hospitalized due to the same kind of poisonous mushroom that killed the TV host. Oh, and you served both men mushrooms shortly before they fell ill. Do you see a common link?'

'I had nothing to do with the mushroom poisoning. I swear I didn't.'

'Which one?'

'Neither of them.'

'Then tell us what you *did* have something to do with,' Reade urged.

Karma Frumm remained silent.

'You're in the middle of a murder investigation and now a possible drug charge. Don't you think it's time you began to come clean, Ms Frumm?'

'You don't understand. I have a brother to look after,' she explained as she gazed imploringly at Tish and Reade.

'We can't help you to protect him if you don't tell us the truth,

Karma,' Tish beseeched. 'We saw Gunnar Randall's journal. We know he gave you a favorable review for a reason, and it had nothing to do with the mushrooms you cooked for him.'

'I can't. I can't tell you. I can't go to jail!'

'Ms Frumm,' Reade answered reassuringly, 'tell me the truth and I will do whatever I can to make sure you can stay with Everest.'

Karma glanced at Tish, who gave her a nod of encouragement. 'OK,' she finally relented.

'OK. So let's start at the beginning. Why did we find psilocybin mushroom mycelium in the soil in the development shed?'

'I can't . . . I can't answer that. You'll only use it against me!'

'Then let's take this in a different direction,' Reade said gently. 'Are there any psilocybin mushrooms on your property right now?'

'No. None. I swear there aren't!'

'Good. Are there any traces – other than the mycelium that we found in the soil – of psilocybin mushrooms on your property?'

'No. None.'

'Good. In order for me to arrest you on drug possession charges, you would need to be in actual physical possession of the mushrooms. The penalty for possession is dictated by the quantity of mushrooms found in your possession. If there are no psilocybin mushrooms physically in your possession, then I can't arrest you for possession.'

Karma's body language relaxed slightly. 'You can't?'

'No. So, unless the search turns up something—'

'It won't,' she assured Reade.

'OK. Now then, did you ever distribute psilocybin mushrooms in exchange for money?'

'No!' she nearly shrieked. 'Never.'

'Good. Then I can't arrest you on drug distribution charges either. Unless, of course, I prove that you're lying.'

'I'm not,' Karma insisted. 'If I were selling drugs, this place would look a whole hell of a lot better than it does.'

Reade cast an appraising eye at the paint peeling from the facade of the office building and the loose hinges on the entrance gate. 'Well, then, the only thing I might be able to arrest you for is growing psilocybin mushrooms, which, of course, is a felony, but, again, that depends upon how much you were growing. So, hypothetically, if we were to find psilocybin mushrooms on your property – hypothetically, mind you – how much would we find?'

'Hypothetically, not very many.'

'Can you be more specific?'

'An area about one foot square. I destroyed them after you came by to question me.'

'So enough for personal use?'

Karma's eyes grew damp. 'Personal, yes, but not mine. They were for Everest.'

'Everest? Why for Everest?' Tish questioned.

'Along with the myriad of physical ailments my brother suffers from, he's also very high on the autism spectrum. My parents tried their best to care for him at home throughout his life, but as they aged and I was no longer in the house, they were forced to send him to a care facility. Everest flourished for a while, but then he slowly retreated into himself. He spoke less and less and finally reached a point where he refused my parents' visits. After they consulted with me about it, as they were both already ill at that time, they decided to pull him out of the care facility and bring him home again – with my help. It was during Everest's first home nurse visit that we saw the marks on his back. Someone, some monster, at the facility had abused him.'

'I'm very sorry,' Tish said.

Reade also offered his sympathies.

'Thanks. We sued the facility and the case was settled out of court, as if money could make up for what happened,' she sneered. 'But we had no choice. My parents and Everest wouldn't have made it through a prolonged trial. Of course, we also sought treatment and therapy for my brother. Everest made tremendous progress, but even with therapy, he was not the same brother I'd known and loved. He was sad and despondent and withdrawn most of the time. Since it's the family business, I've always kept up with the mushroom world – science, farming, you name it. One day, I read about a study done at Imperial College, London, where people with severe depression were given either psilocybin or a conventional antidepressant. Those given the conventional antidepressants noted slight improvement, but those given the psilocybin reported rapid and sustained improvement – improvement substantiated by brain scans which showed neural activity resembling that of a healthy brain.

'I immediately talked to my brother's doctors about it,' Karma continued. 'They were not only skeptical but fearful of losing their licenses because, as you know, Sheriff, psilocybin is illegal.'

'So you decided to take matters into your own hands,' Reade presumed.

'I didn't know what else to do. I wanted Everest to be the way he used to be. I wanted my brother back – all of him. So I cultivated a small patch of mushrooms and, starting with the tiniest of amounts, fed some to Everest as a test. It took some tweaks before I found the right dosage, but when I did, the change was pronounced and almost immediate. Everest was more relaxed, more animated. He talked more and was excited about things again. He picked up his old hobbies and started his part-time job. He wrote the letter to *Taste of America*. My brother was back,' she said with a sob.

'What happened with Gunnar Randall?'

'Gunnar Randall got nosy. He wandered around the farm and eventually stumbled upon the development shed. Most times, it's usually only me around here, so I never used to keep it locked. When I knew a tour was coming through, I'd temporarily move the mushrooms to a higher shelf – one that couldn't be reached without a ladder. No one ever asked about what was growing there because it's called a development shed, so, obviously, I was growing new varieties of mushrooms. I never ever had a problem.'

'Until Randall,' Tish guessed.

'Until Randall,' Karma confirmed. 'I don't know if he knew right off the bat what I was growing or if he needed to Google it, but he saw the mushrooms for Everest and assumed I was growing them to sell. First, he wanted to buy some from me. Naturally, I refused. He must have given it more thought because he then came back to me with a deal. If I cut him in on my mushroom business, he'd give me a rave review.'

'What did you say?'

'No, for the very reason that there was no mushroom business to cut him in on. But Randall was persistent. There was no telling him no, because he didn't believe me. And so he threatened to turn me in to the police if I didn't agree to his deal. I had no other choice than to go along with his deal and try to look surprised at his review.'

'And eventually plant more psychedelic mushrooms,' Tish noted.

'Only Randall didn't live long enough to put that kind of pressure on you,' Reade said.

'I know what you're suggesting, but I didn't kill him,' Karma said emphatically. 'I did not kill him.'

'What happened last night?'

'Last night?' Karma appeared confused by the question.

'Jackson Payne's birthday dinner.'

'I couldn't attend. I needed to take care of some things here on the farm while we still have our long days. After that, I fixed Everest and myself some supper and made sure he had taken his medication before we both headed off to bed.'

'But you did contribute a dish to the party,' Tish prompted.

'Yes, mushroom vol-au-vents. Everyone who's anyone in the Richmond restaurant scene was slated to be there. Letting them sample a variety of mushrooms was a great opportunity to expand my business.'

'So you weren't there to serve the vol-au-vents?' Tish asked, even though she already knew the answer.

'No, I dropped them off during the afternoon and gave instructions to the kitchen staff.'

'Instructions?'

'Yes. The vol-au-vents were unfilled so the puff pastry stayed crisp and flaky. The cook on duty had to heat the mushroom filling and then assemble them.'

'So, unlike the other contributors, you didn't specify that a particular vol-au-vent be served to Jackson Payne?'

'No. Maybe I should have because some of the pastries looked better than others, but I'm a farmer, not a food stylist.'

Before Reade or Tish could ask another question, Clayton approached, shaking his head vigorously. 'Nothing, sir. We've searched the sheds, the compost, and the fields. We've come up empty.'

'OK. Thanks, Clayton. You and the team can head back to the office. Well, Ms Frumm,' he addressed the farmer. 'It looks as if you were telling the truth.'

'I told you I was,' she replied. 'About everything.'

TWENTY-TWO

'I discovered that Gunnar Randall was the guest staying in the Turret Suite two months before he arrived,' Glory Bishop told Tish and Reade over a pot of coffee at the B & B's kitchen table. The staff, meanwhile, had dispersed upstairs to make beds and clean rooms before the wedding party returned from their pre-wedding salon and brunch trips.

'How did you find out?' Tish asked.

'First, I was sent a nondisclosure agreement to sign – never had to sign one for a guest before, so I figured that secret reservation had to be for someone famous. Then, a few days later, I read in the paper that *Taste of America* would be filming in Richmond on the same dates as the reservation. It didn't take too much to piece together.'

'I'm surprised you kept the reservation.'

'I wasn't going to. My first instinct was to email Ms Fisher and tell her to take her reservation and shove—' Glory started and then, eyeing Reade, changed course. 'Toss it out the window. But the spring and early summer had been so cool and rainy that nearly half of my reservations had either canceled or cut their stay short. Having a full house – a confirmed full house – was terribly appealing. Could I rent out the Turret Suite for this weekend? Not to the bride and groom. Their reservation was set elsewhere, with a no-cancelation policy. Someone else might have taken it, but "might" isn't the same as having that money in the bank.

'There was a time, not so many years ago when I would have told Gunnar Randall to walk,' Glory continued. 'But it's no longer just me running this place. There's George, Esmeralda, and the part-time housekeepers to be paid, and all of them are supporting their own families. And then there's food and gas prices rising by what seems like the day. Nope, there was a time when I could turn down a paying guest just because I got a strange feeling from them. Those days are well and truly over.'

'We understand why you took and kept the reservation, Glory, but why didn't you tell us that you knew Gunnar Randall was your "mystery guest" when Shae Fisher checked him in? Why conceal that fact from us?' Tish queried.

'Why conceal it?' she asked with a sardonic laugh. 'To avoid what's happening now. To avoid y'all accusing me of murdering Gunnar Randall.'

'Did you?' Tish asked.

'Did I what?'

'Did you murder Gunnar Randall?'

'No, honey, I didn't. You know I didn't. You said yourself that I couldn't have,' Glory reminded as she patted Tish's hand. 'Randall had already been poisoned when he ate my omelet.'

'That was before we remembered your welcome tray, which would have been waiting in Randall's room the day he was poisoned.'

Glory pulled her hand away from Tish's as if the younger woman might carry some communicable disease. 'The welcome tray has always been a part of my establishment. It's a selling point that other inns in the region have tried to duplicate, but never have,' she stated briskly.

'Yes, it's a brilliant little perk for your guests,' Tish said in an effort to defuse the situation. 'I especially like how you customize it according to the seasons. What's on it now?'

'Oh, some tomato and chili jam, herbed scones, cucumber pickle, butternut squash and . . . um, vegetable Palmiers, ginger cookies, a couple of sachets of soothing chamomile tea, and bottled water.'

'One could easily bypass supper with that.'

'That's the whole point. After a long day – or maybe two – of traveling, sometimes all you want to do is put on your pajamas and relax in your room with a bottle of wine and a good book. We offer wine chillers, too,' Glory told Reade with pride.

'I haven't traveled much recently,' he remarked, 'but the few times I've driven north to visit family, I would have loved to find an inn with a welcome tray like yours. Going out in search of dinner after a long day of driving can be miserable, especially when it's late and the weather is bad.'

'Yes,' Glory excitedly agreed – whether grateful for the vindication of her position or because of the distraction the conversation caused. 'Yes, that's exactly it. Despite the popularity of Door Dash and all these other food delivery services, many of my guests enjoy the slow, homemade goodness of the tray as an alternative to the fast food they consume on a regular basis.'

'Did Gunnar Randall appreciate it?'

'Clever young man, aren't you? Trying to trip me up with a trick question. Not only was Gunnar Randall ill that evening, but – as you already know – he wasn't the type to enjoy or appreciate anything.'

'Did you take note of the tray when you cleaned his room the next morning?'

'Esmeralda cleaned his room,' Glory answered with a sniff.

'But you must have seen it when she brought it down to the kitchen. If you don't tell us, I can ask Esmeralda,' Tish reasoned.

'Yes,' she relented. 'Yes, I saw the tray. I kept a close watch on Mr Randall's room, lest he have reason to complain about something.'

'And the tray?'

'It was empty, but that doesn't mean anything. There was nothing on that tray that would have hurt him. Nothing!'

'Not even the butternut squash and mushroom Palmiers?' Reade put forth. 'I assume that's what you meant when you said "butternut squash and vegetable."'

Glory shot him a look. 'I know Randall was a difficult man, but I had no motive to kill him.'

'Glory, if you kept a close watch on his room, then you probably saw his journal,' Tish ventured.

'N–no, I—'

'He kept it on his dresser. Right out in the open.'

'And that means that I would read it?' Glory was indignant.

'If it were any other guest, no, you wouldn't. But Gunnar Randall might have tried to take down this Bed and Breakfast – your sole passion in life.'

Glory confirmed Tish's suspicions with a slow, steady blink. 'What I feared might happen was about to happen. "Granny Palace." "Who would want to get married here?" If he ever put that on his television show, this place – my place – would be considered a joke by hundreds of thousands of people.'

'So you killed him,' Tish surmised, 'using the Death Caps that were growing outside the root cellar door.'

'I didn't. Please believe me, Tish. I didn't! I thought about it, though. I thought about it long and hard. He was a terrible, terrible man,' she said with a shiver. 'The way he acted. The things he said – not just about me, but about other people – were just plain cruel and vindictive. But then I thought about what would happen to the B and B and my employees if I did kill him. It wasn't worth it. He wasn't worth it. As for the Death Caps on the property, I had no idea what the mushrooms growing outside the root cellar even were. I thought they looked nice – nicer than weeds, at least. As for identifying them, I can hardly keep up with everything inside the house, let alone what's outside of it. And although George is an excellent gardener, he isn't an expert in mycology.'

'What about Jackson Payne?' Reade questioned. 'He fell ill last night. Mushroom poisoning – just like Gunnar Randall.'

'Oh no! The poor man. He's not . . . dead, is he?' she asked, her voice trembling.

'No, but he has been hospitalized.'

Glory gasped. 'How terrible! How did it happen?'

'We're trying to piece that together, so if you could recount your time at the party yesterday, we'd appreciate it.'

'I wasn't at the party. I couldn't possibly attend. Not with an inn full of wedding guests and not after' – her voice dropped to a whisper, as if they hadn't spent the last thirty minutes discussing murder – 'what happened.'

'But your dish was at the party, was it not?'

'Yes, I brought my Palmiers to The Jefferson around three in the afternoon. These were plain mushroom – no squash – because I didn't want them to get soggy before serving. Oh, and they were partially baked, so that they didn't get too brown when the kitchen staff reheated them.'

'Was the Palmier meant for Jackson Payne different in any way?' Tish asked.

'Different? Why, yes, of course. I pointed to the shapeliest Palmier of the batch and told the cook that it was the one to be served to Chef Payne. I'm not sure why you're asking me all of this. If you think I poisoned the man, you couldn't be more wrong. I love Jackson Payne.'

'Yes, he's an American treasure.'

'No, I mean, I *really* love Jackson Payne.' Her face colored.

'It's childish and unladylike, I know, but when I saw his first television show years ago – so long ago that it was in black and white! – I was smitten. He was so handsome, so cosmopolitan, so accomplished. And he loved food and cooking as much as I did. It's ridiculous, I know. I was a grown woman with children, but I sometimes wondered what it would have been like to be married to Jackson Payne or at least someone like him. Someone whose heart leaped at the same things mine did. Someone who had the same passion for food and fine living and wine and art.'

Tears welled in Glory's eyes. 'I never really dated after my divorce. Between the boys and work and the house, I never seemed to have the time. And then, when I had the time, I was doubtful that I'd ever meet anyone who could love me for who I am. But each Saturday evening, when I'd put the kids down for the night or finished turning down the guest beds, there he was – Jackson Payne – right there on my television set, and I'd spend an hour watching him create a French omelet or perfectly sear a steak or use the languishing vegetables in his refrigerator to create a stew. And, at the end of that hour – no matter how my week was, what my hair looked like, or how empty my bank account was – I felt comforted and soothed and empowered and inspired. And that is why I would never, ever dream of hurting Chef Jackson Payne.'

'Is that how *you* feel about Jackson Payne?' Reade asked as he and Tish unloaded two halves of a metal wedding arch from the back of the SUV.

'Minus the romantic angle, yes,' she replied.

'Yeah, I sort of figured that. I was talking about the feeling of being soothed and comforted.'

'It's very much the same as Glory described. Part of it, of course, stems from the fact that I watched his early shows with my mother, but the rest is more about Jackson Payne himself. Unlike my father, Payne is an example of positive masculinity – good manners, good taste, minimal ego, and respectful to the women in his life, including his mother-in-law who was one of the *Mères Lyonnaise*, France's first female chefs. As a cook, I find him inspiring, and his culinary sensibilities are something to which most chefs aspire. Payne understands that cooking and food have the ability to bring people together and he works toward that end. And before you think I'm offering him up for sainthood, I'm not – nor would you if you watched him cook. He's quite human – messy, impatient at times, a bit absent-minded – but quite wonderful.'

'As are you,' Reade replied. He leaned in for a kiss before the two of them carried the arch pieces to the B & B's garden.

'You're not too bad yourself,' she teased.

'Is that all I get?'

'I think I did a pretty good job at flattery earlier this morning. You yourself told me to be careful.'

'And so I did,' he conceded with a smile. 'Are you going to put flowers on these?'

'Not yet.' Tish led him back to the car, where two boxes of used books had been loaded beside the arch.

'Books?' he questioned, grabbing one of the boxes. 'I wondered what these were for.'

'Mm-hmm,' she confirmed, taking hold of the other box and leading the way back to the arbor. Once there, she began threading the books on to the narrow-welded steel pipes.

'You're making a book arbor,' he said in amazement.

'Yes, Daryl Dufour let me rummage through the library's purged books – you know, the ones they usually put outside in a box every so many months – I got these for just a few bucks.'

Reade took note of their titles. 'English literature, mysteries, romance, sci-fi . . .'

'Yes, the bride and groom's favorite reading subjects. I wanted to customize the decorations to their tastes. Then I brought all the books over to Orson Baggett over in Coleton Creek, because he has a drill press in his garage.'

'So he drilled them for you?'

'No, he supervised while I drilled them. It brought me back to my high school shop days.'

'Is there anything you can't do?' he asked appreciatively.

'Run. I can't run. At. all. Full stop. Not only am I ridiculously slow, but I look like I'm having some sort of muscle spasm.'

'Well, let's hope that we never have a case where we need to apprehend a sprinter.'

'That's why we have Clayton, isn't it?' she joked before threading books on to the other side of the arch. 'Now, if you'll help me push them together.'

Reade did as he was instructed. When united, the two parts of the arch formed a beautiful bookish arbor.

'Now for the finishing touches.' She trotted off to the SUV and returned with a box of fresh baby's breath and a spool of white mesh ribbon.

'You're very good at this,' he said as she tucked sprigs of the tiny white flowers at irregular intervals between the spines of the books.

'A caterer wears many hats. I just hope the bride and groom are as impressed as you are.'

'They will be,' he declared as Tish began weaving the sheer ribbon through the books and along the length of the arch. 'Have you . . . have you ever thought about marriage?'

'Yeah, of course. I told you I was married before, didn't I?' she said.

'What I meant to say is have you ever given any thought to marrying again?'

Tish was fixed where she stood. She wanted to express to Clemson how much he and their new life together meant to her. How grateful she was to have him by her side during these challenging times and how excited she was to celebrate happy occasions together in the future. But marriage? The idea had, in fact, flitted across her mind once while they were attending a wedding, but she had swatted it down just as quickly as it had risen. It was too early in their relationship for such talk. Far too early. And yet she didn't want to discourage him completely. No, this was the time for a lengthy conversation and carefully articulated thoughts.

Sadly, all she could muster was 'I, umm . . . umm . . .'

'Guess who's here?' Jules's voice echoed through the garden. 'Your bartender extraordinaire! By the way, Tish, I took your van through that drive-through carwash. It looked like you had parked it in the aviary in the Metro Richmond Zoo. Oops,' he exclaimed, noticing Reade standing at Tish's side, 'am I interrupting something?'

'No,' Reade replied. Then he asked Tish, sotto voce, 'Do you pay him to arrive during critical moments?'

'Nope, just the bartending. The impeccable timing is a bonus – or a curse, depending on the situation. I'm sorry, Clemson. I'd like to continue this conversation at another time. May we?'

'You bet.'

'Thank you.' She threw her arms around his neck and kissed him. He eagerly returned the kiss.

Jules, meanwhile, folded his arms across his chest. 'Hello? I'm ecstatic that the two of you are happy. Really, I am. But I have a chest of ice that needs to find a nice shady home, and Celestine's going to be out here any second, and you know how ornery she gets when she doesn't think there's a plan in place.'

'But there is a plan in place,' Tish emphasized.

'I know that and you know that, but from the minute I deviated from the schedule by going to the car wash, Celestine has been convinced that we're approaching this wedding all higgledy-piggledy. Her phrase, not mine.'

'Yes, I gathered that. Don't worry, Jules. I'll reassure her.'

'Well, you'd better do it quick because—'

'Just what in Sam Hill is going on here, Tish?' Celestine's voice resonated through the heavy summer air. 'First, Jules takes me on a joy ride through the car wash—'

'Come on, that was fun,' Jules insisted.

'—and just now, I go inside to put my wedding cake into the refrigerator and find Glory Bishop holed up in the butler pantry drinkin' sherry. Looked as if she'd been cryin', too.'

'That's my fault,' Reade stated. 'I was questioning her about Gunnar Randall's murder.'

'*We* were questioning her,' Tish corrected. 'We're both equally to blame.'

'Well, y'all had better stop it. There's a weddin' here today. Two young people are vowing to spend their lives together, so, for the day, death is takin' a powder.'

Like naughty schoolchildren, Jules, Reade, and Tish tried their best to stifle their giggles.

'What's goin' on?' Celestine insisted. 'What's so funny? Have y'all lost your marbles?'

'Probably,' Tish conceded. 'But that's not why we're laughing.'

'No? Then why? What's up?'

'Technically, death *is* taking a powder, Celestine,' Jules explained.

'Yeah, that's what I said. Death's takin' a powder today, so y'all stop sassin' me, and let's get to work.'

Tish cleared her throat and settled down to business. 'Jules, you're setting up the bar on the porch. It will provide a nice shady retreat where guests can escape the sun. Also, the wine won't warm and the ice won't melt as quickly. Glory's staff already set up some tables there for you to use, but if you need more, let me know.'

'Gotcha!' Jules dashed off to his station.

'And us?' Celestine asked.

'I'll help you unload the van, and then we'll finish arranging the chairs for the ceremony and decorating the tables for the reception. You brought the book page roses, right?'

'Sure did! They look terrific. The bride and groom are gonna be awfully happy with what you've done.'

'Book roses?' Reade asked.

'Yes, well, in this case, *Reader's Digest* roses. After I made confetti for last night's party, I folded the rest of the pages into petals and used floral tape to adhere them to wire stems,' Tish described.

'You're amazing,' he said, clearly enthralled with his girlfriend's talents.

'That she is,' Celestine agreed. 'I'm glad you recognize it. She also has business to attend to.'

'I think that's my cue,' Reade said to Tish as he started to take his leave.

'Cue? That was an order,' Tish replied as she snuck in a small kiss before an eager Celestine called her to the van.

Despite the blazing late-August sun, the wedding ceremony went off without either a hitch or a swoon, thanks to Tish's last-minute decision to place a tall, oscillating fan and two beverage dispensers filled with ice water and cold lemonade in a discreet, shady location close to where the ceremony took place.

When the service had ended and the wedding party had dispersed to the front lawn to take photographs, the Abbingdon Green staff – under Tish's direction – moved the pre-set and decorated round tables that were hidden in the rear driveway into the garden and rearranged the white lace-festooned chairs from the ceremony around them.

As Tish lit the garlands of fairy lights that encircled the garden and set the table candles alight, Celestine arranged a tray of warm buttermilk biscuits, crocks of honey and whipped butter, and a carving board groaning with the weight of a partially sliced old-fashioned country ham on the buffet table. It was a lavish display – one only to be outdone by the presentation of Celestine's utterly stunning wedding cake later in the day.

'Looks terrific,' Tish complimented before she and Celestine retreated to the kitchen to prepare for the main course. Their retreat was well timed, for the wedding party returned to the garden mere seconds after the pair had disappeared. Tish and Celestine listened at the open door to the 'oohs' and 'ahhs' that ensued.

'Well, that'll keep 'em busy for a while,' Celestine declared with a giggle. 'What a beautiful weddin'! Good food. Friends and family. Not a lot of hoopla. If I ever were to do it again, that's how I'd want it.'

'Celestine Rufus! Are you thinking of marrying Daryl Dufour?' Tish asked in surprise.

'No,' the baker insisted. 'Daryl's like a favorite pair of house slippers. Comfy, makes you feel good, and broken in in all the right places. He's a good friend and companion, and I'm awfully fond of him, but marriage? I don't know if I want all that again. Not right now. What about you and Clem?'

'What about us?' She feigned ignorance and checked on the roasted okra warming in the oven.

'I saw how he was moonin' all over you. There's no better enticement to the altar for a fella than to watch another fella go through with it himself. Did Clem pop the question?'

'No, it was more like he was putting out feelers.'

'Yeah, I saw those feelers when I got here!'

'Celestine,' Tish nearly sang.

'Sorry, honey, that's what happens when you force me to ride with Jules to these things. Before you know it, I'll be carryin' a dog around in my purse and singin' Lady Gaga songs while I'm cookin'.'

'Just what I need!'

Celestine laughed. 'Sorry, again, honey. I understood what you meant. So, what did you say to Clem?'

'Nothing. I completely froze. My brain was functioning, but my mouth wasn't.'

'Well, how do you feel about it?'

'I'm not opposed to it someday, far off in the future. Which is strange because, with Schuyler, the very idea of marriage terrified me.'

'You probably knew, deep down, that he wasn't the right person.'

'Maybe. I know I can visualize Clemson and me together for the long haul. I know that it feels right. And yet I also feel like it's too soon to even discuss it – even if it's only to find out whether or not we're on the same page. I want to enjoy where we are first. I want to enjoy this moment and working together and living together, and, when this case is over, enjoying some down time together. Perhaps it's because I'm being forced to think about the future of my business, but I really don't feel like thinking about the future of my relationship right now. I simply want to feel it and live it and relish every second.'

'Seems your mouth is workin' just fine now.'

'Yeah, now that Clemson's not here,' she said with a sigh.

'You'll be able to talk to him. When the time is right.'

'And what if he becomes angry or disappointed?'

'Honey, Clemson Reade is loaded to the gills with love for you. You two will have your disagreements – all couples do – but you'd have to do something truly horrible for him to ever become so angry or disappointed that he'd end things. Clemson is also a man of integrity. He wouldn't have asked you to move in with him if he wasn't committed to the relationship as it stands, right now.'

'You're right, Celestine. I'll talk to him – when the time is right, like you said.'

'Good for you, honey. Now, how's that okra doin'?'

'Just about ready,' Tish confirmed as she gazed through the oven window.

'Then let's get this show on the road!'

As Celestine set to work tossing the green salad with the chutney dressing and portioning it on to small plates, Tish removed the tray of okra and gave the lobster and oyster pies their final bake. All the while, the word 'integrity' reverberated in her ears.

Integrity. It was a word bandied about by everyone from insurance agents to politicians, but from what Tish could see, real integrity wasn't bold or boastful or vain. It was silent and strong and decent. It was Clemson, covertly playing music and giving away toys at the Interfaith Center's Christmas gathering, seeking not an iota of praise, or participating in the countless multicultural events in Hobson Glen to show that he served all of his constituents. It was Jules, quietly changing his middle name because it represented a painful part of American history. It was Celestine and Mary Jo offering to live modestly so that they could help fund a possible new café.

Integrity. A small word with deep roots and far-reaching implications. With it, one could positively impact the lives of an entire community. Without it, one left a trail of pain and misery. What else was at the heart of the Gunnar Randall case other than a lack of integrity? Randall used and mistreated those around him, and he paid the ultimate price.

Tish frowned. But what, then, about Jackson Payne? Payne was known for his fairness, integrity, and generosity, and yet he nearly shared the same fate as Randall. Although many of the suspects with whom she and Clemson spoke had a motive for wanting both men dead, nothing about the scenario seemed right.

'Got somethin' stuck in your craw?' Celestine guessed.

'Yes, and I can't get it unstuck.'

'I recognize the look on your face. This is about the case, ain't it?'

'It is,' Tish replied as she pensively plated the okra and then covered the dishes to keep them warm.

'Well, you keep workin'. It'll come to you. It always does.'

'I hope so. This case is a bit more complicated.'

'I have faith in you, honey. Keep on workin' and thinkin'. And, in the meantime, the weddin' guests will be fed.'

Tish grinned. 'Yes, Celestine.'

'Hey, between love, murder, and Jules's craziness, someone's gotta keep you on track.'

TWENTY-THREE

As the bride and groom sliced into Celestine's stunning seven-layer chocolate torte with a white chocolate collar printed, in edible ink, with phrases from the couple's favorite books and topped with hydrangeas, Tish and the gang cleaned up the dinner dishes.

'I don't know about the rest of you,' Jules said, 'but I feel like leaving here and plunging right into a swimming pool, clothes and all.'

'I'd say you'd shrink that designer dinner jacket of yours, but it looks a little too small already,' Celestine teased.

'That's the cut, Ms Celly. Suits are far more fitted today.'

'Looks like you're wearing the suit from your first communion.'

'Thanks,' Jules deadpanned as he loaded a tray of dirty glasses into the dishwasher.

'A swimming pool, huh? Are you going to visit Mrs Wilkes down at the retirement home?' Tish asked, citing Jules's eighty-four-year-old friend.

'No, not only are her grandchildren in town but the pool is closed. Apparently, the new pool company let the chlorine level get so high that Mrs Valdez's brand-new, jet-black Miraclesuit turned a light shade of violet. She was absolutely livid.'

'Wow. Can't say that I blame her,' Tish remarked as she prepared a stack of plates to be loaded into the dishwasher's bottom rack. 'Still, if that's the worst bit of news in a community of retirees . . .'

Jules grunted his agreement. 'Oh, speaking of news, I no longer need your baked beans for the party next weekend.'

Tish was so startled that she stopped what she was doing. 'You don't? But you only asked me just a couple of days ago.'

'I know, but I changed my mind. I no longer want it.'

'What? But I always bring baked beans. It's become a tradition,' she said, more than a little disappointed that yet another cozy, familiar element of her life was falling by the wayside.

'Not this year,' he replied matter-of-factly.

'Why? Did you change the menu or the theme of the party or something?'

'Yes.'

'Yes? Yes what?'

'Yes, the food-menu-theme-thingy. It's all different now.'

'Well, what did you change it to?'

'I changed it to a celebration of Tish Tarragon taking the day off. I've been looking for a way to help you and I finally found it.'

'Yes, you've helped me to not make baked beans.' She pushed the top rack of the dishwasher back with a shrug and began loading the bottom rack. 'Celestine, what are you making for the day of the party?'

Celestine, at the sink washing baking pans, cast her eyes heavenward. 'After listenin' to you two, reservations for a Greyhound bus to Yuma.'

'The first meal you make in your new home with Reade shouldn't be baked beans,' Jules argued. 'It's kinda weird and gross.'

'Jules, the party isn't for another two weeks. I'll be cooking plenty of meals during that time,' Tish volleyed.

'Maybe I just want you there as a guest so you can relax and enjoy yourself. Is that such a difficult concept to grasp?' He pulled the top rack of the dishwasher back out.

Tish folded her arms across her chest and drew a deep breath. 'When you put it that way, how can I argue? Thanks, Jules.'

'Aww, you're welcome, honey.'

They each leaned over the dishwasher and awkwardly embraced. 'There is one little thing I need from you, though,' Jules said sheepishly as they returned to their upright positions.

Tish refrained from saying 'I told you so,' but it was written all over her face. 'Oh?'

'I need your boyfriend.'

'You need what?'

'Reade. And his band.'

'What?'

'I need them to provide the music for the party.'

'I don't know if they're available. This is awfully short—' Tish started.

'Oh, I already cleared it with him. He said it would be fine.

And don't worry, they're bringing a sound system where we can connect a phone so we can play recorded music, too. This way, he'll have plenty of time to spend with you.'

'As I sit around with my feet up, not making baked beans,' Tish wisecracked.

Before Jules could retaliate, Glory Bishop entered the kitchen, her mood markedly improved from earlier in the day. 'Tish, I just spoke with the Spencers – the bride's parents – and they are thrilled – simply thrilled – with the food and service they received today.'

'That's terrific news, Glory. I'm so happy they're pleased.'

'Yes, they want to speak with you before you leave – no doubt to praise your work and to give y'all a little tip.'

'Well, we never say no to those,' Tish said with a smile.

'My staff might receive one, too, if the bride's parents are as happy as they seem to be. I tell you, after Randall's passing, I was worried about this wedding, but you really pulled it off! I always knew you were talented, Tish, but you truly exceeded expectations this time. Above and beyond anything I was expecting.'

'Thanks, Glory,' Tish replied with a beatific smile, as Jules and Celestine high-fived each other. But something in Glory's words struck a chord. *Exceeded expectations.*

Tish and the team completed the clean-up job and met with an extremely pleased bride, groom, and both sets of parents before loading up the van and driving back to the café.

'Jules, can you drive?' Tish asked as they piled into the van's front bench seat.

'Sure,' he readily agreed. 'You OK?'

'Yes,' she assured him as they pulled out of the Abbingdon Green driveway and on to the road that led to Hobson Glen. 'But I need a favor.'

'Name it.'

'I need you to drop me off at home.'

'At home?'

'Yes, well, Reade's house. The place I'm living now.'

'Oh, yeah, sure. I'll give you a lift in my car after we drop the van at the café. We're not unloading it, right? I mean everything from today is going into storage.'

'No, I need you to drop me off before we get to the café. I know it's a bit out of the way but—'

'She's got that look,' Celestine noticed. 'You've got it figured out, haven't you, honey?'

'I'm not sure. I have my suspicions, but I need to check something.'

'That means you have it figured out! I knew you'd do it if we let you think through it.'

'And work through it,' Tish joked.

'Hey, we wound up with some highly satisfied customers.'

'That we did.'

'We'll drop you off,' Jules confirmed before pressing the accelerator. 'You can count on us.'

'You needn't speed,' Tish told him. 'Remember, I still have four years of payments to make on this thing.'

He slowed it down a touch. 'Sorry, I want to make sure you catch the bad guy – or girl – before they kill again.'

'Thanks, Jules, but I'm not sure that's a concern in this case,' she absently replied.

Tish bounded through the front door and ran straight upstairs to the bedroom. Tuna gave chase.

'Hey,' Reade shouted after her from the living room. 'I got your text to meet you here. What's wrong?'

'I'll be right down,' she yelled back to him before snatching Randall's journal from her bedside table.

'What's going on? Are you OK?' a concerned Reade asked when she and Tuna both returned to the main floor. 'How did the wedding go?'

'The wedding was perfect. Brilliant. Magical. Everyone's extremely happy.'

'That's great! So what's this all—' He spied the journal in her hand. 'You have a lead on the case?'

'I might. "Exceeded expectations." Do you remember those words?'

'I do, but I can't exactly place them. Randall either wrote them about Karma Frumm or . . .'

'Jackson Payne,' she replied, flipping through the pages of the journal. 'Here it is. "Can't believe this meeting of geniuses almost didn't happen. I could have murdered that stupid tart for her mistake. JP was brilliant. His simple approach to food is magnificent. Expectations exceeded."'

'Yes, I remember it now. What about it?'

'Glory said the same thing about the food and service at today's wedding,' Tish explained. 'You see, until now, Glory had only been a customer of my café. She hadn't actually been present at one of my catering jobs. Nor had she ever tasted the dishes I had created for those events, which tend to be more refined than my café offerings. Glory hired me based strictly upon word-of-mouth and the lunches she had enjoyed at the café.'

'And?'

'The first time I read that passage about Jackson Payne in Randall's journal, I assumed that Randall was talking about their meeting and their conversation.'

'He was,' Reade stated. 'The two chefs had never met before – hence Randall's line about two geniuses – and the meeting, wherein they discussed Payne's simple approach to food, "exceeded expectations."'

'Yes, that was my initial take at first, too, particularly because both Jackson Payne and Nick Latanzza emphasized that no food was cooked during Randall's visit. But what if they're lying? What if Jackson Payne created a dish to welcome Gunnar Randall? Imagine that's the case and reread the last part of that entry: "JP was brilliant. His simple approach to food is magnificent. Expectations exceeded."'

'You're right. His statement applies just as well to the food,' Reade remarked.

'I'd argue that it fits the food even better,' she added. 'From the beginning, everyone – Shae Fisher, Dalbir Singh, and now Zach Farraday – has referred to Randall's meeting with Payne as a lunch date.'

'Because it took place during most people's lunch hour.'

'Or because it actually was a lunch date. Even Jackson Payne referred to it as such.'

Reade looked surprised. 'He did? Was that while you were alone with him?'

Tish shook her head. 'We know Payne referred to it as such because that's how Farraday referred to it as well.'

'And Farraday only learned about the meeting because Payne told him,' Reade deduced.

'Precisely. Farraday was furious that Payne would make and keep a lunch date with someone who treated him and other up-and-coming cooks so terribly.'

'But what about Latanzza? He stated specifically that only store-bought cookies and English tea were served that day.'

'Yes, he did. And yet we also know that Gunnar Randall wasn't a fan of tea. He took only a sip of the tea at Tiffany Harlow's restaurant.'

'Yeah, but that was made from mushrooms.'

'True, but that's just part of the story.' She lifted the journal to her face again. '"Abbingdon Green B and B. Granny Palace. Wallpaper and mothballs. Tea served when you're not sick. Breakfast served before anyone under seventy is even hungry."'

'Equating tea with sickness. Not exactly the kind of guy to share a pot of Earl Grey,' Reade agreed.

'The tea-and-cookies story also doesn't fit with Randall's character. Randall thought he was if not the king of the cooking world, then at least the crown prince. If he were meeting with Jackson Payne, his fellow genius, he'd expect Payne to cook for him. If he were met with packaged cookies and tea, you'd better believe it would have wound up in this journal.' She gave the leather cover a tap.

'Then why would Jackson Payne lie about what was served? To cover up for Latanzza?'

Tish shook her head. 'Being served food made by Latanzza – his rival – would have been more of an affront to Gunnar Randall than the cookies and tea. No, Clemson, Latanzza lied to cover for Jackson Payne.'

TWENTY-FOUR

The heat and humidity of the day had given way to a stormy and cool evening. Tish, a thin raincoat concealing her catering clothes, and Reade arrived at Jackson Payne's understated yet elegant Richmond home at approximately nine o'clock. They were met at the door by Chef Latanzza, who immediately led them to a rear study.

There, in a leather wingback chair positioned in front of a wide bay window, sat Jackson Payne. He was dressed in a chambray shirt and khaki trousers, and he appeared relaxed and content, although he was still a bit wan – most likely a byproduct of his latest health scare. On the elegant mahogany piecrust table beside him rested a large glass of red wine.

'Ms Tarragon. Sheriff Reade,' he greeted. 'As you can see, I have been released from the hospital. I'm uncertain whether Pinot Noir was on the discharging nurse's approved menu, but I figured even she could not say no to a 2015 Louis Latour Chateau Corton Grancey. Won't you please sit down and share a glass with me?'

Reade accepted the seat but refused the drink. 'I'm on duty. Sorry.'

Tish did the same.

'Ah, but you have the heart and soul of a cook, Ms Tarragon, and *Wine Spectator* named this bottle as Red Wine of the Year,' Payne cajoled. 'How about a small glass? Wine like this should be shared with those who can appreciate it. I've also heard it said that it's bad luck to drink alone.'

Tish gave a nod of silent acquiescence.

'Good.' He motioned to Chef Latanzza, who left the room and returned with a crystal balloon glass into which he poured a small amount of the ruby-red liquid. Payne lifted his glass to hers. 'To life.'

Tish raised her glass but failed to drink from it.

'I assure you it's perfectly safe,' he promised.

'Unlike whatever you fed to Gunnar Randall during his visit,' she asserted.

Payne stared down at an undetermined spot on the carpet. 'I am sorry about that. I know it doesn't make up for what has happened, but I am sorry.'

Tish felt her stomach churn. She had come to the house because she suspected Jackson Payne of poisoning Gunnar Randall, but to hear him – one of her cooking heroes – all but confess to the crime was gut-wrenching.

'All I ask is that you listen to my story,' the chef asked. 'I have lived all my life in the public eye and I feel as though I owe it not just to the law but to my students, readers, and my colleagues to know what happened.'

'Go on,' Reade urged.

'You have, by now, probably delved into Chef Randall's background.'

'We have,' Tish confirmed.

'And you have, by now, probably deduced that Chef Randall was a human being completely devoid of morals, conscience, or ethics.'

'He was still a human being,' Reade reminded. 'A human being who was murdered.'

'I understand, Sheriff. I don't offer Randall's lack of character as an excuse – there are no excuses. I offer it only as a partial explanation.'

'And the rest of that explanation?' Tish prompted.

'I'd known the man called Gunnar Randall for nearly thirty years. He was one of the very first students enrolled in my program. He went by the name of George Randall back then and he wasn't at all the type of young person my foundation was established to help. He was wealthy, privileged, and, at age seventeen, had attended – and subsequently been thrown out of – nearly every elite boarding school in the country. His parents were about to ship him to a military academy when they learned about my program and contacted me, because while George reacted badly to sports and team endeavors, he always seemed to enjoy cooking.

'I was torn. I wanted to help underprivileged, disenfranchised youth, not the wealthy, but my wife, Jeanette, convinced me that George was a troubled young man who needed help, and if I could

provide that help, I should. She also reminded me that my foundation was in dire need of a donor who could fund my plan to operate
cooking and life skills classes in Richmond's poorer junior and
senior high schools. And so, after a fat donation from his parents,
I took George into the program.

'George excelled,' Payne continued. 'Excelled is actually an
understatement, for he was truly talented. He learned the elementary knife techniques quite rapidly and he intuitively understood
flavors and how to combine them for maximum impact. He was,
however, undisciplined and unruly – both in the kitchen and outside
of it. He listened to no one. Not his instructors, not his peers. His
thought process was disorderly and his conduct inappropriate. But
worse than all of those things, he was cruel – intentionally and
markedly cruel.'

'Cruel?'

'George would swap students' sugar for salt during baking
lessons. He'd trip his peers while they carried their dishes for
presentation, sending food flying everywhere, but particularly all
over the student presenting. He patted a fellow student – a rival,
in fact – on the back so hard that it sent him falling down a flight
of stairs. And finally – in the act that got him expelled – he
assaulted a female student who wouldn't go on a date to the
movies with him.'

'Did you report these incidents to the police?' Reade asked.

Payne nodded. 'Not the salt swapping, but the other incidents,
yes. And because George was a minor, I called his parents as
well. As is often the case with wealthy individuals, no charges
were pressed – not even by the young lady and her parents.
Everything was swept under the rug, as they say. I, however, had
had enough of George Randall. He was a cancer on the face of
my foundation. How could I teach these young people, who had
already struggled in their short lives, that food and cooking was
an art, an act of love, when they were constantly being terrorized
by someone who both promulgated and fed off fear and hate?
And so I dismissed George from the program. My plans for the
Richmond school system had to wait until I could find another
donor, but I could not allow George Randall to continue in my
program, and I could not, in good conscience, abide by his parents
funding my foundation.'

'How did his parents react?'

'Not well,' Payne replied with a sardonic laugh. 'They thought their son was doing brilliantly – which he was, on a technical level – and they blamed me for taking away their son's best opportunity to build a better life for himself. They bribed me with a bigger donation to keep him on. I refused. There was not enough money in the world to make me change my mind. Eventually, they gave up, but not without making me sign a statement swearing that I would never mention George's enrollment in the program. Stupidly, I signed so I could be rid of him.

'And that, I thought, was the last I would ever see of George Randall, apart from possibly an item on the evening news stating that he'd raped a woman or killed a man. You can imagine my surprise when, years later, I heard whispers of a "genius" young culinary student named Gunnar Randall who was set to graduate from the Culinary Institute with top honors. Ironically, our dear Chef Latanzza graduated second in that same class, but I would not learn that until years later.' Payne smiled at his steadfast friend. 'In any event, the similarities in name and the description of this person's talents left me wondering: could this actually be the same teenage boy who attended my program?

'As stories of his quick temper and arrogance soon surfaced, I thought that this could be no coincidence, so I stopped by the restaurant where he was working to find out. I am friends with many chefs and restaurant owners, so my visit was not looked upon as suspicious. Indeed, I was welcomed most warmly, given a good lunch, and even offered a tour of the kitchen. I declined the tour under the guise of not wanting to make the staff nervous – I often refuse tours for this reason – but in this instance, I did not want this Randall person to see me. On a trip to the men's room, however, I did indulge in a sneak peek through the kitchen door. There he was, standing over the stove, barking orders at a very unhappy staff. He was slightly taller and his hair had been lightened with the platinum streaks that would become his signature, but it was George Randall.'

'What did you do?' Reade questioned.

'Nothing. Sadly, I did nothing. In my mind, there was nothing to do. There were never any charges brought against young George Randall, so I could not say that he had a criminal record or had been wanted by the police. Also, the restaurant owner and head chef understood that they had, on their staff, a brilliant but wild creature who might strike at any moment, so warning them about him seemed moot. And then there was the agreement I signed with the Randalls. If I disclosed how I knew George and that I knew about his weaknesses, I could find myself in court. And so I remained silent.' He shook his head. 'It was easy to do at the time. I thought perhaps George – now Gunnar – might change his ways as he aged and gained more experience in the food industry.'

'We know how that turned out,' Tish remarked. 'When did you see Gunnar again?'

'This past Wednesday. Through the years, I'd kept track of his career and, of course, I knew about the television show. One would have to be living under a rock not to know about that. I made the mistake of tuning in when it first aired. How he treated them!' Payne cried. 'He was a chef in a position of power, and instead of using his power to help the people on his show to become better cooks and to create better products, he humiliated them. He humiliated them for ratings and profit. The fact that the show did so well . . . was disappointing.'

'What happened on Wednesday?'

'I knew Randall was in town. I debated contacting him, but then I asked myself: to what end? There was nothing I could say to him to make him stop. His behavior had made him wealthy and famous and, even more important to him, feared. That fear that he strived to cultivate in his classmates as a teen was now his all the time. All he needed to do was show his face at a restaurant and the staff would start breaking glasses and dropping silverware – the sight and sound of which I'm sure made Randall feel even more powerful.

'I was just feeling confident in my decision not to contact Randall when I received the call from Ms Fisher. She was frantic, distraught. She explained who she was and told me that Randall needed to see me that day at lunchtime. She had called before only to be told I was busy, but she hadn't told Randall because she feared how he'd react to the news. As she was speaking through her tears, I could hear him in the background, berating her, belittling her. He had such anger in his voice – the same anger he had as a boy when he assaulted that girl – I could tell he was about to hit her. Not that he needed to; his words were harsh enough to leave a lifelong bruise. So I told Chef Latanzza to reschedule my noon appointment and agreed to meet Randall.

'I was tempted, after hanging up the phone, to call the police, but then I thought the better of it. I had no proof of a physical altercation other than my suspicions, and sending the police might have only further infuriated Randall, possibly prompting him to seek violence against Ms Shea at a later time. And so, with that thought out of my head, I prepared to meet Randall. I asked Chef Latanzza to put on the usual spread – cookies and tea.'

Tish and Reade both glanced at the chef, who stood off to the side and behind his friend's wing chair.

'Yes, Latanzza was telling you the truth,' Payne confirmed. 'I certainly wasn't about to cook a meal for George – Gunnar . . . whatever he chose to call himself these days. Cooking is something you do for the people you love, not what you do to . . .' Payne broke down and then regained his composure. 'It's not what you do to appease a monster who abuses everyone around him.'

Tish leaned forward in her chair. 'What happened?'

'Randall arrived. He sat in that chair.' The chef gestured to the seat now occupied by Sheriff Reade. 'He looked older than his years and bloated, as if he'd been abusing his body with the same tenacity with which he abused other people. I'm uncertain what prompted his visit. He was loud, boastful, and full of put-downs, yet he still seemed to retain some of his childhood reverence toward me. It was truly a bizarre, unsettling meeting.

'I dismissed Chef Latanzza the moment Randall arrived,' Payne went on. 'I knew their history and thought it best that they didn't spend much time together. My instinct was correct, for moments after his arrival, Randall inquired into the well-being of Chef Latanzza's wife.'

'Chef, please.' Latanzza stepped forward from the shadows.

'Nicolas,' Payne silenced. 'I'm afraid Chef Latanzza lied about his whereabouts during that meeting, Sheriff. He did so to protect me. I do hope you understand and will not press charges.'

Reade glanced between the two men. 'So long as Chef Latanzza is willing to corroborate your latest statement when you've finished, there should be no problem.'

'Chef, please,' Latanzza once again pleaded. 'You need not tell them everything. Not now. Let us call your attorney.'

'Silence, Nicolas,' Payne instructed. 'I need to speak freely, my friend, if I am to find any peace in this world or the next.'

'Chef Latanzza is correct,' Reade stated. 'Before you say anything else, you have the right to have an attorney present.'

'If you're going to call anyone, call a priest. Perhaps he can help to save my soul,' Payne directed.

'I'll note, in the case files, that you've declined legal representation,' Reade responded.

Payne nodded his approval. 'After his unfortunate comment to Latanzza, Randall sat down. He was overblown, full of himself. He proceeded to tell me of his achievements – all of which I already knew about from following him in the news and other circuits. But he listed everything from his grades upon graduation to the amount of earnings entered on his last tax return. It was as if he was trying to prove that I made a mistake by discharging him from the program all those years ago. A big thumb to the nose to say that he didn't need me or my lessons after all – that he did this all by himself.

'I, naturally, reminded him of his early lessons with me. How to hold a knife, how to properly use a knife, how to sauté, how to properly measure ingredients – all those elementary skills that form the foundation of greatness. He grudgingly acknowledged my "small contributions," as he called them, but then condescendingly asked me if I was still writing my "little books." I told him I was working on a compendium of three hundred of the best recipes of my career – the recipes I've turned to repeatedly through the years. Randall referred to the idea as a great "historical work" as it would show what people were eating during the mid- to late twentieth century, as if my methods and techniques had not altered in the last thirty years! He then asked if I was still recording shows for public television or if I'd finally given up hope of breaking into prime time. Well, I'm afraid this was a trigger for me,' Payne chuckled. 'I explained my position on public television and how proud I was that my shows were accessible to everyone because I thought my greatest role as a chef was that of teacher. This was about the time that Chef Latanzza brought in the tea and cookies, both of which Randall refused.'

'He pushed aside his cup the moment I placed it on the table,' Latanzza recalled.

'Chef Latanzza then left us to our meeting,' Payne explained.

'Where did you go?' Reade asked Latanzza.

'The kitchen, to test recipes . . . at first.' He gazed at Chef Payne and then down at the floor.

'Randall was completely self-absorbed, which I expected,' Payne resumed. 'When I told him about my wife – of Jeannette's passing – he didn't offer his condolences. His reaction? "Bummer." Even that I could have overlooked, but then he began to discuss his show. He bragged about how he had not one but two former members of my program on the show he was shooting this week. He described Ms Harlow in the vilest of terms and suggested that she could receive a positive review from him, "if she earned it." Those were the exact words he used. I don't think I need to explain what he meant by them, do I?'

Tish shook her head.

'Randall then moved on to Zach Farraday. Zach had poked fun at Randall during a presentation he made years ago at the facility where Zach was serving time for car theft. Not only did Randall never forget it, but he never got over it. He wanted to humiliate Zach. He wanted to make him pay for questioning his brilliance, so he planned a review that would absolutely destroy him and his pub.' Payne blinked back tears. 'Jeanette and I never had children of our own. To say that the young people who graduated from my program were like family to us – to me – was an understatement. What Randall proposed to do to them – what he *had* done to hundreds of well-meaning, hard-working cooks through the years . . . I'd let him get away with it, all of it, for far too long. I let him get away with it because I wasn't brave enough to stand up and say that what he was doing was wrong.'

'You've always made it clear that you disapproved of Gunnar Randall,' Tish stated.

'Thank you, Ms Tarragon, but did I? Did I really? I'd made it clear that I disapproved of chefs who made cooking into a competition. I'd stated, numerous times, that cooking and food were about love, and there should be no harshness or cruelty in it. But not once did I denounce Gunnar Randall by name. Not once did I tell the world all that I knew about him. Gunnar Randall was guilty of despicable behavior, but I was complicit in his deeds. Complicit in my silence.

'I'm uncertain just when or how the plan came into my mind, but I decided, then and there, to put an end to George/Gunnar Randall the best way I knew how. I appealed to his ego – even as a teenager he couldn't resist, and I wasn't surprised to learn that this trait had only been amplified with age. I apologized for not providing a meal for him, citing the last-minute appointment change and the fact that most of the ingredients in my refrigerator were designated for recipe testing. George had never been impressed by much, even as a teenager, but one recipe of mine that he'd always enjoyed was cream of wild mushroom soup. Recalling the mushrooms that had cropped up on the property, I suggested we take a stroll through the gardens and grounds to see what we might forage. He eagerly agreed.

'I collected a couple of tender leeks, an onion, a bunch of thyme, and a carrot from the garden and then, from deep in the woods, a few champignons and a "hen of the woods" – not to be confused with "chicken of the woods,"' he said, aside, to Tish. 'Randall was pleased with our findings. So pleased, in fact, that he did not see me drop my pocketknife at the edge of the woods. Nor did he see me harvest a large, creamy yellow Death Cap mushroom as I stooped down to collect my knife from the cluster of leaves into which it had fallen.

'The rest was a bit more difficult. I needed to keep Randall from seeing the Death Cap, for he might become suspicious. And so, while I removed the mushroom stems from their caps, I gave Randall the task of retrieving my heavy stockpot from a high shelf in my pantry. He rather enjoyed the prospect that I was too weak and frail to lift the cast aluminum pot myself. Then, when he had retrieved that, I set him to work making the stock for the soup from the stems, while I chopped the caps. Once the mushrooms were chopped, I felt confident I was out of the "danger zone," as it were, so I made the rest of the soup in the same way I have for decades. When it was finished, I ladled it into a large bowl, garnished it with fresh parsley, and served it to Randall with a generous slice of fresh, buttered sourdough. I begged off from eating it. Creamy soups no longer agreed with me, I told him, which was a lie. But the fact that

I could no longer enjoy certain foods also seemed to please him greatly.'

'Your soup was a success,' Tish said. 'Randall raved about it in his journal.'

'Yes, he asked for a second helping. He said it was the most delicious mushroom soup he had ever eaten,' Payne noted with an ironic smile. 'He had no idea what was in it, and even though I watched him, intently, while he ate, looking for any indication of illness or suspicion, I started to doubt that I'd even spiked his food. Given his positive reaction to the meal, it felt as if I had simply made a pot of soup for a friend, just as I have in the past. Of course, I *knew* otherwise, but it didn't seem *real*.

'When Friday arrived and I still hadn't heard any news about Randall, I began to have serious doubts about whether I'd correctly identified the mushroom as a Death Cap. I'd spied a cluster of them beneath a group of older pine trees just a few days before Randall's visit and was highly confident that they fit the description, but the mushroom identification training I received as an apprentice was long ago, and I had no proof that it was an actual Death Cap and not one of the many false Death Cap varieties.'

Payne paused and sipped his wine. 'Then the news came. The glorious, glorious news! I hadn't imagined it at all, as I was beginning to fear. Gunnar Randall was dead in his bed and he would no longer be able to inflict pain upon the world. No more would his ugly countenance and even uglier words poison television screens and young minds. His plans to destroy Tiffany Harlow and Zach Farraday were wicked notions of the past – ones that I hoped would never materialize with the release of the show footage. And Randall's employees, like poor Shae Fisher, would find new jobs working for people who treated them like human beings. Yes, I rejoiced – inwardly, because I could not share my secret – but I rejoiced.

'My relief, however, was short-lived. Gunnar Randall had gotten off easy. I know that sounds terrible, considering how he died, but it's true. He should have been held accountable for his deeds. Those he injured should have had their chance to look him in the eye and tell the world what he had done. He should have been publicly disgraced and had his vast wealth redistributed to those

who needed it. He should have spent his final days in a cage, just
like the cage of fear he built for those around him. No, to have
defeated a man like Randall via legal, ethical means would
have been a source of pride. I, on the other hand, was nothing
more than a common criminal. Although I sought to rid the world
of Randall, I was no better than he was.'

'Is that why you tried to frame someone else by poisoning
yourself at your birthday party?' Reade challenged. 'Because you
felt like a common criminal?'

Latanzza leaped forward. 'No. This is not true! Chef Payne
did not try to blame anyone else for what he did. He ate the
mushrooms himself that day. He ate them because he wanted to
die.'

As Payne buried his face in his hands, Reade urged Latanzza
to tell the rest of the story.

'I had spent the entire day at The Jefferson, setting up for
Chef's birthday party, making sure everything was just so. As the
time for the party drew closer, I called Chef Payne to remind him
to get ready, so my wife and I could pick him up, but there was
no answer. I tried again – no answer. A third time – again, no
answer. By now, I was nervous, so I came here to the house to
check on him. I found him here, right where you see him, tears
in his eyes, a partially eaten dish of mushrooms on toast, and a
glass of wine in front of him. I ask him if he's getting ready for
the party – he tells me no. He does not want a party. He does
not want a birthday. He does not want to live any longer. I had
seen Chef Payne in this state before, after his wife had died, but
this time seemed to me to be more serious. So, I call my wife,
I tell her to stand by in case we have a problem. I walk Chef
around the living room. I tell him who's going to be there. I
describe the food that's arrived. I tell him so many people want
to say hello and wish him well. He says he should probably say
goodbye to everyone and agrees to come to the party. I wanted
to argue with him about the goodbyes, but I figure at least I am
getting him out of the house. It was not until he became ill at the
party that I realized . . .'

'Did you know that he had poisoned Randall?' Reade quizzed.

'I had the suspicions, yes. As you know, I was in the kitchen
during the visit. I was at the sink when I looked up to see Chef

Payne and Randall walking outside in the garden. Then I saw them in the woods. It became clear to me that they were going to cook something, which I found strange, knowing how Chef felt about Randall – how we all felt about Randall. When I found out Randall was dead, I wondered about the meal Chef had prepared. I wondered if he . . .' Latanzza was having visible difficulty completing the sentence. 'When Chef became ill, that is when it all made sense. That is why I called the ambulance as quickly as I did. That is when I knew what he had done.'

Payne reached for Latanzza's hand. 'I'm so sorry, my friend. My loyal, loyal friend.'

Latanzza gripped Payne's hands with both of his. 'You need not apologize, Chef. Anyone who knew Randall, even remotely, knows what he was like. They also know the world is better off without him. If he could provoke someone with your patience and kind view of the world to murder, then none of us were safe around him.'

'I hear your words, but I'm not sure I agree. From watching the news prior to the party, I learned that not everyone viewed Randall's death as a liberation. The tributes from fans who hailed Randall as a visionary and a hero, rather than recognizing him as the cruel vulgarian he truly was, has left me in despair for our world – for the future of cooking.'

Tish spoke up. 'I know it can appear bleak sometimes, Chef. I've had the same doubts myself, but even though there will always be those who enjoy cruelty as entertainment, I believe that most people prefer to live in a world that's kind rather than cold. A world where someone bakes a cake on your birthday or brings you soup when you're sick. We sometimes lose sight of those things, but we circle back to them eventually.'

'I do hope you're right, Ms Tarragon,' Payne uttered, his eyes damp. 'I suppose you're going to bring me in, Sheriff?'

Reade gave a solemn nod. 'I have an officer outside in an unmarked car. There will be no handcuffs and no fanfare.'

'Thank you, but someone will find out what I've done – somewhere, someday, Sheriff. It cannot remain a secret forever. In the meantime, I don't care what happens to me. I am old and tired. I will be marking the days until I can see my wife and friends long gone, and all the dogs and cats we owned through the years. No matter where I am, a prison cell or a hospital, or even here in this house again, working with Latanzza, I will be marking the days until I am back home. Back home with her.'

After bidding farewell to a distraught Latanzza, Tish watched from the passenger seat of the SUV as Clayton drove Jackson Payne to the sheriff's office for processing.

'What will happen to him, Clemson?' she asked.

'Given his age and his mental state, most judges would go easy on him. He'll probably end up in a secured facility where he'll be able to continue to write his books. If he decides that's what he wants to do.' He reached over from the driver's seat and wrapped an arm around her shoulders. 'You OK?'

She shrugged. 'I guess so.'

'We'll get you home,' he promised, removing his arm and starting the engine. 'I didn't eat tonight, did you?'

'No. There wasn't time,' she answered despondently.

'I figured as much. You get showered and I'll whip us up some grilled cheese sandwiches and tomato soup. Then we can binge-watch something on TV.'

'Would you mind if it's one of Jackson Payne's cooking shows?' she asked. 'Although I still respect him greatly, I'd like to remember him as he was, when my mother and I would watch him. I'd also like you to see how great a chef he is.'

He reached over and clasped her hand in his. 'I'd like nothing better.'

TWENTY-FIVE

As had been the case for five years running, the afternoon of the Labor Day party was sunny, hot, and terribly sticky. As per Jules's instructions to 'dress nicely' – which made her wonder if she typically resembled a street urchin – Tish slipped into a cool cotton sundress and a pair of canvas espadrilles and, after feeding the cats, applying a light layer of makeup, and donning a pair of classic Ray-Bans, drove, alone, to the Hobson Glen Recreation Park where, given the decibel level of the crowd and the music, the party was in full swing.

Tish locked her van and wandered to the area where the event was being held. As she drew closer, she was shocked to see that the affair was being catered by Justine's, a seafood restaurant near Richmond's Canal Walk that she and Reade frequented. Tish gave a friendly wave to Shirley, the restaurant's proprietor, and then sought out Jules.

She found him dressed in a magenta T-shirt, rolled-up chinos, and alligator loafers. He was standing outside a rolling whiteboard similar to those used in school classrooms. On the board had been drawn a large thermometer.

'You know, you could have just told me that you hired Shirley to cater your party,' Tish scolded. 'I would have understood. Her food is fabulous! Although I've gotta say, it's quite a step up from hamburgers and hotdogs. Did the TV station give you a raise or a bonus or something?'

'Oh, um, Justine's is free,' Jules explained, trying to conceal both the contents of the whiteboard and the marker in his left hand.

It was too late. Tish's eyes focused on the words *DOLLARS RAISED* written on the side of the thermometer. 'What is this, Jules?'

'Help,' he replied with a worried grin.

'Help?' she questioned. By now a small group of people, including Mary Jo, Celestine, Clayton, and – on a break from the band – Clemson, had gathered.

'I've been asking for weeks how I can help you. How can I help you find a new place? How can I help pack up the old one? How can I help you settle into your home with Reade? How can I help with the case? Every time the answer is "I've got it," so I took the matter into my own hands. This is a fundraiser to help you raise the money you need for a down payment on a new café.'

Tish reeled backward. 'A fundraiser? I couldn't take people's money. I–I just can't.'

'You can and you will,' Jules ordered. 'Shirley is here dishing out food, Celestine has provided the cake, Clemson and his band are supplying the soundtrack, your beverage supplier donated the drinks, MJ and I are working the bar, and everyone in town has been invited. So there's no backing out now.'

Tish blinked back tears. 'I don't know what to say.'

'"Thank you, Jules. I could, in fact, use your help" would be a refreshing change of pace,' he suggested.

She laughed and gave him a hug. 'Thank you, Jules.'

'You're welcome, honey. We'll get you your own place, one way or another.'

Tish made the rounds, greeting everyone nearby, finally culminating with Reade, in his standard ensemble of jeans and T-shirt, on whom she bestowed a great big kiss. 'You knew about all of this?' she asked when she'd finished.

'I did,' he answered proudly.

'So Jules told you he was going to try to raise fifty thousand dollars with a barbecue and it didn't sound insane to you?'

'It did, but it was far less insane than his other ideas, so I went along with it. Oh, and I got Shirley involved, too.'

She laughed. 'Oh, you poor thing. Jules has broken you in, hasn't he?'

'Must be. I seem to be immune to the craziness.' He chuckled and gave her a quick kiss. 'I'm going to get back to it. I see a whole bunch of people arriving and some up-tempo music might make them feel more generous.'

Tish excused him and rushed to the bar, where Mary Jo, working alone while Jules passed the collection hat, was swamped with orders. After several minutes of intense work, the long queue that had formed was gone.

'Thanks, but you're not supposed to be working today,' MJ

chastised, pulling her long dark hair into a bun and securing it with a ballpoint pen.

'If I'm the beneficiary of this fundraiser, pitching in is the least I can do.'

'Yeah, well, don't let Jules find out I allowed you to help. He'll have my head.'

'Um, I don't think he'll be too upset,' Tish said as she noticed an extremely handsome man enter the party area and approach the bar. He was well over six feet tall and was carrying a toddler sporting the latest in noise-canceling baby headphones.

Mary Jo followed Tish's gaze. 'He looks like Lenny Kravitz. Is he Lenny Kravitz?'

'No, it's Jules's friend Maurice. He came into the café one late afternoon when I was working by myself.'

'Maurice, as in the Maurice-who-Jules-changed-his-middle-name-for-Maurice?'

'One and the same,' Tish confirmed.

'Dang! Can't say that I blame Jules. I'd let that man call me anything he liked.'

Celestine, wearing a muumuu and dangling earrings in a not-so-subtle dollar-sign motif, sidled over to the bar. 'Say, who is that fella? Looks like a movie star.'

'That's Maurice,' Mary Jo whispered.

'*The* Maurice?'

'Yes!' Tish shushed. 'Now be quiet or he'll hear . . . Hello, Maurice. How are you?'

'Hey, Tish. I saw the email Julian sent around. I'm real sorry about your café.'

'Thanks. It's, uh, it's definitely been an unexpected challenge.'

'I'm sure you'll come through it just fine. At least, if Julian has anything to say about it.'

'He is tenacious,' she noted with a laugh.

'Yeah, but in a good way.'

'Absolutely,' she agreed. 'I appreciate you coming out here on what's usually a family day.'

'Yeah, well, this is my family now.' He pointed to the child in his arms. 'My husband and I split up a little while ago. Seems he wasn't quite as ready for fatherhood as he claimed.'

'Oh, I'm so sorry, Maurice.'

'You mean you're single now?' Mary Jo eagerly blurted, prompting Tish to give her a swift kick in the shin. 'I mean, how terrible. How absolutely terrible.'

'Yeah, it's been rough, but Cassius and l will make it through.'

'Aww, I'm sure you will, and Cassius is just adorable,' Mary Jo cooed.

'Thanks. He's pretty cool, isn't he?' Maurice boasted.

'That he is,' Tish agreed.

'Yes,' Mary Jo rushed to the other side of the bar. 'And I know who would love to see him. And you. Jules!'

Tish and Celestine watched as Mary Jo whisked Maurice and Cassius through the crowd.

'She always been that transparent?' Celestine asked Tish once the trio was out of earshot.

'Let's just say Jules and I nicknamed her "Cellophane" in college,' Tish answered, much to the baker's delight.

While Mary Jo played matchmaker, Celestine and Tish took turns greeting guests and tending the bar. They had fallen into a pleasant rhythm when a familiar face appeared on the edge of the party grounds.

'Chef Latanzza,' Tish called in greeting. Having only previously seen him in a tuxedo or chef whites, she nearly didn't recognize the linen-clad figure.

'Ah, Ms Tarragon.' The chef stepped forward and gave her a very continental kiss on each cheek. 'Your friend has done an excellent job with the party.'

'Yes, he has. Will you join us for some food?' she invited. 'Or a cold drink?'

'I would love to, but this is not a social call.'

'It isn't?'

'No, I'm here on business.' He produced an envelope from the inside of his white jacket. 'As the new director of the Jackson Payne Foundation, it's my pleasure to give you this.'

With Celestine peering eagerly over her shoulder, Tish opened the envelope with trembling fingers. Inside was a check for one hundred thousand dollars.

As Celestine whooped and hollered, Tish brought her hand to her mouth in disbelief. 'No . . . this can't . . . this can't be for me.'

'*Sì*,' Latanzza confirmed. 'It is.'

'But I–I helped to put Chef Payne in prison.'

'Chef Payne said to tell you that the only person responsible for him being in prison is him. As for me, you saved my best friend's life. It sounds strange to say, I know, but it is true. If left alone, Chef would have tried suicide again and the next time he might have succeeded. The transition has not been entirely easy on him, but he has a comfortable room, he is allowed a pet cat, and he has his work to which he has returned with renewed energy.'

'And he has you,' Tish added.

'*Sì*. My family and I are going to visit him now.' Latanzza reached into his other jacket pocket for his wallet and extracted a fifty-dollar bill. 'And this is from me. Add it to the collection.'

'Oh, no. You don't have to—'

'Yes, I do,' he said with a smile. 'The check is for the building. The cash is for your first supply order. Looks like you're going to have a lot of people to feed.'

Tish gave Latanzza a hug and bid him farewell. Meanwhile, Celestine's whoops of joy had garnered the attention of everyone gathered there.

'What is it? What happened?' Jules asked.

'Yeah, what is it?' Reade questioned as he jumped from the stage.

Tish held the check above her head. 'One hundred thousand dollars. Hobson Glen Bar and Grill, here we come!'

There was a celebratory cheer from the crowd. As one of Reade's bandmates struck up the recorded version of 'Everybody's Free (To Feel Good),' Tish was bombarded with high-fives, embraces, congratulations, and, finally, a passionate kiss from Reade.

However, not everyone was in a celebratory mood.

'You have some nerve showing your face here,' Mary Jo challenged a sheepish Schuyler Thompson as he watched the dancing crowd – and specifically an affectionate Tish and Reade – from the perimeter of the grounds.

'I, um, I came to give Tish this.' He took a folded check from his front suit pocket.

'A donation? Trying to save face? Tired of everyone ragging on you for shutting down their favorite breakfast spot? Afraid your re-election efforts might be in jeopardy if you're not seen making a conciliatory gesture?'

'No, I was . . . I was wrong. I shouldn't have evicted Tish. I was a jerk in pain because of our breakup and I lashed out.'

'You were a jerk, all right. But you don't get to play the victim card here. Tish loved and trusted you, but you became so obsessed with your career and the election that she didn't recognize you any longer. And as for Jules and me, the moment Tish became your girlfriend, we accepted you and loved you as a friend. You played basketball with my son after his father left. You arranged for me to rent the apartment above the café at a discount so my kids and I had a place to live. You helped to care for Biscuit until Jules adopted him. And Celestine . . . well, she's known and cared about you since you were a kid. When's the last time you even checked in with her?'

Schuyler stared down at his shoes.

'No, Schuyler, the pain you described was caused by you. Now, I think it's best you leave before you ruin anyone's good time,' Mary Jo advised. 'But before you go . . .' She held her palm out.

Schuyler deposited the check into it.

Without looking at it, Mary Jo tore it into pieces and ground those pieces into the grass with a sandaled foot.

'That check was—' Schuyler began to argue.

'—written to assuage your conscience,' Mary Jo completed the sentence. 'Now, get out of here. And on your way home, I suggest you take a good hard look at yourself in your rearview mirror, because this person you've become is going to get you into trouble someday.'

While Schuyler bid a hasty retreat, Tish and Reade swayed to the band's version of the Beatles' 'And I Love Her,' blissfully unaware of the mayor's presence.

'Aren't you needed on stage?' Tish asked.

'Nah, they're handling those bongos just fine. When they need the full kit, I'll be there. For now, I'm enjoying my time with the woman of the hour.' He pulled her closer. 'I told you you'd do it.'

'The Jackson Payne Foundation did it. Nick Latanzza did it,' she corrected. 'I'm just a lucky beneficiary.'

'Luck had nothing to with it. You were your own wonderful,

beautiful, caring, intelligent self, and that's why the foundation decided to help you. End of discussion.'

'You know I hate to lose an argument,' she teased.

'Sorry, you've already lost this one.'

Content to lose this particular battle, she leaned her head on his shoulder. 'You know, I believe I still owe you an answer from the other day,' she said softly in his ear.

Reade stopped swaying and pulled back to look at her. 'You don't have to answer that. I'm ashamed that I sprung it on you in the middle of a catering job in the middle of a case.'

'It did take me by surprise,' she confessed as they reconnected and continued their dance. 'But the answer is no.'

Reade stopped dancing again. 'No?' he repeated in surprise.

'No, I hadn't given any thought to remarrying, but since we've been together, I have thought about marrying you.'

Reade's face broke into a wide smile. 'You have?'

'Yes. Not now, of course, but in the future, down the road, when the moment is right, and we've had our first argument, and my belongings have had a chance to collect a little dust, yes.'

He pulled her close and kissed her. 'When the moment is right, you let me know and I'll put a ring on your finger faster than Jules can un-tag himself in an unflattering Facebook photo.'

Tish laughed and leaned her head back on his shoulder. 'Don't worry,' she promised. 'I will.'

Tish's Southern Marinated Shrimp

This makes a terrific first course on a hot summer day.

½ cup/125 ml extra virgin olive oil
1 small bunch fresh parsley, minced
3 tablespoons/45 ml red wine vinegar
3 tablespoons/45 ml fresh lemon juice (about the juice of
  three lemons)
2 garlic cloves, minced
1 bay leaf
1 tablespoon/15 ml fresh basil, minced
1 teaspoon sea salt
1 teaspoon Coleman's mustard powder
¼ teaspoon freshly ground pepper
1 medium red onion, sliced into rings
2 medium lemons, sliced
2 pounds/1 kg cooked medium shrimp

Mix the first ten ingredients in a bowl or airtight container. Blend
until thoroughly combined. Add the onion, lemons, and shrimp.
Stir to coat.

Cover and refrigerate for 24 hours before serving.

Mushroom Palmiers

Makes 40

    2 tablespoons/30 grams unsalted butter
    ¾ pound/340 grams fresh mushrooms (white or brown)
       chopped
    2 medium shallots, finely chopped
    1 teaspoon fresh thyme, minced
    ¾ teaspoon lemon juice
    ¾ teaspoon hot sauce (I use Frank's)
    ¼ teaspoon salt
    1 pack frozen puff pastry (two sheets), thawed
    1 large egg
    2 teaspoons water

Preheat the oven to 400°F/200°C.

In a large skillet, melt the butter over medium heat. Add mushrooms and shallots and cook, stirring, until tender. Stir in thyme, lemon juice, hot sauce, and salt. Remove from the heat and allow to cool completely.

Unfold one pastry sheet and place it on a greased or parchment-lined baking sheet.

Place half the mushroom mixture in the middle of the pastry and spread to within ½ inch/1.25 cm of the edges. Roll up both sides, width-wise, until the rolls meet in the middle. Repeat with the second puff pastry sheet and mushrooms.

Cut both rolled pastry sheets into approximately 20 slices.

In a small bowl, whisk egg and water. Brush over pastries.

Bake for 15–20 minutes or until puffed and golden brown.

Serve warm or at room temperature.